going on, but she was short and couldn't push to the front helplessly from the outside. Sun Yu enthusiastically called her over to stand in front of him, but she refused with a red face.

Eunuch Cao glanced arrogantly at Loud Mouth. I'm not sure if he was still keeping track of the time he got beat up by Loud Mouth over the case files he made.

"What are you looking at? Hurry up and tell me." Loud Mouth's thunderous voice reverberated around the class and Eunuch Cao instantly shriveled back.

"It's just& master Ye and my dad are filming a martial arts short film series. It's acted with real kung fu, real men, and a really smart dog."

"A dog who can act?" The class leader was interested.

Loud Mouth didn't really believe him, "It's all empty words, you can even say you guys filmed Titanic. Do you have any proof?"

It was as if Eunuch Cao was waiting for those words. He placed his phone in the middle of a desk and beckoned everyone over.

"It's actually a short film called 'Bloody Battle of Jin Ling'. It's been out for almost two months, but there aren't many citizens left with martial arts spirit in times of peace. That's why this film hasn't been noticed much, but that's the reason why we shot a controversial video to promote our film."

As expected, Eunuch Cao was planning on passing off the main antagonist of the film as me.

We do look a bit similar, but he is much older than me. Will we be able to deceive them, besides& why do I feel like it's not really a good idea to show them scenes from this movie&

Eunuch Cao had pressed the play button before I could react. He let everyone enjoy the first episode of 'Bloody Battle of Jin Ling' on his 5-inch screen. (they only have one episode currently)

The opening title was very short and had 'Director: Cao Jing' written under the bloody title.

"Cao Jing is my dad." Eunuch Cao said complacently.

Don't worry, no one's going to steal him. Everyone knows your his biological son based on your identical appearance and personality.

I've briefly summarized before what 'Bloody Battle of Jin Ling' was about:

Before the main protagonist's master went to seclude himself in the mountains, he was at an influential family and taught martial arts to Jin Ling Young Thug.

While Jin Ling Young Thug may have been a terrible person, he had an insane amount of innate talent. Even the master couldn't reach level nine on 'Xue Sha Xiu Luo Gong', but Jin Ling Young Thug was able to master it. And what did he do after mastering it, he started looking for experts to kill for fun.

After he killed all the expert and skilled people in his city, he landed his sights on his master. He found the place where his master secluded himself and killed him too.

Afterward, the story was about the main protagonist suffering through many ordeals before defeating Jin Ling Young Thug to get revenge for his master and obtaining a happy ending with the female protagonist.

It sounds like an extremely normal wuxia movie, but since it was filmed and directed by Director Cao, it was filled with anecdotes and discordant scenes.

The first episode didn't even really show the main protagonist, it was Jin Ling Young Thug who appeared more often. As he appeared on screen with a nasty evil grin, Eunuch Cao pointed at the screen and said:

"That's my master. Now, do you believe me?"

Loud Mouth stared until her eyes bulged out.

"Huh, they do look similar, but& he looks too old."

"What do you know?" Eunuch Cao clicked his tongue, "That's makeup! You can easily change someone's age, but& for a fat girl like you, you won't be able to turn skinnier even if we use makeup&"

Loud Mouth had her hands around his neck before he even completed his sentence. He would have lost his life if the class leader didn't intrude.

"Ah, the clothing tags are coming out from the outfits of the servants standing behind Jin Ling Young Thug."

Xiong YaoYue always pays attention to different places than other people.

"Ye Lin isn't good at acting." Little Smart said indistinctly, "Jin Ling Young Thug is obviously a bossy and domineering person, so his eyes shouldn't look depressed."

Damn, that's some god-like observation skills! How can you even tell Wu Sheng has depression on such a small screen. Man, you guys don't even need to come to school anymore. Just open up a detective agency with Loud Mouth and specialize in solving those complex or unsolvable cases.

"Is this really you?" The class leader looked at the screen, then looked back at me with skepticism.

"It is my master!" Eunuch Cao shrieked, "He has depressed eyes because he originally wanted to play the main protagonist!"

"Don't insert yourself into the conversation." The class leader glared angrily at Eunuch Cao.

But Eunuch Cao became more excited and repeatedly very pervertedly: "Okay, I won't insert myself."

"How could I be the one to insert myself when my master is present? If anyone, he should be the one to insert&."

The class leader had an ice-cold expression and said to Loud Mouth, "You can choke him to death, I won't stop you this time."

Wow, her expression is vicious. Why does it feel like anyone who marries the class leader will end up being dominated by her?

Take me for example, even if I'm a Spartan, I still might not be able to defeat the Justice Devil as my wife. If you do anything wrong, you'll have to kneel on a washing board as punishment.

I don't want to do anything that embarrassing! I want to be the head of the house. You're not allowed to become a crime detective, just stay home and be a housewife. All you have to do is cook for me when I return home exhausted and provide me with a lap pillow.

When we reached the point in the movie where Jin Ling Young Thug rips his master in half with his bare hands, the class leader trembled and said:

"I can't believe they let you put this violent movie online&"

"It's kind of his own fault." Xiong YaoYue held the empty popsicle stick in her mouth, "If you already know he has a terrible personality, don't teach him your real skills. It's not like cats would teach tigers how to climb a tree."

At this point in time, Loud Mouth was choking Eunuch Cao to the point where he was on his last breath.

Then, the white dog that accompanies Jin Ling Young Thug that the class leader was waiting for finally appeared.

But it was more accurate to say it was closer to a wolf than a dog. It definitely shares lineage from the Mongolian wolf and will howl at the moon at night.

The class leader made a hard to notice smile with a bit of envy when Jin Ling Young Thug patted the white wolf.

Is she envious that there's a dog willing to follow someone as evil as Jin Ling Young Thug?

Don't be mistaken, that's a wolf! According to Director Cao, the beast tamer accounts for ten percent of the filming fees!

But the class leader's complexion changed as she kept watching.

Jin Ling Young Thug ordered the white wold to eat his master's corpse. He's taking huge bites and eating it deliciously. Class leader, why are you staring at me? It's not like I was the one who wrote the script. Besides, the actor is Wu Sheng, not me, so don't blame me.

"Animals get hooked on human meat once they get a taste."

Little Smart provided a piece of trivia in an untimely manner.

The short film was nearing the end. I quickly picked up the phone and wanted to close the video, but Xiong YaoYue stopped me, "Wait, there's still a preview of the next episode!"

That's exactly why I want to turn it off! I remember the next episode was basically an AV!

The orphan female protagonist was living a poor and simple life at the temple in her village, but Jin Ling Young Thug broke in! I mean there aren't even any martial art experts here, so it's not even in his character to come here! Director Cao, if you want to film AVs, then go back to Japan!

Ah, damn, Xiong YaoYue snatched the phone away from me and the class leader also saw the next episode preview. The main content of the next episode: The female protagonist and all the other orphan girls will all be raped by Jin Ling Young Thug!

The class leader's eyes turned into black holes.

"Huh, did Ye Lin act in the nude? I can't see."

Loud Mouth tossed the gasping Eunuch Cao to the side and came closer.

What do you want to see? Wu Sheng doesn't wear a top in the film, but if you've ever seen my muscles, you would know it's not me. I can show it to you if you don't believe me.

Also, the supposed rape scenes was only a montage of dark and blurry pictures to let the audience imagine what happened& regardless of how brave Director Cao is, he wouldn't have the guts to upload a pornographic video.

"I can't believe you would act in such an immoral video&" the class leader said hatefully.

A more immoral scene occurred before she could say another sentence. As Jin Ling Young Thug was raping the orphan girls, his white wolf comrade also brutally raped a cat the girls were raising.

A dog is synchronous with its owner. They both looked at each other and smiled, the class leader was about to burst with anger.

"How could you treat that cat&"

"Hahahaha~~~" Xiong YaoYue abruptly began to laugh, "It got exposed! The dog is clearly female, how could it even rape the cat?"

"It's indeed female." Little Smart nodded along.

Only then was the class leader able to slightly alleviate her anger.

Did you forget it was all acting? Or did you actually believe the cat and girls were raped?

The actor isn't even me, it's Wu Sheng. And I didn't even know the white wolf was a female dog! The tamer is amazing for being able to teach a female dog to act like a male and rape the cat! Did you also teach the cat to stay under the dog without moving?

In the credits at the end of the film, the words Jin Ling Young Thug - Wu Sheng appeared.

"Huh, how come it's not your name?" Loud Mouth asked.

Eunuch Cao, who had just revived, got up and said after clearing his throat:

"Wu Sheng is my master and my master is Wu Sheng. It's his stage name."

"The name doesn't have any personality?" Little Smart evaluated.

"That's right." Xiong YaoYue patted the desk, "If you're going to make a stage name, why not make it bolder like 'Proud Sky Dragon'."

Currently, Bloody Battle of Jin Ling had become a hot topic in class. The students in our class all told the story to the ones who came back from lunch break:

"Did you know Ye Lin acted in a movie, how interesting."

What do you even find interesting? Do you like watching people getting raped?

"Ye Lin's a perfect fit for villain roles. Now our school can add another member to the renowned actor list, rapist Ye Lin&"

Who's a rapist? You can call me a murderer or an arsonist, but don't call me a rapist!

Not good, I can't admit I acted Jin Ling Young Thug for the sake of my reputation (plus I really wasn't the actor)

So I cleared my throat and said to the crowd around me:

"Eunuch Cao wasn't telling the truth, Wu Sheng isn't my stage name. He only looks like me, but he's a student from the film school."

Loud Mouth and Xiong YaoYue frowned, "Wait, what's going on, you're confusing us."

"So, it's not you." The class leader had challenging eyesight, but felt slightly better as I admitted the truth.

Huh, how did she realize it wasn't me? Did she see Wu Sheng's body and realize he wasn't as muscular as me? Was it because I was wore a tight vest at Xiao Qin's house, so you were able to deduce it wasn't me?

I never thought the class leader would have such a deep understanding of me.

Then I called everyone who was interested over and told them Wu Sheng was the one who acted in the film and his nickname was Depressed Bro. He's a pretty well known person at film school, so you can ask anyone who goes there about him. He only looks a bit like me, but he doesn't have any connections with me.

The students who began to believe my words began to have their questions:

"Then does that mean the fight with the underwear thief wasn't a promotional event?"

"So, it was still because you guys couldn't split the loot evenly?"

Wait& I haven't even finished speaking yet. I called out before they could spread even more odd rumors.

"Although I wasn't acting as Jin Ling Young Thug, I've still acted as a body double for him. I was the one who stood in for him when he did somersaults in the film."

My words weren't a complete lie, since I did substitute Wu Sheng to do a Rolex product placement in one of the scenes.

"Oh, that's why I thought the figure looked a lot like Ye Lin."

A lot of people said after the fact due to hind sight bias.

What figure? I don't even think he did a somersault in the film! That's why it's so easy being a politician because it's so easy to trick people!

The class leader wasn't able to overlook certain aspects: "What does being a substitute have anything to do with fighting while wearing underwear over your head?"

My expression didn't change: "Of course it's related. What's so strange about me appearing in promotional videos as a substitute? Besides, the person I was fighting wasn't even the underwear thief, he was the protagonist for the film, you can't really see clearly due to the low-resolution video."

Since I'm already at this stage, I might as well play along.

"Why do you have to use such a shameless video to promote the film?" The class leader couldn't understand our thoughts.

"Because nowadays poeple have poor taste." Eunuch Cao followed up.

"That's why my dad made a plan for master and the protagonist of the film to attract attention with underwear over their heads and promote the next film in the series!"

"It's a sacrifice for art! You have to try and understand!"

The bell rang at this time. Because the lies were more believable than last time, the class leader returned to her seat.

After a short period of time, the entire school found out I acted as a substitute in a minor film.

"Why didn't they just make Ye Lin the villain?" Someone asked, "He was born to be a villain with a face like his!"

"I'm assuming it's because Ye Lin isn't educated enough and couldn't read the script."

Even if I miswrite words frequently, I'm great at recognizing words. I really want to thank my dad's old wuxia novels. I was able to read The Seven Heroes and Five Gallants when I was in grade three!

Xiong YaoYue met me secretly after class. She prodded me with her elbow and said with a sly smile:

"No wonder you stood up for Shu Zhe, it's because you were also stealing underwear."

Huh, didn't you guarantee I didn't steal the underwear to jack off, so why are you saying this now?

"Hmph, since your gay, I still don't think you stole the underwear to jack off. I mean you would have to use a guy's underwear if you wanted to jack off."

"Are you too stressed because no one understands your love, so you stole underwear to wear?"

Why did you come to another weird conclusion?

"Please don't do it anymore in the future. Actually, it's normal for good female friends to exchange clothes, if you want to wear female clothes again, you can come ask me. You can also lend me the female clothes you buy."

Damn, who wants to swap clothes with you? I'll never be able to keep living if I was caught by the class leader or Xiao Qin.

The unexpected part was that Gong CaiCai spoke to me when we bumped into each other in the hall:

"Ye Lin classmate, you're so brave. I really respect that you have the courage to act in a movie."

"Are you not scared when you're in front of a camera? I get the shivers when I'm in a photo studio to get my picture taken&"

"Sometimes, I wish I wouldn't be afraid of anything like you&."

Turning back the time a bit around the time Xiao Qin got back from the math teacher's office. Xiao Qin wasn't really mad about being scolded for her poor grades. Instead, she claimed she was bored and secretly drew a picture with the math teacher as the model.

I took her pad with a bad feeling. Our math teacher is chubby and looks like he had a sense of responsibility, but he turned from this

m

n

mn

```
n

m4  $n

OOï

p,  o

_____

into this:

(__)

oo_____

\\--\

\\

_____*

_YY
```

I mean it's not even the same person! I mean, I only drew a picture as an example and still did it a thousand times better than you! The guy's face you drew is basically composed of potatoes and eggplants!

When Xiao Qin heard I acted in a film, she also watched the Bloody Battle of Jin Ling along with the panties video.

"Ye Lin classmate isn't even in this film." Xiao Qin said with certainty, but the one with the underwear over his head is definitely Ye Lin& but whose underwear is it? Even if you couldn't beat your opponent and needed to transform, you should at least use your girlfriend's& use my underwear.

Xiao Qin kept pestering me about whose underwear I was wearing on my head. I insisted that I was filming a promotional video with Director Cao and the underwear were only props.

She was paranoid and refused to believe me, until I threatened her by saying she would no longer be my girlfriend if she keeps asking anymore questions.

I had to endure the various rumors spreading around the school while trying to provide explanations to as many people as possible. This Tuesday was the most unendurable day I have experienced.

In particular, due to the many misunderstandings, I feel like my reputation in the class leader's eyes has fallen below zero. So, I got out some of the coupons Xu JinSheng gave me for the dojang and asked the class leader if she was interested in Taekwondo.

"This dojang is owned by the family of the guy who filmed the promotional video with me." I blabbered, "Class leader, if you want to join the criminal police division, it would be advantageous to learn some Taekwondo."

The class leader glared at me. She must have not liked it when I try to bribe her.

"I don't like to fight. Besides, we're currently in the age of firearms."

Are you already determined to be a marksman? Do you not place an importance on close-quartered combat because you think you would get assigned a gun and one hit KO people even at close range?

It's kind of like Ai Mi's bodyguard, Vasya, who killed 6 of his colleagues with a gun for humiliating him. It seems like the 'Katyusha' nickname Ai Mi gave her actually might be pretty fitting.

"But there are times when firearms aren't reliable." I persuaded her, "What if it rains and the gunpowder got wet?"

"What time period are you talking about?" The class leader asked in return, "The Napoleonic era?"

I replied abashedly: "No one's using these coupons and they're almost expired&"

"Stop using the expiry date to trick me." The class leader got a bit upset, "Last time you already tricked me with a nearly expired coupon, do you think I would fall for the same trick?"

Why did you say I tricked you? I only brought you along to have a meal, it's not like I tricked you into booking a hotel room together&

"Um, class leader, since you don't really need Taekwondo to improve your stamina, what about Shu Zhe?"

The class leader hesitated for a bit, "Are you saying he should learn Taekwondo?"

"That's right." I emphasized my statements as I saw a weak point to attack, "Doesn't Shu Zhe like Korean culture? He might like Taekwondo since it originates from Korea. If he trains in Taekwondo, his PE grades will also definitely improve."

The class leader sank into deep thought.

"Won't you get injured if you practice Taekwondo?"

"No, you won't." I guaranteed her without an ounce of basis, "Taekwondo actually has weak attack power. Besides, all beginners wear a full suit of protective gear, so nothing bad would happen to Shu Zhe."

Though, I'm not going to mention which 'weak' martial art it was that's still making my body sore.

But I guess the main reason my body aches is because I used Berserk mode. And Xu TianMing wasn't even using pure Taekwondo.

"These coupons were given to me personally by the owner of the dojang. If you go to the main dojang, you might even receive some personal guidance from the owner."

"Shu Zhe's smart, so if he has a good teacher, he might be soon able to develop a healthy body and become a manly man."

"Class leader, if you don't believe me then you can go with your brother. Also, if you don't use these coupons, they will be useless&"

The class leader couldn't fight against my persuasion and nodded.

"Okay, I'll think about it."

Then, she reminded me:

"But, don't misunderstand. I'm doing this for Xiao Zhe, it has nothing to do with you."

"If you really want to give me the coupons, then I'll give you something in return."

Huh, what is she going to do in return, maybe& a kiss? Last time was an accident and I didn't get to enjoy it enough.

"Bring your clothes tomorrow." The class leader said expressionlessly.

"Clothes, what clothes?"

"Of course, I'm talking about Qing Zi Academy's uniform." the class leader sighed, "The buttons probably all fell off since you wore it in a fight."

"Bring it to school tomorrow and I'll help you fix it. But you should carry it in an opaque bag and don't let Xiao Qin see when you give it to me&"

It was like the class leader had a large internal struggle as she said those words.

I was really happy, even though I knew the basics of sewing, I would end up with crooked buttons or prick my fingers until they bleed.

"I would appreciate it, but no one helped me pick up the buttons this time& they got lost in the alley."

"No problem. I usually collect a lot of buttons, so I should have some similar ones, just bring the clothes over&"

Then, she began to act cold towards me like usual as if it was an entirely different person who agreed to help me sew on my buttons.

And she didn't even take the Taekwondo coupons. Perhaps she wants to go with me instead of her brother?

That should be fine, but I have a lot of coupons, so we can actually bring more people.

The problem is which dojang should we go to?

The dojang in the west district is closer, but it seems their amenities are a bit lacking. And the west district might have great facilities, but the owner often appears and He Ling, the female student I beat, also goes there.

Well, let's just see where it goes from here. I still don't even know if Shu Zhe wants to go or not.

My body had pretty much recovered on Wednesday. I feel like I wouldn't lose even if I fought Xu TianMing right now.

I have to thank the Little Tyrant for my quick recovery abilities.

It was pouring rain when I woke up the next morning.

I thought it would pass by quickly, but it actually got bigger and formed a river on the streets.

I then received a text from the weather forecast office: "Due to the sudden rainstorm, Er Huan Road and San Huan Road have all been closed. Please try to stay at home."

Then it was a group message from teacher Yu: "Rainstorm is too big so school is closed for the day. Everyone should self-study at home."

Right when I was happy about the sudden one day break, I received a call from Ai Mi:

"Hey manservant, we can't film today since the set turned into a pool. How about you come over and let's take a walk together?"

Take a walk? Where are we going in this rain?

I don't want to admit it, but it's likely both Ai Mi and I inherited Ai ShuQiao's crazy genes.

Ai Mi actually invited me to go for a walk in Dong Shan city's central street in the middle of a rainstorm.

Speaking about central street, the municipal government actually put in a lot of effort and money into it when I was in grade five. (Around the time when Xiao Qin and my living complex got torn down and we were no longer neighbors) The construction style mimicked the central streets from other cities.

The tried to copy too many different ones, so it only seems out of place.

My dad once brought me here to stroll around on a blazing hot day. He pointed to a row of buildings near us and said those are Baroque style, those over there are Gothic style, and the ones on the left are classical French style, the ones on the right are postmodernist style, and we're about to pass buildings with Romanticism style&

I ate my one dollar ice cream cone while telling my dad that I wasn't interested. But I thought about how humans were not the only ones classified by socialism or capitalism, even architecture have different ideologies. When night falls, would the buildings rise up like Optimus Prime and fight over their different ideologies?

I would always accompany my sister for a walk and buy her as many ice cream cones she wants, but don't choose a day with awful weather! Er Huan Road and San Huan Road have already been submerged, even if central street is located above sea level at the highest point in Dong Shan City, the water level would still be at your ankles!

"Ai Mi, can we go on a different day?" I tried to negotiate.

"No." Ai Mi firmly declined, "Do you think it's easy for me to get a day of break? You said you loved me a few days ago, but you're not even willing to go on a walk with me?"

"But it's pouring outside, none of the stores would even be open!"

"Who wants to buy things from those shitty stores?" Ai Mi said with disdain, "I only want to go for a walk."

"Um& Dong Shan City doesn't open the lights during the day to cut down on expenses." I reminded her, "There's a lot of dark clouds today, and since there's no streetlights or sunlight, what if you fall&."

"That's why I need my manservant to accompany me!" Ai Mi became impatient, "Besides I love it when there's no sunlight, did you forget I was sensitive to UV rays? I love cloudy days and rain. Anyway, hurry up and get ready. I'll be there soon in the RV to pick you up."

"You like cloudy days and rain?" I covered my mouth and laughed, "Are you a frog?"

"No, you're the one who's a frog." She said angrily, "And you're the type that would never transform into a prince even if you were kissed a million times."

Whatever, from a genetics standpoint, it wouldn't be good for either of us if one of us was a frog.

I had no other alternative but to agree to Ai Mi's unreasonable request. I put on waterproof clothes with rain boots to prevent getting soaked by the torrential rain.

I wondered how Ai Mi was going to pick me up in her RV if Er Huan Road and San Huan Road were both blocked. Or do Americans have some super-tech that allows her RV to fly.

The truth showed I was way off the mark. This American made RV from South Carolina costs around 2 millions USD and was an amphibious vehicle.

It can't compete with the air force, but it can compete with the navy when traveling on flooded roads.

Once it enters water, a change would occur to the luxury bus. Two inflatable sacks would protrude from the outside and turn it into a luxurious yacht.

Peng TouSi arrived in front of my house with the RV. When he told me to get one the car (boat), an auntie who was standing in front of the building was stunned. After I jumped on, I seemed to have heard the auntie say: "It would be nice if I could play mahjong once on that&"

So the first thing on your mind when you get on a 2 million USD car is to play mahjong? Please don't get too addicted.

Right when I was thinking about how the car could transform, Ai Mi caught me unaware as she arrived behind me.

She was wearing a white camisole with her double ponytails tied behind her head. She also had on a pair of red sandals and she looked very relaxed.

"Why are you dressed so burdensomely." Ai Mi was unsatisfied when she saw my waterproof outfit along with my rain boots.

"You have to dress casually when going out for a stroll. You're going to affect my mood dressed like that."

"But it's to cover myself from the rain." I explained, "You should wear more too, at least a pair of rain boots& There's a lot of coal factories near Dong Shan city, so the rain is not clean, you might even get blisters on your feet."

I would always go out to play when I was a kid and run all over the place including into dirty water. It caused me to get a lot of uncomfortable blisters on my feet.

My dad wanted to pop them with a needle sanitized with a flame, but I wouldn't let him and continued to run out and play with blisters on my feet.

But I ended up getting caught by the Little Tyrant. She told the other kids to hold me down while she popped all my blisters with a nearby stalk of straw!

It was torture. If I knew it was going to happen, I would have let my dad pop them.

But because she got pus sprayed on her, the Little Tyrant also got some blisters on her the next day. I heard she even cried in front of her mom.

She deserved it, who knew she would be so squeamish. I felt great at the time so I ate an extra half a bowl of food at every meal.

Wait, was she afraid of turning ugly? Did she already care a lot about her appearance at that time? If she cared a lot about her own face, then why did she keep hitting mines?

I get angry whenever I think about the past. Although I'm already 14 and I don't like playing with toy robots, but hurry and return my Optimus Prime!

After I warned her about wearing sandals, Ai Mi completely disregarded it and said:

"I'm not afraid. I can even rest if I get sick."

Not only did she ignore my advice, she even forced me to take off my rain clothes and I was left wearing a short white shirt.

I guess if my feeble sister isn't afraid of getting sick, then there's no reason for her Spartan brother to have a full suit of gear.

After I took off my top, AI Mi laid her sights on my waterproof pants and rain boots.

"We have to get wet when taking a stroll in the rain, so take off your pants too."

I said awkwardly: "I only have underwear under it&"

Ai Mi reluctantly agreed to let me accompany her with waterproof pants and rain boots after a lot of persuasion.

As we traveled down the flooded Er Huan Road, there were numerous drivers who were stuck in the middle of the road. They cursed at the weather forecasting office as they sighed and gazed into the sky.

"Hahaha~~~" Ai Mi spoke gleefully, "It looks like China's sewer systems are really behind. If America's marine corps invaded, Dong Shan city wouldn't even be able to deploy their troops properly."

Who do you think you are, the US president? It's really not up to you if they invade or not.

Also, you're not going to be able to stand on the sidelines and watch the fun while eating chips if America and China actually went to war. The Americans would treat you extremely poorly since you have Oriental blood.

You probably haven't even learned it in American History class. I heard from my dad that after the Pearl Harbor incident, America was afraid American citizens of Japanese descent would act as spies for Japan. So, they forced them to sell off their houses and businesses and sent them all to concentration camps.

A total of over 110,000 Japanese-Americans were forced into ten concentration camps. Quite a few became insane and committed suicide.

If China and America actually went to war, your scope of movement would be even more limited. If you are still a singer at the time, your songs would first have to be approved by the government to ensure there are no coded messages for China. And don't even think about coming to China, even if the government does let you come, it would be to the front lines.

No, I won't let anyone discriminate against my sister, not even the White House or the Pentagon. If a war breaks out between America and China, the first thing I would do is you keep you confined in China. Then, I would order all your lolicon American fans to immediately surrender to China. (But it seems those types of people would be useless to America anyway)

At this point, all the drivers who were trapped on the flooded road watched our amphibious RV leisurely pass by.

"Rich people are so pretentious." A BMW driver cursed from afar.

Even though the rain was really loud, his words didn't escape Ai Mi's ears.

"Stop the car and turn around." Ai Mi gave an order to her bodyguards.

Peng TouSi understood her intentions and pulled a U arc around and cause a huge layer of mud to be caked on the BMW's windows.

After punishing the one who showed her disrespect, Ai Mi placed her hand on the railing of the deck and commanded to continue our journey.

I walked next to Ai Mi and used the handrails as support. It's not often I could witness a rainstorm from this point of view.

The gushing water rolled around in front of the deck and would sometimes be carrying all sorts of trash.

There were some slippers, plastic flower pots, plush toys, and even a blow-up doll.

Damn, was this something our store sold? Why does it look a bit familiar?

After we passed the deepest section of water, the RV's eight wheels once again hit the land.

There were stalled cars and pedestrians running in every direction. Ai Mi watched the current disaster with delight.

She then began to sing a song. As someone who was not proficient in music, I believed it to be a soft rock song.

Of course, the lyrics were all in English. How could I understand an English song if I can't even have a simple conversation in English? So, I asked 005 who was standing nearby and holding an umbrella for us: "What's Ai Mi singing, is it one of her own songs?"

Since 005 has been in China for a while, his Chinese has improved drastically. He properly did his duty of holding a large umbrella over us as he replied:

"It's not Miss Ai Mi'er's own song, I believe it's called ."

"Huh, what's that?" I frowned.

"Umm& it's one of the songs played in Vampire Diaries."

Based on 005's translation, the song goes like this:

I'm only happy when it rains~

I'm only happy when it's complicated~

And though I know you can't appreciate it~

I'm only happy when it rains~

You know I love it when the news is bad&

What the hell, it's basically a song celebrating misfortune. It's actually a fitting song for this situation. You're riding an RV with a someone holding an umbrella for you& while everyone else is so misfortunate. Did you see that KFC delivery driver crash his motorbike onto those bushes? I mean who's even ordering takeout during a rainstorm?

But this was the first time I was able to appreciate a song sung with Ai Mi's sweet voice that actually makes her happy.

There was no musical accompaniment or a stage. Ai Mi was able to drift off into her own musical world as she sang a song that wasn't written by her.

I leaned on top of the railing and stared in awe at my sister.

"What are you smiling at?" Ai Mi suddenly stopped singing and said, "Is it because I was off-key?"

I only then noticed the smile on my face.

"I've never even heard the original, so I wouldn't know if you were off tune."

"Then why are you smiling."

"From what you told me before, it seemed like you hated to sing. But now, that doesn't seem to be the case."

"What exactly are you trying to say?" Ai Mi seems to detest ambiguity and she stared at me with her cat-like blue eyes.

"I, I just think you have a pretty good sense of music. I think you're talented and a lot of people like you, not just because they're lolicons."

My compliment seemed to have worked well, but she deliberately turned away.

"I don't need a manservant to acknowledge me, and don't think I would be happy."

After a while, it seems she thought of something troubling and said:

"I don't like a single one of the songs my mom had people write for me. I once wrote my own song, but my mom ripped it up after reading only two lines. I can't believe she called it childish, I mean doesn't she love hiring people to write childish songs for me?"

"I really want to sing songs I like without jumping around on stage. I just want to be able to hide in a place where nobody would see me and sing in peace&"

Eh, that's a strange request. But didn't this happen in the 2008 Olympics where one of the singers was lip-syncing while the actual singer was behind the curtains? Do you want to become a singer's assistant after already becoming famous?

I ate a French-style breakfast in the RV on the way to central street. I didn't know what it was called, but it was a fried golden patty with fried egg wrapped with bacon and lettuce. It was all really appetizing and increased my stamina.

Ai Mi sat across from me and watched me ravenously wolf down my food. She only ate some fruits and half a croissant.

"It's good, right? I bet you've never had it before." Ai Mi teased as she stabbed a thousand holes in her bread with a fork.

Even though I've already acknowledged the French chef's skills, but I had to a bit stubborn as a citizen of a country with thousands of years of cuisine history.

"It's okay." I said, "It's because we were taught every grain of food counts in elementary school, so I reluctantly finished it."

Ai Mi didn't really seem to believe me and continued to poke her bread.

"Stop poking. It's a crime to waste food, there are tons of people starving out there. If you're not going to eat, then I'll help you finish it."

I said as I grabbed the remaining half of the croissant and tossed it in my mouth.

It had a slight taste of honey. I heard they would add natural honey in the baking process, how extravagant, completely different than the croissants you get in supermarkets.

Ai Mi kicked me from under the table.

"Don't you have any manners? Who said I would reward you that piece of bread?"

"I already ate it, just be glad I didn't find you dirty."

"I'm dirty?" Ai Mi licked her lips provocatively, "You've probably already had your sights set on the piece of bread that's been blessed by my lips. How did it taste? Was my saliva sweet?"

It's only sweet because of the honey. If your bodily fluid was sweet, then you would be eaten by ants in the middle of the night.

"So you're not replying? I won't forgive you even if you stay silent? How should you be punished for eating my toy?"

"How can you treat food as a toy&" I mumbled, "I guess I'll be your toy."

Ai Mi instantly jumped up excitedly. She held a sharp fork in her right hand and she wanted to crawl across the table, but her knee bumped into a plate of desserts and got covered with some cream.

Are you trying to kill your own brother? Keep that sharp fork away from me!

In the end, it was the French chef who saved my life.

The method he used to save me was to run out onto the deck and wave his arms while yelling: "I don't want to live anymore! Don't try to stop me, let me die!"

t

It turns out the French chef heard 005's translation when I said his food was just okay. He was hurt and immediately wanted to jump off and kill himself. What an amazing sense of self-respect, Chinese chefs completely lose in this regard. In the end, two bodyguards had to stop him while I personally apologized and said his food was actually delicious.

A respectful reminder for you. If you ever have the chance to visit a French restaurant, please don't criticize the chef. I heard from my dad that French chefs seem to have a tradition of committing suicide. During a banquet for Louis XIV, there was a chef who killed himself with his own sword because he was distraught over the lateness of the food. Between 1996 and 2003, there were two famous French chefs who killed themselves over bad reviews. (I only remember this because the cartoon Ratatouille used one of the chefs as the basis for one of the characters)

I guess the more romantic you are, the more sentimental you are. In France, a chef who doesn't want to kill themselves isn't a good chef!

After repeatedly entering the water, coming back on to the land, entering water, and getting back on to land, the RV finally arrived at a pedestrian entrance.

The walkway was paved with square stones about the same size of a slice of bread. They protruded out a bit so it was fine for people to walk over, but it would rock your vehicle if you tried to drive over it.

Even though the RV had great shock absorbers, Ai Mi still ordered them to park far away. All the bodyguards, including Peng TouSi, were instructed to keep watch on the RV and to not interfere with our 'walk'.

What do you mean walk? We clearly have to trudge through a rainstorm, and if 005 is not there to hold the umbrella, then that means I have to carry it.

I held a large umbrella that had a size comparable to a satellite dish and walked forward against the wind. I tried to use the umbrella and my body to block the rain heading towards Ai Mi.

Ai Mi wasn't satisfied even when she had such a diligent brother.

"Manservant, move your arm. I'm trying to enjoy the scenery, so don't block my view, just focus on holding the umbrella."

My arm is there to help block the rain! Do you not see how my sleeves are soaked? Besides, you can't even distinguish if something is a person or an object ten meters away in this heavy rain, so how do you even enjoy the scenery?

Ai Mi quickly found her own joy and began walking jubilantly on the walkway. The rain between the paved stones were sent flying everywhere by her sandals.

It's a good thing I'm still wearing my waterproof pants, otherwise it would have been turned into a splash art painting.

Even though I would always jump in puddles whenever I wore rain boots as a child, I decided against it today since it was embarrassing enough having your younger sister jump around.

I also had to drop my speed to prevent splashing water onto Ai Mi's clothes.

"Ai Mi, slow down." I called from behind, "You'll catch a cold if you get soaked."

"What's so bad about a cold? I don't even care even if I get pneumonia."

Do you hate your acting work that you would rather get pneumonia than go to work?

All the stores and restaurants on the two sides of the pedestrian walkway were empty. There would usually be a lot of couples feeding each other on the benches near the brass sculpture, but it was empty today.

I mean, if anyone actually came out to do those stuff in a rainstorm, they should be sent to a research center to be investigated.

It seems the owner of a souvenir shop had stayed overnight in his store. He couldn't head home in the morning and he's not going to get any customers, so he began cleaning.

The store owner had a frightened expression as he saw me and Ai Mi pass his store while braving the rain. He almost knocked over a nearby matryoshka doll with the duster in his hand.

He must have thought Ai Mi was crazy. But as a family member, I had no choice but to follow along and be crazy together with her.

Through the store window's reflection, I noticed 004 and 005 peek their heads out from around the street corner before going into hiding again.

It's true that bodyguards shouldn't follow too closely. They have some flaws, but it's acceptable for them to follow along if they don't feel at ease.

Ai Mi was originally enjoying her rain baptism, but her expression changed when she noticed 004 and 005.

"Didn't I tell you to not follow us!" Ai Mi was furious, she took off a jade bracelet from her wrist and threw it on the ground. The yellow jade was blown into powder once it hit the ground and was washed away by the rain.

005 stuck out his head a bit: "Miss, there's not a single person on the street. How would we protect you if we don't follow you."

Ai Mi pointed and scolded them: "It's safer because there's no one around! I hate having people around me, the manservant is enough, so get lost!"

004 shivered and discussed it a bit with 005.

Seeing as they didn't follow her orders, Ai Mi wanted to find something to throw and vent her anger. But she realized she had nothing to throw, so she shifted her sights on me.

"Manservant, give me your phone."

"Do you want to make a call?"

"No, I want to break it."

No, don't break it, even if it's a counterfeit and the screen is cracked, but it's easy for me to use. With your temper, you probably break as much stuff as we sell in a year.

Ai Mi came over to grab my phone when I didn't listen to her. I tried to balance the umbrella while keeping her away with one hand:

"Don't break my phone, it's not worth anything. It wouldn't be as impressive as when you broke your bracelet."

"I just like breaking things." Ai Mi searched my body while I was inconvenienced by the umbrella. "You already said you loved me, but you won't even let me break your phone?"

"Stop, it's really ticklish&"

"Then hand over your phone. Also, hold the umbrella properly, don't let my shoulders get wet."

Didn't you just say you like getting wet, but now you want me to block the rain? I would have already threw away the umbrella if you weren't my sister.

004 and 005 decided to back off, so I guess it means they saved my cellphone from its untimely fate.

The rain got bigger and bigger as if it was to celebrate Ai Mi's victory.

Ai Mi wandered around in the rain and her dress was already see-through, but she didn't mind and began to hum the Only Happy When It Rains song.

I felt my phone vibrate and saw it was a text from Xiao Qin:

"Please don't go outside today in this weather. Just lie in bed thinking about me, that's how I'm passing my time while thinking about you~(@^_^@)~"

Ai Mi glanced at my phone. I was afraid she would break it, so I put it back in my pockets and guarded it with my hand.

"Who's it from?" Although it's not an accurate comparison, it feels like I'm being questioned by my jealous wife.

"It's Xiao Qin, she told me to not go outside."

"Hmph, are you still putting up with that violent girl?" Ai Mi mocked, "When are you going to break up with her? Don't forget to call me when it happens, I want to watch her cry while eating chips."

Every word in the sentence was filled with malicious intent. I thought your relationship got better after the food battle, but you still unilaterally want Xiao Qin to have bad luck.

I laughed inside: You wouldn't get any benefits even if I break up with Xiao Qin.

Ai Mi was dissatisfied with my smile, "What are you smiling at? Did I say anything wrong? Or are you in a serious relationship with the violent girl?"

"How could I be in a serious relationship with Xiao Qin?" I denied it in a hurry, "But it doesn't concern you whether or not she is my real girlfriend&"

"How does it not concern me?" Ai Mi's eyebrows stood up at its ends, "As the lowest level of manservant, since you already said you'll love me forever, that means you have to set clear boundaries with other girls."

"Although& I won't ever return your feelings, and I might like someone else, but you still have to endure it and stay as my manservant. You have to hide your unrequited feelings of love deep down inside while faking a happy smile!"

"Watching me be happy will make you happy. You should be able to achieve at least that if you said you love me."

Wow, you really know how to oppress people. It's a good thing I'm your brother and the only love between us is sibling love.

Ai Mi seemed to yearn for that kind of future. She put her hands behind her head and said while kicking at a puddle:

"If you're going to stay by my side, then you can't do anything to me either, otherwise it means you don't really love me."

"What's up with that awkward smile, do you think it's too cruel?"

"Since you already chose to love me, then it means you picked a difficult road to walk. Get prepared to use the rest of your life to keep your promise."

"If you move me with your loyalty, then I might graciously bestow you a reward. So hold on to that tiny bit of hope and progress towards your goal, because one day&."

The rain got louder and drowned out the rest of her sentence, but then I faintly heard some different sounds coming from the side of the road.

Along with a nearby clap of thunder, the wind picked up, and the rain transitioned from a vertical descent to a frontal assault. The umbrella became completely useless and almost flew out of my hands a number of times.

I was relatively fine because I had waterproof pants, but Ai Mi was already soaked from head to toe and an outline of her underwear was visible.

Of course, I looked away and tried to contend against the force of nature while trying to block as much rain as possible.

Ai Mi was not the least bit grateful. She raised her head and let the rain pour down as she enjoyed the feeling of rain trickling down her limbs.

"It's better if the sun never comes out again." She yelled.

Do you really think you're a vampire? I mean would there even be a vampire as weak as you? You would probably starve to death if you had to attack people with your strength. But if you beg me while crying, I might spare a bit of my blood.

It happened all of a sudden when a different crackling sound appeared. Before I realized what happened, a huge fracture split the sky, then a large black building began toppling towards us.

No, it wasn't a building, it was a large tree. I'm not sure if it was because the tree's roots were rotten, but it began falling towards me and Ai Mi.

Shit, does the tree want to commit double homicide? Did you have a grudge on me in your past life, then waited for me for five hundred years after reincarnating as a tree? Why did you have to fall right now? How come someone who's destined to become a harem king be flattened by a mere plant?

The tree snapped near the bottom, but the bark still held on for a bit which delayed its speed.

Ai Mi was thoughtlessly standing in front of me. When she heard the sound of the tree breaking and the large black shadow descending from the sky, she froze and couldn't even scream for help.

Martial arts, especially Yin Yang Sanshou, is about anticipation and quick reactions. I instantly estimated the amount of time it would take for the tree to fall and compared it against the time it would take for us to dodge.

It's a bit dangerous, I would only have 0.1 seconds of margin if I don't make any mistakes. Let's get my sister out of the way first.

I snapped forward and shouted "watch out!" and shoved her to the side before she could react.

It might have been a bit barbaric, but it's better than being squashed by a tree.

Ai Mi stumbled backwards, but couldn't stand still and sat down on the rain-covered stone street. But it was better to land with her butt than with the back of her head, the worst case would be a slightly wetter dress.

After being positive my sister was out of danger, I let go of the umbrella and let it be blown away so it wouldn't slow me down.

The rain poured down on me without any obstructions, but it didn't matter since my sister was in the same situation. Rather, I felt pleasure at returning back to nature.

If a martial artist focuses their concentration, especially with the help of adrenaline, they would see their enemies in slow motion, like the tree that was falling towards me.

I could have avoided it unscathed, but I suddenly had a thought, which was in short a mistake.

Although gramps have already told me the wuxia moves you see in on TV or in novels are all bullshit& but subconsciously I still thought they existed.

Especially when gramps praised my improvement, it inevitably made me a bit cocky.

So I had an impossibly stupid idea, which was to use Yin Yang Sanshou to change the force from the tree and shift it towards another direction. Then Ai Mi would be safer and she would also respect me more.

"So my brother is even more incredible than superman! I've acted inconsiderate towards you before, but please excuse your immature sister."

Would she say something like that?

I wasted the tiny amount of margin time I had when I was having stupid thoughts.

As the black shadow began to drop on my face, my body ordered me: Dodge it, you idiot. You watched way too many wuxia movies. If you don't dodge it, you're going to die in front of your sister.

I quickly turned my heels around and ran towards Ai Mi. But since I wasn't used to wearing rain boots, paired with the fact the ground was wet and slippery, I made a mistake and slipped.

Then, the tree that was thick enough to be enveloped by one person's arms, fell onto my back.

"It's over." That's what I thought at the time, but I tried my best to disperse as much of its force as I could. I tried to act like a cotton ball and move along with the flow and not go against the force.

There was a 'CLANG' followed by a 'BANG'. I thought all my innards had leaked out after my ribs were crushed into a pulp. I couldn't help feeling a bit of sorrow.

I had such a miserable death even though I haven't done anything bad. Congratulations tree, you were able to get your revenge after five hundred years. now you can go ahead and reincarnate in peace.

Wait, I think the clang earlier was made by something metallic. I don't think I have anything metal on my body. Unless I'm actually a robot made by my dad, and he's been progressively giving me an aging body so I didn't notice anything.

Wait, that doesn't sound right. What kind of shitty robot wouldn't even be able to beat Little Tyrant? I'm a defective robot, I don't have the courage to face brother Optimus Prime anymore.

After feeling around a bit, I realized my ribs weren't broken even though I was under the tree.

It seems the clang from earlier was the tree knocking down and flattening a nearby garbage can.

I was actually saved by a garbage can! I have to take the remains back home and worship it, then pass it down to my descendants. Its noble sacrifice created a tiny space between the tree and the road. My life wasn't in any danger, but I was pressed against the road tightly so I couldn't crawl out.

It kind of seems like I'm not going to make it.

They say those who survive a catastrophe are bound to have good luck later on, so I have to go and buy the lottery! Ai Mi, why are you just staring blankly? Hurry up and call the bodyguards. The space seems to be stable for now, but who knows how long it would hold.

Hey, why& are you crying?

In the midst of a downpour, it was hard to differentiate if it was tears of rain flowing down her cheeks. But based on her sad expression, she was definitely weeping.

"Manservant, you can't die."

Ai Mi shouted with a trembling voice.

The rain fell heartlessly on her head and turned the celebrity in front of me into a drowned rat. But in my opinion, her sorry figure actually makes her cuter.

She began to shiver, but I'm not sure if it was because of the cold.

"It wasn't easy finding someone to play with me&"

"Whywhywhywhywhy&"

Ai Mi's sudden raise in voice made me jump in surprise. It's a good thing I was underneath the tree and couldn't actually jump up.

She sat in the rain and looked like a stray dog. Tears flowed out of her deep blue eyes and at the same time it contained her anger towards the world.

She tightly clenched her fists, and her already pale skin turned even whiter around her knuckles.

"Why& why does everyone I like have to die."

"Grandpa died, Vasya also died, and is even the manservant going to leave me?"

"God& god is an awful person. He's always thinking of new ways to torment me."

"Don't die." She seemed to have realized that I was still alive, so she focused her attention on me, "Manservant, you have to survive, you can't lose to god."

I was stuck under the tree with only some superficial wounds, but I was moved at the fact my sister shed tears over my safety.

"I can't defeat a last BOSS like god, but don't worry I won't die."

It was hard for me to speak with something pressed against my chest cavity, but I forced a smile for Ai Mi.

"You're lying, you guys always lie." Ai Mi cried harder, "You can't be fine after being struck by a thick tree. I hate it when you guys always smile to me before death."

Oh, are you referring to Vasya? He was clearly a cold-blooded sniper who aimed his weapon at his master, so why would he smile at Ai Mi before his death? It's really hard to understand the thoughts of a psycho.

"I'm fine, I really won't die. Look."

I pointed at the flattened garbage can. Since central street was an important area for the city, even the garbage cans were incomparably hard. So, it was able to absorb most of the force from the tree.

Ai Mi, who definitely didn't pass physics, thought the chances of me surviving was even slimmer if the metal garbage can wasn't able to escape its fate.

She began to bawl her eyes out and I couldn't get her to stop.

It may be a bad time, but there was a dark part of me that didn't want Ai Mi to stop crying. She's usually so proud, so it was currently a great time for her to frankly express her feelings.

I'm clearly not simply a manservant, and Peng TouSi isn't simply a bodyguard to her. She clearly values us, but why doesn't she just admit it.

I said a lot of words to persuade Ai Mi to stop crying, so I was currently gasping for air and my face may have been a bit pale.

A streak of lightning flashed in the distance, but luckily there was no sound of thunder. Ai Mi stopped crying and froze as if she had just fallen asleep and was dragged into this nightmare with no warning.

She had streaks of tears on her face and her first expression was despair. She clenched her teeth and began crawling towards me.

After the downpour, Ai Mi's dress was already translucent and one of the shoulder straps began slipping down.

I frowned and reminded her: "Hey, watch your image, you're revealing yourself."

Ai Mi ignored my warning and even left behind her left sandal as she crawled toward me.

"You can't die. I'm ordering you to not die." Her eyes glittered with persistence and madness, "Didn't you say you loved me? Didn't you say you wanted to stay with me for the rest of your life? You can't die before you fulfill your promise or you're a liar."

"I didn't lie and I won't die." I smiled bitterly, "If you have the time, you might as well give Peng TouSi a call&"

I then remembered Ai Mi probably didn't bring a cell phone, otherwise, she would have smashed it after she smashed her bracelet. And I can't take my phone out of my pockets either&

Ai Mi frantically felt her body for a phone but didn't find anything.

Stop searching, your whole top is already translucent. I could see the color of your bra and underwear, but I can't see any phones.

Ai Mi looked around but didn't see 004 or 005.

"Useless bodyguards, where did you go when I need you? Hurry up and come!"

Only the pitter-patter of rain on the empty street could be heard in response.

Actually, when Ai Mi was crying earlier, I believe I saw a person in black clothing running towards the RV.

It was either 004 or 005. They saw I was crushed under the tree but could still speak, so they probably went to find a medic.

It's the same thing after an earthquake. If you don't have any first aid knowledge, then you shouldn't remove debris off injured people, because they may have had internal bleed which was being stopped by the pressure from the debris.

That should be common knowledge for Ai Mi's bodyguards, so that means a medic should arrive here soon.

As I was looking for the medic, Ai Mi caught me off guard and brought her face really close to mines and made me nervous.

"Don't move the tree." I reminded her, "You won't be able to move it with your strength. If a mishap occurred, then I would actually die."

Ai Mi stared into my eyes like she was trying to pass her own life force to me with her eyes.

"Manservant, hold on there. Peng TouSi will be here soon to help. You have to hold on."

Well, that's all you can do for now. Can you also pull your shoulder straps up? Your dress straps and bra straps are all slipping off!

My face reddened and I looked away. Ai Mi misunderstood and thought her naked shoulder brought color back to my face.

"Don't die, you can't die." She placed her hand on her shoulder strap. I thought she would adjust it, but she pulled it down even more.

Shit, don't show that vulgar scene to your brother. The pink rose bud on her chest was already beginning to peek out.

"Did you see it? There's still a ton of beautiful things in the world, so you can't die."

Are you planning to use this tactic to make me reluctant to leave? It's completely unnecessary as my injuries aren't even as bad as the time the Little Tyrant kicked me into the river.

Unfitting of a brother, I began to unconsciously compare Ai Mi and Xiao Qin's breast size.

In terms of overall volume, Ai Mi's might be a bit smaller, but if Xiao Qin was the same height as Ai Mi, then Ai Mi definitely developed better. Ai Mi could also be in a swimsuit commercial without the need to pad her breasts.

"Stop, stop& being so dumb." I urged Ai Mi to stop, "I'm really fine, you'll find out soon enough&"

I choked and began coughing at a bad time.

"I'm not dumb, you're going to die if I don't do anything." Ai Mi anxiously half-revealed her breast and said seductively:

"Look, this is what all lolicons dream of& I'll let you kiss it if you survive."

Damn, I'm going to have a nosebleed. Don't give your brother such a vulgar proposal, even if I'm about to die.

Also, who are you calling a lolicon? Don't put me in the same group as Director Cao! I heard he put your underwear in a golden gilded wooden box.

I waved my hand at Ai Mi, "Now&"

"I can't let you kiss it now." Ai Mi evaded, "You'll definitely die with a smile if I fulfill your final wish."

Who said my sister's breasts is my greatest wish, can you let me finish my sentence?

"& As long as you survive." Ai Mi called me impatiently as if she was afraid I would lose consciousness, "As long as you survive, I'll let you kiss it as many times as you want."

Calm down, even though I can't stop her, I can still close my eyes.

"Don't close your eyes. Don't go to god, stay with me."

"As long as you survive, I'll let you kiss other places beside my breasts too."

"Didn't you promise you will love me forever&"

Ai Mi began to sob again. I opened my eyes and saw her disheveled appearance and thought it was laughable.

"Ai Mi, don't misunderstand. I've never had any improper thoughts towards you."

"Didn't you also say it's not real love if I had any thoughts about your body?"

"Even if I was actually about to die, I would never make an outrageous request like kissing your breasts&"

"I'm relieved that you're not injured, it was really my own fault I'm stuck down here&"

"Can& you come closer?"

Since I said a lot of words, Ai Mi fell further into despair. She must have thought I was telling her my last words.

As if to satisfy my final desire, Ai Mi lifted her naked left breast and brought it closer to my face like she was performing a holy act.

Shit, don't feed your brother your tit milk! I didn't tell you to come closer to do that. If I actually kissed your breasts then survived, then you would kill me!

Of course, I didn't kiss her breast. I grabbed her hand and pulled her lower.

She cooperated with me and her usual arrogance was gone.

Finally, I kissed her on the cheeks.

I kissed my sister's ice-cold cheek.

"Don't worry." I promised next to her ear, "I'll always love you."

Ai Mi, who was kissed on the cheeks by me, was at a loss as if she would feel more comfortable if I kissed her breasts.

"Why, it's clearly your last chance, you damn lolicon&"

Ai Mi looked at me incomprehensibly as the cold air made her jaws chatter.

"Hurry and get dressed so you don't catch a cold."

"Do you think it's worth it?" She asked me seriously.

"Why is it not worth it?" I responded, "I'll regret it for the rest of my life if you were the one who was stuck under the tree."

"So, you don't regret it?"

"Yeah, I won't regret it even if the same thing happens again&"

In an instant, Ai Mi's blue eyes were filled with ashes and she spoke in a calm and frightening tone:

"Can the three of you wait for me on the other side?"

Damn, don't scare me. Also, which three? Your grandpa, me, and Vasya? I don't want to be lumped together with that psycho! What if one day he thinks my appearance was an insult to him, then I would have to die again!

Besides, what do you mean wait for you? You're only 12 years old and still have the rest of your life in front of you, don't continue your life with a pessimistic outlook! Why do you remind me of the 81-year-old gramps who said most of his dear friends had already passed away. Are you saying although you have a lot of fans, the ones most important to you are your grandfather, father, Peng TouSi, me, and Vasya?

Is Vasya included even though he almost killed you? So, in total there's only 5 people and as expected Ai ShuQiao is not included.

If I also died, then three of us would no longer be with you. Then, the only one left beside you all the time would be Peng TouSi, but he could also be called back by Ai ShuQiao at any time.

No wonder you would lose interest in life. It's like gramps who's not afraid of death, but it's actually something he looks forward to. Please don't have the same outlook on life as a dying man at such a young age.

Even if the three of us waited for you, what can we do even if you join us, play mahjong? So, does that mean the three of us would just be staring at each other before you arrive?

I feel like Ai Mi needs a more positive outlook on life regardless if I die or not.

So I tried to persuade her: "Hey, even if I do die one day, you can't commit suicide. Didn't you believe in god? You will go to hell if you commit suicide!"

Ai Mi clicked her tongue: "No, that's an Islamic belief. Besides, God doesn't care if you live or die."

She seemed to think that I was having my last flash as a dying man, and since she believed I would be waiting for her in the other world, she spoke to me as if we would meet again.

"I won't commit suicide because suicide is painful." Ai Mi had an unfathomable smile.

"There's a lot of ways to leave this world, some of them are even pleasant ways&"

"From tomorrow on, I'll make sure to do everything my mom forbids me from doing."

"I want to do everything all other celebrities do."

"Whether it's drugs or sleeping around, I'll make sure to film everything and piss my mom to death."

"If I spend everyday indulging in these pleasures, I'll probably die quickly."

Ai Mi seemed to have painted a very depraved future for herself.

I frowned, "Hey, don't do drugs or sleep around."

"What's wrong with sleeping around?" Ai Mi looked at me provocatively, "Will you despise me because I slept around? Didn't you say you would love me no matter what?"

"That's true&" Right when I was worrying about our strange conversation, I saw Peng TouSi walking towards us with 004 and 005 following behind him.

004 was holding an umbrella in his left hand and a first aid kit in his right hand. 005 was holding a military knife in his hands, not really sure how he would use that.

Peng TouSi took off his suit as he walked closer. His sturdy body of muscles riddled with bullet holes gave off a majestic aura.

Peng TouSi requested Ai Mi to give him some space. Ai Mi regained her composure in front of the bodyguards. She wore her clothes properly and stood under the umbrella while speaking from a bit further away:

"Check if the manservant can still be saved. If he can't be saved, make sure to keep his body intact so I can keep him preserved in a crystal coffin."

"I'll keep the coffin in the mansion's living room, that way the manservant will be able to see whatever I do."

Are you not going to let me rest even after I die?

Peng TouSi squatted in front of me and checked out my complexion, then he stuck out a single finger and asked:

"How many fingers am I holding up?"

"One. Damn homo, stop joking around and hurry up and pulled me out."

Peng TouSi put his finger on my neck and felt my pulse.

"He won't die." Peng TouSi turned and said to Ai Mi, "I've never seen such an energetic person before death."

Ai Mi didn't really believe him, "Stop lying. He's my manservant, so that means even when he's dying, he would be cooler than everyone else."

"Why didn't you bring a doctor?" Even though I knew I didn't need a doctor, I still wanted to ask.

"We usually always have a private doctor nearby." Peng TouSi said, "But the last doctor made the Miss unhappy, so he was fired two days ago&"

"Miss Ai Mi'er's personal doctor is a job that has the highest turnover rate. To date, thirty-two doctors have already quit& I've been learning medicine in my spare time to fill up the empty times when we don't have a doctor nearby&"

Peng TouSi gave me a straight forward smile, "The med kit 004 brought is for me to use to help you out."

After monitoring my vitals for a while, Peng TouSi ordered 005 to cut away a few branches.

"Everyone get out of the way." Peng TouSi warned.

Ai Mi walked to a safe location under 004's protection.

"Make sure to keep his corpse intact." Ai Mi was prepared for the fact I would instantly die after the tree gets moved out of the way.

I thought Peng TouSi would use some lifting equipment to help, but all I saw was him take a deep breath and his muscles immediately swell up in size. Then, he clasped his arms around the trunk of the tree, paused for a moment, and suddenly shouted "up".

Damn, it actually raised up. He raised the tree and even moved it a few steps before placing it down where no one would trip on it.

He came to check on me after placing the tree down. In order to show I was fine, I quickly jumped up and waved at Ai Mi.

Ai Mi was shocked, delighted, and dumbfounded.

Peng TouSi stopped me from intense movements and said I still needed to be inspected. Thus he took out a simple stretcher from the med kit and asked 004 and 005 to carry me to the first aid room in the RV.

To make sure Ai Mi kept up, Peng TouSi seated her on his wide shoulders and held the umbrella higher to cover from the rain.

Ai Mi's eyes were flickering and she kept asking Peng TouSi:

"Is the manservant really going to live? Is he really not going to die?"

Peng TouSi responded with a smile: "He won't die."

It was the first time I entered the first aid room in the RV. It was a bit smaller than hospital rooms, but it was fully equipped.

It had X-ray machines, ultrasound scanners, UV disinfection lights, and even a surgical bed and surgical lights&

I laid on the surgical table as Peng TouSi inspected me with various devices.

Other than a few scratches on my back and a ripped shirt, there were no other problems.

Peng TouSi didn't give up and wanted me to take off my clothes so he could check my body.

Color returned to Ai Mi's face after she heard I had no problems.

She was accompanying me the whole time while still wearing her wet clothes.

Ai Mi had her mouth wide open now that I was alive and well, and even asked the French chef for some dessert. She started to believe that she was being played by me earlier.

"You're the worst." Ai Mi angrily flung her towel on the ground and stamped on it.

"You're clearly fine, but you feigned death to scare me."

I already said I was fine, you were the one who thought I was about to die.

Ai Mi's face gradually turned as red as an apple. Her body temperature was raising high to a point where she could practically steam dry her wet dress.

"And& I was lying when I said you could kiss my breasts. You can't take advantage of me by deceiving me."

"I got it." I said, "I won't covet your body& but, you weren't lying when you cried out of concern for me, right?"

Ai Mi stayed quiet for two to three minutes before shouting out loud:

"I wasn't crying because I was worried about you, did you already forget I'm afraid of lighting? I could hear the sound of thunder before the tree collapsed& that's what made me cry."

I knew Ai Mi wasn't being frank, but I still accepted her makeshift excuse and replied:

"Okay, okay, I know you don't even care about the lives of your subordinates. You probably wouldn't even shed a single tear even if both Peng TouSi and I died."

Peng TouSi and I looked at each other and smiled, then I shuddered because I felt it was a bad omen to be aligned in thought with a homo like him.

"You guys won't die." Ai Mi said stubbornly, "You guys are like cockroaches and would even survive a nuclear war. At the time, you guys have to protect me and you can't lose to the zombies!"

A post-apocalyptic era, the same setting as Fist of the North Star?

As Peng TouSi and I escort Ai Mi and step onto the barren lands vaporized by nuclear weapons, will there also be an enigmatic narrator reading out some strange opening lines?

For example:

"In 20XX, the entire world was enveloped by nuclear bombs and almost all living things became extinct, but the human race did not perish."

"There's a hidden assassination technique with over 2000 years of history known as Yin Yang Sanshou. It uses the sun and moon as a basis, and it can also bring out your maximum potential if you wear a pair of underwear on your head."

"Tragedy continues to strike the Yin Yang Sanshou practitioner who only has one successor in every generation."

"Peng TouSi is a huge man with over 70 different scars littered across his body. He was known as the boxing champion in the underground Russian boxing rings."

"Ye Lin might not even be able to defeat Peng TouSi's pinky, but he has good luck and knows how to act cute, that's why he became the successor of gramps' Yin Yan Sanshou techniques."

"Tune in to find out what happens to these two who will be swept up by a multitude of battles&"

These narrators should just drop dead. Why did I imagine it being spoken in the voice of Kyle's old translator, is it because he likes this kind of stuff?

After confirming I wouldn't drop dead, Ai Mi went to take an hour long hot water bath. Peng TouSi and I could only use the single person standing shower to quickly rinse off with some warm water.

"The RV has limited resources, so I get priority." Ai Mi declared shamelessly, "You subordinates can just use my leftovers."

She wore a pair of white pyjamas and blow dried her hair. Then, her belly began to growl so she ordered the chef to quickly prepare lunch.

Perhaps it was to override my insult of calling his food 'okay' from lunch, the French chef made an exceedingly decadent lunch.

There were butter sauteed mushrooms, escargot, foie gras, cream of asparagus soup, and many other appetizing dishes.

The French chef told us since the kitchen didn't have truffles or caviar for the time being, the only famous french dish he could cook was foie gras and hoped we wouldn't mind.

How could I mind? You're currently sitting kneeled in front of us with a katana over your knees and your hair chest exposed. It looks like you're planning on committing harakiri if one of us says it doesn't taste good.

I don't need that much psychological pressure when I'm eating a meal! I heard the katana was a souvenir from the time when you learned how to handle puffer fish from a Japanese master. Please don't use a souvenir in this manner, otherwise it would be like he provided you with a murder weapon. Or did the Japanese master also teach you how to commit harakiri at the same time?

Obviously he affected the taste of the food by sitting next to us and threatening to commit suicide, but I could only say it tastes delicious.

I was soaked in the rain for a long time just like Ai Mi. I was fine, but it seems Ai Mi caught a bit of a cold as she kept on sneezing during the meal.

With some persuasion from Peng TouSi, Ai Mi decided to rest early to prevent actually getting pneumonia.

The streets were still backed up with water. After Peng TouSi dropped me off, Ai Mi coughed and used her eyes to bid farewell as I got off.

"I'll visit a later day." I promised and watched the RV ride away on the waves.

At home, I finished yesterday's unfinished homework and used the computer to manage the online store for a while. Other than a few normal client inquiries, Shu Zhe sent me a message with his 'Southland Red Berries' account and urged me to quickly hand over the bikini or he can't deliver the goods on time.

With his reminder, I also remembered the class leader promised to sew the buttons for my Qing Zi Academy uniform. So I got one of my dad's old paper bags and placed the Qing Zi Academy uniform and the unopened bikini into the bag.

I planned on first handing the bikini to Shu Zhe, then the clothes to the class leader.

But I accidentally messed up the order.

I suddenly remembered I forgot something important after I put the bikini and the uniform in the bag.

The class leader never said she would sew my buttons for free! It's not like my buttons fell off because I was protecting her, so I should use the Taekwondo coupons as an exchange.

I flipped through the drawers and pulled out twenty something coupons and stuffed it into the Qing Zi Academy uniform's pockets.

This way the class leader would be surprised when sewing the buttons Akin to hiding a wedding ring inside the cake, this way of giving presents is much more romantic.

On Thursday, everyone watched the receding flood with disappointment as they had to return to school.

"Did Ye Lin classmate think of me yesterday?" Xiao Qin laughed foolishly and greeted me.

"I didn't have the time to think of you." I answered rudely.

"Ye Lin classmate must have heard something from a bad person, so you're suddenly treating me worse. Did the class leader say something bad about me?"

I didn't even meet the class leader yesterday, and why would she say anything bad about you? Yesterday, I acted crazy with Ai Mi.

Xiao Qin placed her hand on her chest and sighed in relief.

"Oh, so you were with your sister, as long as it's not the class leader&"

"But in modern times, it's not like there aren't any perverts who want to push down their own sisters&."

"But there's no way Ye Lin classmate is that perverted to the point where he would want to marry his own sister, right?"

"No shit." I said sternly, "How could I marry my own sister? I only like her as a brother."

Xiao Qin bit her finger with unease, "Then& do you swear?"

"I swear."

"Swear to your girlfriend that you won't develop any abnormal relationship with your sister and it will always be pure sibling love."

"That's easy." I raised my right hand, "I swear in the name of the martyrs: My sister will always be my sister. I will never look at her as a woman and will never develop a taboo relationship with her."

"Why are you swearing on the name of martyrs?" Xiao Qin said with dissatisfaction, "Don't people usually swear in the name of powerful entities like God or Mother Mary?"

I scoffed at her.

"Fine, I'll do another vow if you want me to swear in the name of God."

"&I promise to uphold my previous promise in the name of the Monkey King."

"Why is it a monkey? Can you be a bit more serious?"

"Fine, fine." I stopped the argument, "Basically, it doesn't matter if it's my current sister or any other sisters who appear later on, I will always maintain a proper distance as siblings."

After seeing my resolution, Xiao Qin swallowed her doubts, but then she asked with suspicions:

"What do you mean by other sisters? Is Uncle Ye going to remarry? Even if that's the case, you won't necessarily get a younger sister!"

Hehehe, I chuckled inside. The sister I'm referring to is you. Even though I'm disturbed about the fact my dad and Auntie Ren hooked up, but I would have to make the best of it if it ended in the worst possible outcome. I'll make sure you also get a taste of my pure brotherly love.

During our conversation, Xiao Qin also kept staring at the paper bag I was carrying.

"What's in there, is it a gift for me?"

Xiao Qin closed her eyes.

I ignored her. She opened her eyes after a minute, but her awaited gift wasn't in front of her.

"Did I open my eyes too early?"

Xiao Qin said as she closed her eyes again.

You won't get a present even if you close your eyes for a thousand years.

I still didn't feel at ease even after repeatedly telling Xiao Qin she would no longer be my girlfriend if she looked in the bag. That's why after the first class, I told Xiao Qin to buy me a bottle of water so I could secretly bring the bag to the class leader.

The class leader was sitting at her desk writing something. I felt she purposely stayed at her spot to wait for me.

I put the bag on her desk and said: "I've brought the stuff, sorry to trouble you."

"No need to be sorry." The class leader didn't stop writing, but she used her other hand to quickly stuff the bag into her desk as if she was afraid of being spotted.

I used a common tactic boys use to act cute and scratched the back of my head.

"Since the class leader has a lot of work every day, you have to manage the class, do homework, cook for your brother, volunteer at the pet hospital& and now you have to help me sew on buttons, I feel a bit bad&"

The class leader had a slightly sorrowed expression when I mentioned the pet hospital, but she quickly livened up and stuck out her hands:

"Give me the taekwondo coupons."

"Huh?"

"What are you standing there for? Did you think I'm helping you sew buttons because I care about you? Please don't misunderstand, I'm doing it in exchange for the coupons."

Why do you have to be so frank? You already know I would have given you the coupons even if you didn't help me fix the uniform.

Thus I said to her:

"Well, as for the coupons& I put it somewhere safe. Take another look when you get home and you should find it easily."

The class leader looked at me suspiciously, I wasn't sure if she already guessed I put it in the pockets.

Xiao Qin's leg strength was indeed impressive as she returned shortly holding a bottle of water. A girl who's usually so sickly ran back to the classroom all of a sudden left Niu ShiLi in a daze.

The class leader immediately straightened her back, then she looked away to pretend we didn't just have an exchange.

Xiao Qin brought the bottle of water to me while panting heavily.

"Phew& phew& since it's hot today, this was the last bottle of water left. Even the third year school beauty had her eyes on it, but she gave it to me after some friendly persuasion, what a good person."

I'm not sure what Xiao Qin meant by 'friendly persuasion', but later on the school beauty would always avoid Xiao Qin every time she saw her.

"Hehe&." Xiao Qin looked at the class leader with a crafty gaze, "What are you guys talking about, it looks like you guys are having fun&"

"We, we're talking about the basketball tournament." The class leader replied with a rare lie.

"Hmph, your nose will grow longer if you lie." Xiao Qin placed the chilled bottle of water on the class leader's neck without warning. Even if her hair was on top, it still made the class leader shriek in surprise.

"It's cold, Xiao Qin, what are you doing?"

"I'm helping you cool down. I'm a slightly better person than the school beauty."

The class leader got up and wanted to tickle Xiao Qin as payback, but she sat back down when she considered the fact someone might see the bag in her desk.

The bell finally rang and I was able to get out of the awkward situation.

I don't even know why I was so nervous because I want Xiao Qin to hate me.

After another class, the class leader actually came looking for me when Xiao Qin and Loud Mouth went to the washroom.

I was watching Niu ShiLi practice basketball from afar while keeping cool under a bayan tree.

The class leader walked right up to me angrily.

She was carrying the bag I gave her in class.

"Ye Lin, what are you trying to say with the thing you put with your uniform"

Oh, did you find the coupons? Of course, it's for you and Shu Zhe to use. Did she think I gave her too much, it was free anyway.

Thus I signaled with my hands that it wasn't a big deal.

"It's a gift for you. You can try it out when you have time."

The class leader's face was flushed red with anger.

"You, you want me to use this?"

"That's right." I was curious about the class leader's reaction, "If you don't have time on weekdays because of school, you can try it out on the weekends."

"You& do you always fantasize about me wearing these shameful clothes?"

Huh, why would it be shameful wearing a martial arts uniform? Even though the collars and sleeves might be a bit wide, nothing would be revealed if you wear underwear properly.

But I guess I've actually imagined the class leader in a uniform. She should look much cooler than He Ling.

I'm assuming I showed a lecherous appearance as I was thinking about the class leader in an uniform and she became angrier.

"Do you think I would be happy getting this as a present?"

"Well, you don't have to get this upset. If you don't like it, you can give it to Shu Zhe&"

"What? You want my brother to wear it?"

Shu Zhe wouldn't seem formidable even if he puts on a taekwondo uniform. Why is the class leader staring daggers at me, the coupons are a sign of my good intentions!

"Hey, class leader, didn't we already discuss previously that it's mainly for your brother? I mean with your body, it doesn't really matter if you use it or not&"

"What's wrong with my body? Are you saying Xiao Zhe is more suited for it?"

The class leader had a look of disbelief and her long black hair began trembling from anger.

I added another sentence: "Haha, don't forget to show it off to me once you guys make some progress.

Slap.

A loud slap.

The class leader pulled out the bikini I accidentally left in the bag and slapped it on my face.

The class leader left the bag under the tree and walked away without looking back.

"You can ask whoever likes wearing those shameful clothes to help fix your uniform."

Ah, shit& it's all because of Xiao Qin, I forgot that was in there.

I thought the class leader was talking about the coupons, so I said too much and made her misunderstand I really wanted to give her a bikini.

I even told her to wear it together with her brother and show it to me.

An awful misunderstanding. Even though the bikini is actually for your brother, but he would never help me fix my uniform!

It looks like my reputation with the class leader dropped again. Why is it so hard to raise my reputation in the one place where I actually want to increase it?

In any case, keeping a bikini is like a hot potato. I should hand it over to Shu Zhe as soon as possible.

The worst part was that the break was almost over. During biology class, Xiao Qin began telling me a joke.

"Ye Lin classmate, I've been collecting a lot of source materials to draw manga and some of them have some pretty good jokes."

"I could tell you one that's really funny, but make sure to not laugh out loud in class."

She began to speak without caring if I even wanted to hear it:

"A hunter went hunting in a forest and suddenly saw a black bear."

"He raised his gun and fired a shot at the bear, but he missed and got caught by the bear."

Xiao Qin already began laughing while clutching her belly after she only said two lines.

"Hahaha& then the bear said: I'll give you two choices. One, get eaten by me or two, give me a blow job." (TN: In Chinese, the literal line says blow a trumpet, which is slang for blow job)

"The hunter thought: It's good as long as he could stay alive, so he gave the bear a blow job&"

What's up with this dirty joke, please stop saying anymore. Don't you have any principles?

The rest of the joke was basically talking about how every time the hunter brought more firepower to take down the bear, he would get caught and made to give the bear a blow job. Finally, the bear asked in bewilderment:

"Do you come to hunt or to give blow jobs?"

Xiao Qin kept laughing non-stop after telling me the joke. She would have been admonished by the teacher if she didn't hide behind a textbook.

I had a serious face and didn't know what was so funny.

"Haha& why aren't you laughing? It's so funny&"

"How is it funny?"

"It's funny& because& the hunter goes hunting, but why does he carry a trumpet with him everywhere? The bear knows how to talk and is even a music lover& what a nonsensical joke."

Damn, so after all that time, you still don't know what they mean when they say blowing a trumpet? I thought your head was already filled with erotic thoughts after spending so much time with Chen YingRan.

After class, Xiao Qin also told the joke to the class leader. The class leader quickly covered her mouth halfway through the joke, then she looked at me angrily as if I was the one who taught it to her.

It seems like Xiao Qin exists purely to distract me so I would make mistakes. I can't forget to hand over the bikini this time.

I called Shu Zhe out next to the school garden. He took the bikini while grumbling about how I cost him money.

"Stop blabbering." I said, "Make sure your sister doesn't see this underwear or we're both dead meat."

Shu Zhe was baffled: "I can't show any of the underwear to my sister."

It's not the same for this pair. If the class leader sees a different pair, I could still push it off as Shu Zhe's hobby, but if the class leader sees the bikini, she would immediately know I was the one who gave it to Shu Zhe!

The sister didn't accept it, so I gave it to her brother. The class leader would definitely think I'm a massive pervert and blow my brains out.

After I finished the underwear business, I remembered about the balloon business recommended by Uncle Fireball.

I've already bought the balloons and lipstick, so the only thing missing is Shu Zhe.

I wanted Shu Zhe to go to my house to blow balloons, but wasn't sure how to split the money. I haven't thought it through fully yet so I hesitated a bit.

At this time, Loud Mouth came near us and said:

"You guys have a pretty good relationship, I've seen you guys together a lot lately."

Shu Zhe immediately began entering his kiss ass mode:

"Oh it's sis Yu Hong, it seems you lost some weight."

Loud Mouth didn't take his flattery seriously and left with a laugh.

I thought inside: You talk to her so affectionately, but you still call her Loud Mouth behind her back.

I originally wanted to say: "Come to my house after school to blow balloons", but because Loud Mouth came by, plus Xiao Qin's joke from earlier, I accidentally said:

"Come to my house after school to give me a blow job."

Shu Zhe was shocked and terrified and almost swallowed his chewing gum.

"Ye, bro Ye Lin, what did you say?"

The sun was shining especially bright and I was kind of dizzy, so I didn't even realize I misspoke.

"Giving me a blow job, don't you need the money?"

"Even if you pay me&"

"It's a surprise that you aren't willing&" I raised my eyebrow, "I thought you were already used to working for me."

"Do all your employees& have to do it?"

"Is it that hard? Even elementary school students can do it."

Shu Zhe began to tremble.

"How do you know they can do it&. did you& make them do it?"

"I've seen them do it before." I said confidently, "But they weren't blowing it for me, they were just blowing it for fun among themselves."

"Blowing it for fun?" Shu Zhe felt he was already out of touch with the current younger generation. He wanted to run, but I held him down by the shoulders since it was disrespectful to leave before his boss finished speaking.

"Bro Ye Lin, let me go. I won't do it, no matter what."

"Why not, isn't it really simple?"

"It's not simple and it's way too perverted."

"Do you have the right to say it's perverted when you wear a bikini to school? I'll give you ¥50 for blowing once, so it's easy money."

"What, only ¥50?"

I can't believe he thinks ¥50 is too less for blowing a balloon&

"Oh right, you only get ¥50 if you put on lipstick, otherwise it's only ¥20&"

"¥20? Are you looking down on me?"

"Well, you need to leave a lip print to get ¥50."

"You want me to leave lip prints on that&?"

Shu Zhe tried his best to break free of my grip, but to no avail.

"I'm not going. I won't do it even if I die."

"Huh, do you have any negative feelings towards my house? Then, we could find a place with no one around and you can secretly blow it for me."

"At& school?" Shu Zhe's panicked expression looks as if he just escaped from the sinking Titanic.

Shu Zhe was on the verge of tears after he realized he couldn't escape from my grasps.

"Bro Ye Lin, please forgive me& you should let my sister do that kind of stuff for you&"

I snorted, "How? There's no way she would agree."

"Yea& normally it would be impossible, that's why you have to build up a relationship with her first&"

Huh, why would we build a relationship to blow a balloon?

"And never mention this in front of her. And you have to listen to my sister and think of her first&"

It's only blowing a balloon, why does it have to be so complicated?

"Then when my sister thinks you deserve a reward and asks what you want to eat or what you want, you would pretend to be troubled and wait for her to talk with you&"

Damn, that's complicated. Is this accumulated from your years of experience from dealing with your sister?

"Then at this time, you should abashedly say that your friend's girlfriends all blow it for them&"

Ah, my friends are mostly from the basketball team. Do their families all run adult goods stores?

"My sister would be upset after you tell her, but don't argue with her. You have to blame yourself and call yourself a pervert. Then you call your friends all perverts and say you have to stop being friends with them."

"Other than blaming yourself, you have to show my sister your devotion. You have to say you were weak and fell prey to the temptations of society&"

"It might not be a 100% success rate, but as long as you invoke her motherly instincts, it would be possible&"

What would be possible? Why would blowing a balloon be more annoying than getting a wife? I could blow it myself, but I don't want to lie to the customers.

"Hey, you're making me confused. The customers won't be happy if it's not you blowing it."

"Customers?" Shu Zhe widened his eyes, "You want me to blow customers for only ¥50?"

"There's no way I would agree. Cilantro Buns said he would give me ¥4000 to go to a hotel with him, but I refused."

No shit, you're a trap, so you would get revealed.

"Bro Ye Lin, you're awful&"

Shu Zhe began to sob for some reason.

"Hey, what's going on? Do you have to be that sad for blowing a balloon?"

"Blowing a balloon, didn't you say a blow job?"

"Huh, did I say blow job?"

"Is it a real balloon or is it slang for something else?"

"Of course, it's a real balloon&"

"Ye Lin, you pissed me off."

Shu Zhe hit my chest as hard as he could and ran off.

Ah, it doesn't hurt at all. But why is nothing going my way today&?

I was a bit sullen because nothing went my way and looked a bit gloomy.

As I was walking back into the school building, I bumped into Xiong YaoYue who was coming back from volleyball practice.

"Ah, it looks like you're in a bad mood."

Xiong YaoYue asked with a frown.

"Yeah, because I can't seem to run into happy situations&"

"Well, happy situations would hide from you if you look so bitter. Be a bit happier."

She patted my shoulders without restraint.

"You make it sound easy. How can you be happy just by saying you want to be happy&"

Xiong YaoYue clutched her chin and began to ponder:

"So you want to get rid of your bad mood first, then how about&"

"Giving me a beating."

"What?"

"You'll feel much better after giving me a beating. Don't look down on me, I'm someone who's willing to sacrifice myself to help a friend out."

She stuck up her thumb to signify it was not a big deal. She had a clear and bright smile and the and the sun rays reflected off her two small canine teeth.

It's too bright, it hurts my eyes just looking at her. You're such a good friend that you would be willing to take a beating just to make your friend feel better.

But even if you don't mind, there's no way I can hit a girl. I can't even hit Xiao Qin who bullied me for many years, so there's no way I can hit you.

I'm grateful for your good intentions, but you should try learning how to act cute from Xiao Qin to lose your manliness so you can marry a good man in the future.

After I returned to the classroom, I saw Xiao Qin secretly sneaking glances into my bag to see what was inside.

I purposely hung the bag on the left side of my desk to keep it as far away from Xiao Qin as possible. The class leader originally agreed to help me fix the uniform, but t looks like I have to do it myself.

I feigned to be angry and said: "Didn't I say you won't be my girlfriend anymore if you go through my bag?"

Xiao Qin trembled and tried to explain:

"I& didn't look through it, I only accidentally peeked a bit."

"You can't accidentally look either." I said with a serious expression, since you broke our promise, from today onward, you will no longer be my girlfriend.

Xiao Qin clenched her teeth and had a deathly pale face, then she suddenly pointed to an open window.

It's the second floor, are you trying to threaten me with suicide? It seems you already mastered the three techniques of woman: crying, screaming, and hanging. It must have been hard since you used to be a tomboy, so you had to learn everything by reading shoujo manga. It looks like Xiong YaoYue should call you a teacher and learn from you.

"Please teach me, Celery-sensei."

Shouldn't Xiong YaoYue bow down to you with sincerity and ask you to teach her how to 'un-man' herself?

Although I believed Xiao Qin would survive even if she jumped down for the second floor, but I still took my words back just in case.

"Did you prepare the Qing Zi Academy uniform so you can visit Ai Mi?"

Xiao Qin asked after she calmed down.

"That's right." I said in a bad mood, "But now all the buttons are gone, so I might not be able to get past the security guard."

"Um& if you don't mind, I can help you fix it."

Xiao Qin suggested passionately.

"You?" I was skeptical towards her sewing skills. Also the class leader said she collected a lot of buttons, so she might have some similar ones to the original, but where would Xiao Qin find them?

"It's fine if you leave it with me. It's one of my biggest wishes to help Ye Lin classmate fix your clothes, so I hope you can meet my needs."

"(^__^) Hehe& I should also mention my other wishes are to get married to Ye Lin classmate, travel the world with Ye Lin classmate, and have kids with Ye Lin classmate&"

It's enough to only realize your wish of helping me fix my clothes. I'll let the other wishes exist only in your dreams.

I handed the bag over to Xiao Qin and she accepted it happily.

"I'll definitely fix it filled with love."

Xiao Qin made a solemn vow, then she turned to the class leader, who was studying intently, and made a face at her.

Did you think you won because you could fix my clothes? Don't feel too good about yourself, because the class leader wouldn't help fix it even if I begged her.

But Niu ShiLi thought the face was made towards him and it made him jump.

"Xiao Qin classmate, you&"

Niu ShiLi only said a few words, but Xiao Qin's androphobia had kicked in. She turned back around and pretended to be reading earnestly.

It caused Niu ShiLi to become restless for the remainder of the class.

It was pretty hot today, so no one wanted to leave the school, so the cafeteria was packed with people during lunch. Xiao Qin, Xiong YaoYue, Gong CaiCai, Loud Mouth, and Little Smart ended up at the same table as me.

The class leader was discussing something with teacher Yu, but even if she was here, she probably wouldn't want to sit at the same table with me.

It is indeed a bit awkward staying close to a boy who always imagines you in a bikini.

Plus, I wasn't 100% innocent, since the class leader's brother has been wearing the thong for the past few days because of me.

Xiao Qin was on my left and Little Smart was on my right. Gong CaiCai was across from me, right in between Xiong YaoYue and Loud Mouth.

Gong CaiCai usually isn't willing to sit next to Xiong YaoYue. But there were not other spots in the cafeteria, and she couldn't fight against Xiong YaoYue pulling her, so she sat down obediently.

Then she would lower her head and take small bites of her food. Occasionally, she would look up at me, but quickly evade her gaze if I noticed, like she was doing something wrong.

There was bound to be some gossip with this many girls sitting at one table.

Loud Mouth was the first to speak:

"Yue Yue, do you think the girls can take number one in our grade for the volleyball tournament? It seems the class leader is taking it seriously."

"Of course." Xiong YaoYue said proudly, "There's nothing special being at the top of our grade, our goal is to place first in the entire school!"

"Ah, that might be hard. I heard the 3-3 class, the class with the school beauty, has a lot of students who's amazing at volleyball."

"That's nothing. There's no one who can block against the class leader and my perfect team work and smashes. Hmph, if the class leader listened to me and cut her hair short, we could increase our effectiveness by 20%&"

Don't give those kinds of suggestions to the class leader! A girl's hair is precious, especially since the class leader started growing it from elementary school. As a girl, you should at least try and relate a bit to her.

Xiao Qin was relaxed since everyone other than me was a girl. She spoke to Little Smart who was on my right while taking the opportunity to stick closer to me.

"Um, I've been reading some novels. Little Smart, you must have read quite a bit can you recommend me some good ones?"

Rudely calling her by her nickname&. but I really have no right to say anything because I can't remember Little Smart's real name either.

Little Smart said: "I've read quite a bit, but I still prefer novels with Guo JingMing pressed under Han Han's body."

Isn't that BL? Damn fujoshi, don't give Xiao Qin any weird ideas.

"I just noticed." Loud Mouth said while picking out a grain of rice stuck on her hair, "Since Ye Lin is the only boy in this table, shouldn't he be treating us to this meal"

I refused: "Why should I treat you guys?"

Loud Mouth said playfully: "Don't you secretly feel happy with so many girls accompanying you?"

"Hmph, it's not like I invited you." I continued to shovel food in my mouth.

"That's true." Xiong YaoYue suddenly interrupted, "How about this Ye Lin. I'll let you touch Gong CaiCai's breasts and you can treat all of us to some yogurt?"

And she even gave me a wink after she finished speaking.

Damn, so you think it would be fine for me to touch her breasts because I'm gay? And that way everyone gets some free yogurt while my mood would also get better? Is something wrong with your brain? If I was actually gay, touching her breasts wouldn't make me feel any better.

Besides, you already have a bottle of yogurt next to you. Is one bottle not enough?

Loud Mouth was the first one to get excited from Xiong YaoYue's suggestion. Gong CaiCai's face flushed red and she lowered her head.

Xiong YaoYue raised Gong CaiCai's chin and forced her to raise her head while also rudely slapping her chest.

"Genuine goods, available to all." Xiong YaoYue said like a merchant, "Also, Gong CaiCai, don't look so down, smile a bit at the customer. All our yogurt is riding on your shoulders."

Xiao Qin suddenly said: "Ye Lin classmate can't touch it, but if I can touch it, I'll treat everyone to yogurt."

Huh, what's up with that suggestion? Do you think your flat chest would be able to finally grow after you touch her large breasts?

Gong CaiCai begged pitifully:

"Can& you not touch me? As long as you don't touch me, I'll buy yogurt for all of you&"

"Ah whatever, Gong CaiCai, you have no sense of humor." Xiong YaoYue saw Gong CaiCai was taking her seriously, so she stopped playing around.

Xiao Qin still didn't stop trying to attack her breasts, and it almost caused Gong CaiCai to hide under the table.

After a warning from me, Xiao Qin started to act well-behaved again. But the she followed up quickly: "How about I tell everyone a joke?"

"There once was a hunter who went hunting in a forest, then he met a bear&"

This dirty joke again? Aren't you getting tired of telling the same joke? The class leader already said good kids shouldn't tell these jokes.

Xiao Qin continued to speak and ignored me: "The hunter shot at the bear, but the bear was agile and nimbly avoided it."

Loud Mouth looked a bit awkward as it seems she's heard the joke before.

"Xiao Qin, tell a different one, don't say this one in front of Ye Lin or it would make us girls seem perverted&"

Little Smart, on the other hand, was full of interest, "I like this story, the hunter must have fell in love with the bear&"

Get lost you damn fujoshi! Are you treating this as a story instead of a joke? In your eyes, the bear must be the attacker and the hunter must be the receiver, right? It must be a sad and inspriign story of love between a bear and a person. I guess human relationships aren't enough for you any more and you have to extend your BL love onto animals.

When Xiao Qin told the part where the bear avoided the gun shot, Xiong YaoYue had already finished eating and was drinking the bottle of yogurt, but then she suddenly burst out laughing and spit everything out. What's even so funny?

It's fine if you laugh, but you sprayed yogurt everywhere, it's even running out of your nose! Gong CaiCai who was sitting unprepared next to you got covered in white and sticky yogurt! It's now all over her hair, eyebrows, and top like she got bukakked!

Not only did Xiong YaoYue not apologize, she even pointed at Gong CaiCai and laughed and made sure to take some photos to keeps as a souvenir.

"Hahaha, look, doesn't she look like an actor in a Japanese AV?"

She instantly admitted she watches AVs without an ounce of shame. I'm assuming she found it on the hard drives on the computers at the net cafe when playing LOL with her teammates. If you were a guy, this would definitely be considered as sexual harrassment.

Xiao Qin took out her phone like she thought the chaotic wasn't chaotic enough, "I, I also want a photo."

Why are you trying to join in? Have you always been harboring bad feelings for her because her breasts are multiple times larger than yours? Or is it because the spirit of the Little Tyrant is still inside of your and it would only give up when you bully someone.

"How could you do this&."

Gong CaiCai sobbed sadly, then she took a pack of napkins out of her pockets to wipe her face.

"Haha, confiscated." Xiong YaoYue heartlessly snatched away the pack of napkins.

Gong CaiCai wanted to get it back, but Xiong YaoYue pressed down on her head with a single hand and kept her seated. Gong CaiCai could only stare hopelessly at the pack of napkins.

"Return it, I'm& going to get mad."

Gong CaiCai's threat was completely unconvincing, and the white fluid rolling down her cheeks made me have some bad thoughts.

"I'll return it if you call me husband." Xiong YaoYue said with a giggle.

Xiao Qin took the chance to take a picture of Gong CaiCai while they were arguing.

Then she lifted the corners of her mouth with an evil expression on her face.

"Hehehe, now to send this to Eunuch Cao&"

What does this have to do with Eunuch Cao? Or does he already listen to your commands because he recognizes you as my wife? Are you planning to hand that photo to him to make an even more wicked photo to ruin her reputation? What did she ever do to you?

Loud Mouth went to stop Xiong YaoYue while Little Smart put her hand on her breast with an empty expression.

So, it's a bloodbath caused by breast size? Since Loud Mouth had decent sized breasts she got in between the fight of the largest and third largest in the class. But Little Smart who was flat like Xiao Qin stood as a bystander.

"Xiao Xiong, you're going overboard." I smacked the table to get her attention. Since she considers herself as one of my bros, then I have to point it out when my bros make a mistake.

"Huh, really?" Xiong YaoYue scratched her head, "I think it's fine~~"

But what you think is fine is especially awful for Gong CaiCai! It might be a joke you could handle, but Gong CaiCai is almost about to cry!

I took out a pack of napkins from my pocket and handed it to Gong CaiCai.

"Use this to wipe it first, otherwise it would be hard to wipe up the yogurt when it dries."

Gong CaiCai paused for a bit. She was abnormally embarrassed and gratefully received the napkins.

Then I ordered Xiao Qin:

"Delete the photo you just took."

Xiao Qin feigned ignorance: "Huh, I was taking a picture of the cafeteria lady. She looked a lot like Rong MoMo, so I wanted to show my mom."

Lying through your teeth& I mean what's the point of showing your mom even if she does look like Rong MoMo.

I took Xiao Qin's phone and quickly deleted the photo.

Damn, what a wicked photo! If Eunuch Cao made it into an actual cover of an AV, then it could actually be passed as genuine!

When I took a closer look, I found a lot of pictures of me on Xiao Qin's phone. Some of them were of me sleeping on my desk, some were of me playing basketball, and some were of me drinking water in the shade& when did you take all of these! There were about about a couple hundred on her phone alone, so I have no idea how many she took in total.

I angrily deleted all the photos she took of me without my permission.

Xiao Qin couldn't even stop me in time, so she sprawled out on the table and began sobbing but I knew it was fake.

"Boo hoo hoo~~~ Ye Lin classmate&.."

After Gong CaiCai finally cleaned her face and was planning on returning my napkins, but she saw Xiao Qin crying.

Would she think of me as someone who hurts their childhood friend just to help her?

"I'm sorry." Gong CaiCai bowed deeply and apologized to Xiao Qin, "Please stop crying, or I& I&"

It was already hard enough for her to stop crying, but once she heard Xiao Qin cry, she was about to shed tears again.

Xiao Qin raised her head when she heard Gong CaiCai's apologize wihtout a single drop of tears on her face.

"I'll stop crying if you return my breasts."

"Um& that&"

Gong CaiCai actually thought earnestly about Xiao Qin's unreasonable request.

"I'm sorry, I can't do it."

Since Xiong YaoYue didn't actually take a photo of Gong CaiCai, the case was finally dropped.

After some advice from me, 'her best friend', Xiong YaoYue relaized her mistake and bought a bottle of yogurt as an apology. She even said sincerely to her:

"If you're still mad, you can spray it on my face too."

Then she closed her eyes and stood there.

Of course, Gong CaiCai wouldn't actually do it and she said feebly:

"As long as you bully me less later on&"

After lunch, I received a call from Director Cao.

I was originally worried he would want me to steal Ai Mi's underwear again. This time I would have to reject him no matter what even if he offers thirty thousand.

But if you're not especially picky, you can easily get a pair of underwear from Obama with some dog food. But that's not something I would share with Director Cao.

But Director Cao didn't even mention underwear, instead, he wanted to discuss about turning the viral underwear on my head video into advertisement for his series.

I thought Eunuch Cao only said it randomly as a cover up.

"Xiao Ye Zi, my son wasn't only saying it randomly. He might be young but he has a business mindset like me."

That's true, I mean he made a ton of money selling those PS photos.

"I'm planning to officially announcing you as Wu Sheng's substitute actor and invite you to talk on Little People, Big Dreams."

Oh, isn't that the show that invited Su Qiao to talk about the path from a minor actor. It has pretty high viewer ratings.

"Who cares about ratings, it's all about the content. I'm going to also invite your opponent and have both of you wear underwear over your heads, then the ratings would skyrocket."

If I actually did that, I wouldn't have the face to return to 28 Middle anymore.

Director Cao kept hounding me on who the other person was and asked how much money did he have to pay so he would come onto the show.

He's not lacking any money since he's the young master of the entire chain of dojangs! He would never appear on the show or his father's business would take a huge dive!

I refused Director Cao's request and said I didn't know who he was. And I said I wouldn't do it even for two million and he should do it himself.

"I'm fine with wearing underwear over my head. I've already done it on a Japanese game show before& but it's useless if I do it, because only the involved party (you) doing it will attract everyone's attention."

Then Director Cao wanted me to be the main protagonist for his next film, but I suspected it was an AV and directly refused.

The next day was Friday and Xiao Qin reverently returned my Qing Zi Academy uniform with the buttons sewed back on.

What shocked me the most were that the buttons were identical to the original ones. Where did she even get this, it's clearly authentic buttons.

She even sewed the school uniform emblem back onto the chest area. Did she wait in front of Qing Zi Academy and force someone to hand over their buttons and emblem?

Since Xiao Qin has androphobia, then she might have mugged a girl. It makes me feel uneasy thinking I could be wearing buttons stolen from a girl.

Even though the buttons may be identical to the originals, Xiao Qin's needlework is clearly inferior to the class leader's.

Well it's still better than if I had done it myself. At least all the buttons line up.

I wanted to compliment her, but I discovered blood stains underneath multiple buttons.

Then I saw Xiao Qin had band aids on four of the fingers on her left hand.

I mean, don't try to sew if you don't have the proper equipment. And you even said helping me sew clothes was one of your top ten wishes, but you haven't done any practice at all.

Xiao Qin began to pout when I said she lacked practice.

"I'm excited because it's my first time sewing. Why would I practice beforehand, that will only ruin the mood. One of my other biggest wishes is to have Ye Lin classmate's children, and I'm not planning on practicing beforehand."

How the hell would you even practice having kids??

"(*^__^*) Hehe& I accidentally left some blood behind on your uniform. I was originally planning on washing it, but I was afraid it wouldn't dry in time and you would hit me if I didn't bring it on time&"

She said as she covered her face with her arms as if she was afraid of being hit while peeking out at me from the crevice between her arms.

"Whatever." I said, "You already did a great job sewing the buttons, I could wash the blood off myself."

As I saw Xiao Qin's band-aid covered fingers, I couldn't help but ask: "Does it still hurt?"

"It doesn't hurt anymore." Xiao Qin abruptly raised her voice, "Although I bled because of Ye Lin classmate last night and it also hurt, I don't regret it."

Niu ShiLi, who was secretly drinking water behind a textbook, almost choked when he heard her words.

Of course, he was called to go to the blackboard to answer a question.

Damn, don't say something that's so easily misunderstood. At most you only poked yourself with a needle, do you really need to talk about whether you regret it or not?

Xiao Qin asked with a smile:

"Ye Lin classmate, did I do a good job completing the task you gave me?"

"You did okay."

"Then&" Xiao Qin became excited and her eyes were flickering with hearts.

"Shouldn't I get a reward for completing the task?"

Hey, do you think you're playing an online game? Do I even look like an NPC who hands out quests? I'm the protagonist!

"Hmph, what do you want as a reward? I'll treat you to lunch."

"Oh, that would cause too much trouble for you&" Xiao Qin chuckled and waved her hands, but then she turned serious: "As long as Ye Lin classmate marries me."

Marriage? Is marriage less troubling than eating lunch in your eyes? Stop being naive, neither of us are at an legal age where the government would even let us get married. Even if you only wanted to host a wedding reception, that would still be many times more annoying than eating lunch.

When I said I wouldn't get married to her, Xiao Qin asked for a different reward.

"Then how about my second wish& come to my house tonight to practice having a child."

I mean she has dirty thoughts, but she has no courage and she's going to run away again halfway.

In the case where you don't run away, I still can't actually push you down. Although I might want to push you down when my body is burning with desire, I know it will lead to an endless amount of trouble after I calm down. Especially because of what happened between my dad and Auntie Ren&

Xiao Qin called me stingy when I wouldn't have kids with her and she kept pestering me for the rest of the class for other things.

I walked down the hallway towards the washroom with Xiao Qin following closely behind and tugging on my clothes.

"A reward~ reward~, I want a reward (gt;_lt;). It could be exp or equipment, hurry and give me something."

Are you actually treating me as an NPC now? Have you even seen an NPC use the washroom? Do you think I'm just carrying around exp in my pockets?

I stopped near the flight of stairs going up to the third floor and looked around for people, then I patted Xiao Qin's head.

Since I always pet animals on their head as a reward, it should work for someone with low intelligence like Xiao Qin.

I've always thought that girls had colder hair than guys.

Xiao Qin's hair felt as smooth as silk in my hands and it lowered the temperature of my palms.

At first, she thought I was about to hit her so she closed her eyes in fear. But she calmed down after I only patted her head and began to enjoy it.

"I think that's good enough as a reward."

"It's not enough." Xiao Qin had a yearning expression after I stopped patting her.

"Ye Lin classmate has to kiss me as compensation for not marrying me immediately."

She said as she offered her cherry pink lips. She stood on her tip toes and waited for me to kiss her.

Kissing at school? Looks like your getting bolder.

A teacher came out from the male bathroom after catching a few kids who were smoking. He saw Xiao Qin and I standing together intimately but ignored it.

Xiao Qin closed her eyes and stood on her tip toes for at least five minutes and began quivering.

She's definitely faking because she should have a strong core after all her training and wouldn't shake so easily.

But why can't I steel my heart against her pitiful expression.

Shit, I'll kiss since it's not like you'll get pregnant. I mean we've already done a French kiss, so another kiss is nothing.

I grabbed onto Xiao Qin's waist and firmly planted my lips against hers.

Strange. Even in summer, a girl's lips are cooler than mines.

Of course, it's softer too. My hands that was around her waist grabbed on to her even tighter unknowingly.

To an outsider, we would look like two real lovers kissing.

Suddenly, I felt a sucking feeling coming from between Xiao Qin's lips.

What are you doing? Are you trying to drink my saliva? Stop doing something so disgusting. Last time we kissed, I thought your saliva was sweet, but mines is definitely not sweet. Don't drink something so disgusting.

Before having more of my saliva extracted, I grabbed her head and forcibly separated us.

As if she was afraid I would confiscate the saliva she took, Xiao Qin quickly swallowed it with a gulp.

"I'm indebted to Ye Lin classmate's hospitality." Xiao Qin bowed timidly towards me as if she was showing thanks for a delicious meal.

Xiao Qin, your methods of expressing your love are becoming more and more perverted.

I was thinking about how to scold Xiao Qin, but I saw a large breasted girl holding some books who was completely frozen on the stairs because she saw our kiss.

It was Gong CaiCai. Did she see our passionate kiss and even the part where Xiao Qin swallowed my saliva? Last time she saw me kiss the class leader and this time she caught me kissing Xiao Qin. Her ability at catching people kissing is already at a master grade.

"I'm sorry." After a brief pause, Gong CaiCai apologized, "I wasn't watching on purpose, please forgive me."

Xiao Qin, on the other hand, didn't mind being seen. She saw it was Gong CaiCai and said with a giggle:

"No worries, it's not the first time we've done it either& right, Ye Lin classmate?"

I didn't respond. Instead, I interpreted Gong CaiCai's flustered appearance in a different manner.

The last time I helped Gong CaiCai on the bridge with the rabbit sellers and she treated me to McDonald's, she had already stated she hopes I wouldn't cheat. So since she thinks I'm already in a relationship with the class leader, then I shouldn't be acting intimate with Xiao Qin anymore.

But she caught us kissing soon after. And based on Xiao Qin's mannerisms, it looks as if I had conditioned her to swallow my fluids. Gong CaiCai must think that I betrayed the class leader. And when she ran off in a hurry this time, she didn't promise she wouldn't tell anyone.

Is she going to report it to the class leader? Since the class leader always protects her, then she can't stand watching me deceive the class leader.

You the order completely wrong! You should have reported it to Xiao Qin when you saw me kiss the class leader! My womanizer plan was meant to lower my position in Xiao Qin's eyes, not the class leader!

Gong CaiCai, please don't end up getting me killed with your good intentions. Should I ask her to have a talk alone?

As we got closer to the men's washroom, there were more boys appearing in the hallway. Xiao Qin couldn't endure it anymore and ran off when we were ten steps away from the washroom.

"There's nothing special about the men's washroom." Xiao Qin said hatefully as she escaped, "I've been in there many times since I was young."

This reminds me that when we were younger, the Little Tyrant would always go into a cubicle by himself whenever we went to the washroom. I always thought it was because he shit a lot, but I guess it was to hide the fact he didn't have a schlong.

Please stop retelling your embarrassing past as if it's something to be proud of.

In the washroom, I chose the most inner urinal. It's mainly because most boys in 28 Middle would never use the urinal next to me because they think I'm a bad tempered boss who would push them into a toilet if they make me mad. If I choose the innermost one, there would be more urinals for the other people to use.

Today, someone strolled right next to me and pulled down his zipper.

I didn't even need to turn around to know it was someone I knew.

As expected, it was the idol-like Shen ShaoYi. I knew him quite well, but the one point I couldn't stand about him was that he looked cool even when taking a piss.

"Ye Lin, I heard you became the PE committee member for class 2-3."

"Yeah. It seems you're slow on the news, I've already been one for a while now."

"Tsk, why would I take notice of your news? It's only because the captain has been training Niu ShiLi lately so I found out you were the PE committee member. You even made your own team and want to do well in the basketball tournament."

"What?" I laughed, "Is class 2-2 afraid now?"

"Stop joking." Shen YaoYi gestured at me as f to say step aside, "I've been in a lot of tournaments along with Liu HuaiShui. A team you slapped together in a hurry is not our opponent."

I provoked him: "Didn't brother Tao tell you Niu ShiLi is progressing insanely quickly?"

"So what. He's not flexible enough, I can easily get by him with some feints."

"You might be able to handle him by himself." I taunted him, "But if the two of us guarded the net together, do you think you could score?"

Shen ShaoYi rolled his eyes, "Why would two of you guard me, and I can also shoot three pointers."

Because of our competitive nature, the two of us began walking in the hallway together after bragging about our own class.

Shen ShaoYi suddenly stopped, put his hands in his pockets and asked me hesitantly:

"Didn't your class have a female PE committee member. Did she stop after you got the role?"

"No." I also stuck my hands in my pockets but I couldn't even be a tenth as cool as him.

Damn it. Once I become the leader of the world, all men cooler than me has to die.

"We use a two role system where I'm in charge of the boys and Xiao Xiong is in charge of the girls. You have already seen us during gym class, so why did you ask?"

Shen YaoYi shook his medium-cut hair with worry and a few girls in the distance were love struck.

"Does everyone in your class call her Xiao Xiong?"

"That's right. She doesn't like being called her full name, some people also call her Yue Yue."

Shen ShaoYi stopped in front of a window and gazed out at the basketball court. I thought there would be someone really good, so I stopped to watch with him.

But there wasn't even any one good playing. Shen Shao Yi watched the boring game of basketball, then cleared his throat and asked:

"Do you come into contact with Xiao Xiong more after becoming a PE committee member?"

"I guess&" I wasn't really sure what he was fretting about. Was he actually scared of Niu ShiLi and me?

"Ye Lin, do you think Xiao Xiong& has a boyfriend?"

"Hahahaha." I laughed out loud and slapped his back and almost caused his head to hit the window.

"How would Xiao Xiong have a boyfriend? It would make more sense for her to have a girlfriend."

"She has a good appearance and body& but she's too manly, she can't make a guy want to instinctively protect her. Her hobbies are also really masculine, so I would think anyone who wants Xiao Xiong as a girlfriend could be leaning towards the gay side."

Shen ShaoYi's face flushed red, then he glared at me and said irately:

"Don't& say bad things about Xiao Xiong behind her back."

"And I don't have any gay tendencies. I also don't know who said I was a couple with brother Tao, but if I find them, I'll strangle them."

"So&. did you get what I was trying to say?"

Shen ShaoYi returned his gaze to the court and his was red.

Ehhhhhhhhhh.

What's up with this situation? I mean other than the death threat against Little Smart, he also gave a lot of other situation.

Are you saying you like Xiao Xiong and want her as your girlfriend?

And since I'm the PE committee member for class 2-3 and has a pretty good relationship with Xiao Xiong, so you want me to be a mediator?

It's my first big commission befitting of my status as Xiao Xiong's best friend.

I patted Shen ShaoYi with a nasty grin, "Young man, you're finally in heat."

Shen ShaoYi pushed my hand aside, "You're the one who's in heat."

I crossed my arms in front of my chest and said languidly:

"Hey, hey, hey, is that the tone to use with your matchmaker? If you don't respect me, I'll tell Xiao Xiong you said she has a big butt."

"You&" Shen ShaoYi was in a panic, "Nonsense, her butt is a perfect size."

Do you secretly look at her ass or something? It looks like you've been thinking about her for a while.

"Call me brother Ye."

"What& did you say."

"I mean you're already younger than me if you go by birthdays, so it's fine if you call me brother Ye. What, you don't want me to help set you up?"

Shen ShaoYi wanted my help, so he could only helplessly say in a quiet voice: "Brother Ye."

I cupped my hands around my ear and pretended I couldn't hear him.

"Louder, did you not eat breakfast?"

"Brother Ye& is that good."

Shen ShaoYi was panting like he just finished a 100m sprint after he screamed it out loud.

"That's better." I said complacently, "Little brother Shao Yi, you can tell your requests to your big brother Ye."

Shen ShaoYi told me a lot of useless stuff before the bell rang. It was mainly about how he really likes Xiong YaoYue, how he wants to go on a date with her to the ice cream store on the weekends and chat with her or something.

Does he want to confess at the ice cream store? I might not have any experience, but it's true Xiong YaoYue loves ice cream, so he definitely did his research.

Thus I promised Shen ShaoYi I would do my best to invite Xiao Xiong out, but I can't guarantee what happens afterwards.

"It's fine as long as you make her come. I'll definitely be able to move her."

Shen ShaoYi had an expectant gaze like a young girl experiencing her first love.

It seems you still get nervous in front of someone you actually like. I see how you usually coolly reject those crazy fans of yours who fling themselves at you, but why are you stammering now?

After agreeing to pull some strings for him, I returned to class 2-3 while thinking about how to tell Xiong YaoYue. But I saw the class leader walk seriously behind the lectern to announce a class meeting during the self study period.

The topic was: should we buy a class outfit. If so, what designs should we put on the tshirt.

Class outfits are very DIY and emphasizes the personality of a class. Last year, the class next to us got matching outfits, but the class leader felt it was a waste of money since we already had school uniforms.

But this year, when we're watching the volleyball and basketball tournament, matching outfits would give the other students in our class a better sense of belonging. That's why this topic came up again.

There's also a clothing factory that's renting a place in our school that wants to stay competitive with online stores, so it's targeting special promotions at students at low prices while guaranteeing quality.

It's because last year, the class next to us definitely seemed more in sync with their matching outfits, so the class leader brought it up again to get other opinions.

t

Since the class outfit is only a white T-shirt with a pattern, it only costs 35, which isn't even enough for a meal at KFC. That's why all 45 students in our class agreed to buy it.

The main problem was what to write on the shirt, as everyone had different ideas.

"We should have a picture of Luffy hugging Boa Hancock." One person suggested.

"You don't need Luffy, Boa Hancock alone is enough." another person responded.

The class leader's face sank: "We're discussing our class outfits. What does Luffy have to do with class 2-3?"

"We all have to live with rubber." Someone mumbled.

The class leader knocked on the lectern to make everyone quiet down, then she wrote the word 'pattern' on the left side of the blackboard, and the word 'words' on the right side of the blackboard.

The words written in chalk were dignified and graceful and had a calming effect.

"Raise your hand if you have a suggestion. Stop shouting it out randomly."

"I'll write all the patterns and words on the board, then we can vote for the best one."

She might have remembered that her main role was to keep order, so she would be missing a person to count the votes. Thus, she looked at Gong CaiCai who was nearby.

"Cai Cai, you come help me count the votes."

"Me?" Gong CaiCai was reluctant as if the class leader told her to strip in front of the class.

"Yes, you're the learning committee member, and you can write neatly with chalk, so you're the best option."

Gong CaiCai could only walk abashedly next to the class leader. Standing next to the class leader made her appear even shorter.

"Oh right, let me know if you have any good ideas."

"I& I can't think of any good ideas&" Gong CaiCai's voice was as quiet as a mosquito, "I can't say it even if I do think of something&"

The class leader sighed, "If there's anyone as shy as Gong CaiCai, you can pass up your suggestion in a paper slip and we'll help you read it out loud."

There were a lot of unreasonable suggestions for the pattern like Spongebob, Kung Fu Panda, and one person even suggested Che Guevara.

Apparently, because Spongebob had holes all over his body, it made people think of acne, so all the girls vehemently refused. The other ideas like Kung Fu Panda were called unoriginal, but the class leader wrote down all the options on the board.

Xiao Qin expressed her ideas like Doraemon and Hello Kitty through a paper slip. Although it received a lot of support from the girls, the boys were strongly against it, so it was dropped.

The class leader furrowed her brows and looked at the nearly empty blackboard, "Are there any more suggestions for a pattern? It's better if it's related to class 2-3&"

Little Smart raised her hand without spirit: "Why not draw the Star of David and put a 3 in the middle."

"What's the Star of David?" The class leader asked.

"Oh, it's basically a hexagram used in Judaism, and occasionally in some curses&"

Little Smart explained as she glanced at me with hate.

"A hexagram is good, at least it's even&" The class leader mumbled, "Then, does the 3 refer to class 2-3?"

"That's right, and it can still be used even when we enter our third year&"

Little Smart's words made the class leader's eyes light up.

As expected, she thinks like a housewife and tries to save whenever possible. It's worth it if you can wear a ¥35 for two years. It's really sad how your brother likes to show off in front of your girlfriend, 35 USD might not even be enough for his daily expenditures.

"Sounds good." Eunuch Cao suddenly jumped up and said, "Let's use the hexagram, it's awesome."

Everyone looked at Eunuch Cao with doubt as they waited for him to continue.

"Jie jie jie jie& Have you guys seen the Da Vinci Code? In the Da Vinci Code, it says hexagrams are composed of two triangles. The one pointing up represents men and the one pointing down represents women. So our class outfits represent men hooking up with women."

"As for the 3 in the hexagram, it could represent class 2-3 or it could represent the fact we don't mind 3somes&."

"Cao JingShen, shut up." The class leader's cold gaze made Eunuch Cao quickly sit back down.

But the hexagram idea was completely destroyed by Eunuch Cao, but everyone agreed to keep the number 3.

"How about this." Niu ShiLi, "We can use a bigger 3 then add a crown on top of the 3."

Everyone thought it was a good suggestion, and someone suggested: "Make the crown slanted, it would seem more charming."

We orginally thought we were getting closer to the final design, but it looked like the class leader's eyes were being pricked by a needle.

Then, everyone remembered the class leader had OCD. Apparently, the world heritage site she destests the most is the Leaning Tower of Pisa. If one day the tower falls over, the class leader would mercilessly light up a lantern in celebration as all the Italians mourn.

That's why it would be torture to make the class leader wear a shirt with a slanted crown.

The class leader was never willing to admit she had a serious case of OCD, so she tried to have a discussion with an unnatural expression:

"Um& wouldn't it be to informal to have a slanted crown. I mean if we do win, we want to place the crown properly, so it doesn't fall down&"

Although no one said anything, we all knew we would drive the class leader crazy if we made her wear the shirt, so we unanimously decided to adjust the crown.

The class leader sighed in relief and thanked everyone for their understanding.

After deciding on a pattern, we had to decide on what words to write.

Someone suggested "Our class" written in grids.

"Class 2 is already using it, isn't it embarrassing copying them?" Loud Mouth was against it.

The skinny and pale literature class representative stood up and said, "Let's use, Let your dreams fly or Hand in Hand with connected hearts."

"It sounds alright&" someone said, but a portion of people thought it was too cheesy.

We might as well use 'Our Youth'.

The English class representative was a serious girl. She raised her hand and stood up and said:

"We might as well write girl for girls and boy for boys."

"Umm& are you afraid people can't recognize your gender or something?"

A few people sneered at her.

The other suggestions became more and more outrageous, like 'Don't annoy me', or 'It's so hot'&

At this point, someone passed up a noted slip. Gong CaiCai read it out loud:

"Today we're classmates, tomorrow we'll be roommates&"

Her face turned red like an apple in an instant. If it was the class leader, she would have definitely skimmed it before reading it aloud. Everyone already knows it must have been Eunuch Cao who wrote the message. He must feel so proud after teasing her.

"Cao JingShen." The class leader said coldly, "Do you think I can't recognize your writing? Next time we're doing a cleanup, you're in charge of scrubbing the tiles in the hallway."

"Jie jie jie jie, it's still worth it."

Eunuch Cao laughed with no regrets.

Xiong YaoYue suddenly raised her hand and stood up.

"Ban Ban, I have something to say."

"Ban Ban." The class leader frowned, "What did you call me?"

"Hehe&" Xiong YaoYue scratched the back of her head, "Because you always called me Xiao Xiong, so I felt it's more fair if I also give you a nickname. Or maybe I should call you Xiao Ban Ban."

The class leader's face darkened and couldn't find words to say. Why did you stand up if weren't going to contribute to the topic at hand?

I can't believe the most handsome guy in school likes someone who derails a conversation as much as you.

I feel like I don't have a high chance of being the match maker for her.

Some students couldn't hold back a snicker when they heard Xiong YaoYue call her 'Xiao Ban Ban'.

"Xiao Ban Ban& I feel like the class leader loses her threatening aura&"

"That's right, we could even write Xiao Ban Ban and Us on our outfits."

The nickname made the class leader red with anxiety. She bit down on her lips and announced solemnly:

"I have never been in support of giving classmates nicknames, so I won't accept it. If anyone calls me by that name, I'll ignore them. In short, I won't allow anyone to call me by that name."

"Okay, okay~~" Xiong YaoYue replied unenergetically, "It took me a while to think of it, so I thought you would be happy."

She plopped back down in her seat with regret.

In the end, we decided to write 'We were together that year', but the words would go on the back with only the 3 with a crown on the front.

Even if the class leader didn't like the nickname, there were still some naughty girls like Loud Mouth who would purposely use the wrong name when calling the class leader& like "Ban& class leader". Every time this happens, the class leader would grind her teeth and try to ignore the ones who did it.

I couldn't help but imagine class leader in elementary school where her nickname was actually Xiao Ban Ban.

Whenever I think of a little and young class leader, I can't help but regret at not attending the same elementary school as her.

After we finished our class meeting, Xiao Qin showed me the class outfit she designed.

Of course, it was another potato. This time, it was a smooth potato with the number 3 written on top of it.

"It's too simplistic." I gave my opinions, "The crown should stand out more&"

Xiao Qin added a few scribbles and drew a crude crown on top of the potato with my advice.

"Now it stands out more." Xiao Qin awaited my approval with expectancy.

"Tsk, if you had a lot of ideas, why didn't you mention them in the meeting?"

"It's because there are too many boys in our class. I can't walk to the front of the class and write it on the board in front of all the boys, but I'm afraid they won't be able to understand the deep implications behind my design if I pass it up with a slip of paper&"

What deep implications? Besides, the idea of the 3 with the crown was someone else's idea. The only original aspect you added is the potato!

During lunch break, I wanted to have a chat alone with Gong CaiCai and tell her not to tell the class leader about how I kissed Xiao Qin. But she was always with other girls and became afraid whenever I got close, so I could only put my plans on hold.

Since I can't complete this task, then I would have to focus on my other task.

Which was to let Xiong YaoYue know that the most handsome guy in the school, Shen ShaoYi, wants to date you.

I don't think Xiao Xiong would mind if I get straight to the point.

I found her rinsing her foot in the sink near the exercise fields because she had sand in her shoes.

"The water's pretty damn cold." Xiong YaoYue muttered to herself.

"It's because Dong Shan city uses deep groundwater." I followed up on her words.

"Oh, it's you. You scared me." Xiong YaoYue said, "I thought it was the head teacher, if I got caught by her rinsing my feet in the sink, she would send a warning and scold me again."

"I mean it's not a big deal, but the class leader would be furious if our class dropped points and my ears would have to suffer."

So you were trying to get back at her by calling her Xiao Ban Ban behind her back? If you're afraid of getting your ears pulled, then stop rinsing your feet here! This is where all the dudes usually come to wash their feet, so a girl being here by herself is really graceless.

After taking a closer look, even though her skin was tanned golden brown, her feet was still their original color. Her skin might not be as white as Gong CaiCai, the class leader, Xiao Qin, but it's definitely whiter than mines.

There was a clear line of distinction separating the two colors. So Xiong YaoYue wasn't naturally dark-skinned.

"Did you need me for something?"

Xiong YaoYue didn't mind it when I stared at her feet for quite a while.

Of course, I wanted to let you know Shen ShaoYi wanted to go on a date with you, or did you think I came here to watch you wash your feet?

"Xiao Xiong, did you know, Shen ShaoYi, he&."

Xiong YaoYue laughed out loud before I finished my sentence.

"I know, hahaha it's already been spread between all the girls. One of them even posted it in our school's newspaper and named it 'Uncovering the secret of Shen ShaoYi's relationship, he loved someone he shouldn't love'. It was hilarious."

Huh, did it get leaked? Did his female fans hear because I was speaking too loudly with him? But, why are you laughing, the person he likes is you! Even if you don't have any intentions of getting into a relationship, you will still be a target for over half of the girls in 28 Middle.

"Xiao Xiong, be serious. He's planning on having a serious relationship."

At this time, Xiong YaoYue had already washed the sand off her feet. She wore her shoes and socks and hopped in place a bit before saying:

"Let's not waste time. I'm going to run a few laps around the track, we can talk while running."

I could only run along with her at a medium pace bracing the winds:

"Xiao Xiong, if you already know about it, then you should give him a reply."

Xiong YaoYue seemed to be happy while exercising. She picked up her pace while yelling into the wind:

"You, should, call me Winnie."

"What?"

"Because Winnie sounds fashionable and high end. I want everyone to call me by that name."

Another evasive answer? I can kind of understand how the class leader felt on the lectern now. I was asking if you agree to go on a date with Shen ShaoYi.

"Okay, I'll call you Winne. But you have to honestly answer my question." I surrendered to her and said: "What do you plan to do about Shen ShaoYi?"

"Eh, what does Shen ShaoYi have to do with me?"

Xiong YaoYue exclaimed.

"Are& you trying to piss me off? Didn't you say you already knew everything? If you already know everything, then you should give a reply."

"Why do I have to give him a reply?"

Are you going to ignore him and give him some neglect play? I never knew Xiong YaoYue would know this tactic.

Shen ShaoYi was still one of the members of the basketball team, so I decided to put in some more effort.

"Winnie, Shen ShaoYi already expressed his feelings, so you should at least&"

"Ye Lin, what's going on? Why are you making it as if I have some sort of relationship with Shen ShaoYi&"

"Well, you guys don't have one right now, but we can't say anything for the future&"

"We won't have a relationship in the future either. I hate it when he flicks his hair and I have no interest in pretty boys. Besides, doesn't he belong to you?"

"Wait, what did you say?"

Xiong YaoYue stopped by the sand pits and looked back at me strangely.

"Ye Lin, you're really dishonest. I mean even the school news people know about it, but you're still trying to keep it a secret. We're supposed to be brothers."

I stood there blankly as she criticized me because I had no clue what she was talking about.

After seeing my face full of grievances, Xiong YaoYue ran back and patted my shoulder to comfort me.

"Don't worry about it. I'm assuming you're a bit embarrassed, so your older sister Winnie will forgive you."

Who's my sister? Let me repeat myself, I'm older than you.

"I was only guessing before that your lover was from our school& but I never expected it to be Shen ShaoYi. No wonder Shen ShaoYi ignores all the girls who show him affection, it's because he's your partner. I see you guys quarrelling on the basketball courts, but I guess you were actually flirting."

My god I'm pissed. What are you talking about? The one Shen ShaoYi likes is you! Even if he was actually gay, his partner would be captain Guo SongTao, not me!

Did you hear that rumor from Little Smart? I can't believe it already spread across the entire school in one morning.

Xiong YaoYue did some stretches while asking:

"But according to them, it seems you were on the attacking side. I thought you were on the receiving side before, or are you alright with being both?"

Who's the one spreading these baseless rumors?!! I mean it can't be Little Smart because she always supports captain Guo SongTao with Shen ShaoYi.

I tried to calm down a bit before speaking to her again:

"You& can't be more wrong. Shen ShaoYi likes you, so he asked me help him pull some strings with you."

Xiong YaoYue burst out laughing as if she heard the funniest joke in the world.

"Ahahaha, why would that pretty boy like me, I don't even know him."

He only likes you because he doesn't know you. Haven't you heard the phrase 'distance makes the heart grow fonder'? Xiao Qin and I are too familiar with each other that we've even used the washroom together. I would never fall in love with someone who would crawl into my cubicle after he's done using the washroom and snatch the toilet paper.

I kept retelling her Shen ShaoYi's words until she felt I wasn't joking anymore.

"Isn't he your lover, why would he ask you to speak with me?"

"I'm not gay, how many times do I have to tell you that?"

"I understand." Xiong YaoYue clasped her hands together, "Is Shen ShaoYi dumping you?"

What did you understand? What kind of twisted logic is that?

"Isn't it obvious? He wants his own lover to play the matchmaker, you must be so hurt to be forced to play as the matchmaker."

Nope, you're overthinking it. I'm not hurt at all, but I already gave up on your intelligence level.

Xiong YaoYue clenched her fists and cursed:

"Shen ShaoYi is awful. He clearly likes me, but he would use me as an excuse to dump you. As expected, all pretty boys lacks a good conscience."

"I mean I don't even like him, but even if I did, I would never betray my best friend. Tell Shen ShaoYi that I would never steal my best friend's lover."

She once again patted my shoulders to comfort me.

"Don't be down. Even if you were unlucky and ran into scum, you will still meet your true love in the future. I'll always be there to support you."

"Um& actually my captain for our game team is a pretty elegant man, should I introduce him to you?"

No, but thanks for your good intentions. I feel like I'm too tired right now to ever love again.

I returned in low spirits to pass on the bad message to Shen ShaoYi.

"Why." Shen ShaoYi clenched his fists, "Why won't she even give me a chance?"

"Accept your fate&" I advised, "Actually Winnie might be misunderstanding something about you&"

"Winnie, who's Winnie?"

"Ah, it's Xiao Xiong, it's a new nickname she likes& the reason she rejected is because she thinks you like men&."

Shen YaoYi's face distorted and he kicked a basketball rack, "I don't like men, it's all baseless rumors. There's nothing going on between me and the captain."

No, actually the recent rumors already paired us together, but I'm too ashamed to tell you.

"Anyway, Winnie will ignore until you clear up the misunderstanding& so the priority is to prove you're not gay&"

"How would I prove it?"

"Um& I don't know either& how about you accept one of the female's who's chasing you and get together in front of Winnie&"

"How could you even think of that? She might not think I'm gay, but she would definitely think I'm a playboy."

We had a lengthy debate on the basketball court on how to prove we weren't gay and it troubled us for the entire afternoon.

In the afternoon's language class, we got back the essay we wrote in class yesterday.

The topic of the essay was 'My FatherMother'. Even the topics the teachers think of are more progressive and consider people like me who only have a single parent.

Although Ai ShuQiao's story would be much more odd and interesting, there's no way I could write about her.

Thus, this was how I started my essay:

"My father, Ye YuanFeng, is a noble man who's detached from poor taste hobbies."

You can't say running an adults goods store is considered a poor taste because all we're doing is helping lonely men and women in releasing their stress and reducing sex crimes. I think other than the police, we're also partially responsible for keeping peace. I think it's already good enough we're not asking for payments from the government.

But the parents of my classmates should have normal jobs. Even a person who sells noodles is more impressive. (I'm not looking down on people who sell noodles. When I was in the third grade, one of the student's parents sold noodles but they went to vacation in the Maldives every summer.)

Should I have to write about how my dad always conducts business honestly. For example, he would never substitute a Japanese AV vibrator motor with a Chinese one. Even all the complimentary gifts (lotion, condoms, etc&) he gave away were all quality goods with none of them past the expiry dates.

It would be way too embarrassing if I write that. In class 2-3, Xiao Qin and Eunuch Cao are probably the only ones who know what my family shop sells. The other students only heard my family runs an online store.

Besides, if the language teacher, old man Zhang, finds out, he would look down on me even more. He already looks down on me because of my ugly handwriting.

So I decided to freestyle, it's actually one area I'm pretty good at in writing.

I raised my pencil and began to write:

"My father was the lead designer of the Shenzhou 10. The spaceship he designed has lasers, magnetic cannons, particle cannons, atomic cannons, etc&"

"The American government was scared witless, so they sent female spies into China to seduce my dad to handing over the secrets. But he was a noble man and rejected them, thus earning praise from his colleagues&"

"My dad single-handedly protected our country and he was crowned a captain like Li ShuangJiang. Now all our neighbours refer to my dad as general Ye&"

"So I'm general Ye's son. If you don't give me a good grade, I might end up doing something like Li TianYi&"

"Basically, my dad's awesome. I'm already at the word count, so the end&"

Now that I look at it, the essay I wrote was a complete mess. I think I wasn't in a good mood because I accidentally gave the bikini to the class leader. I wonder what kind of criticism I received.

I took a look and old man Zhang drew a big X at the end of my essay and said:

"All utter nonsense."

"First of all, Zhang BoNan was the designer for the Shenzhou 10, it has nothing to do with your father."

"Also, Li ShuangJiang isn't even a general. China has never had a civil general, don't believe everything you see online."

Damn, why did you have to correct this many times in a 400 word essay?

I wasn't sure if I was the only one who made up lies on the essay, but old man Zhang wanted us to go home and have our parents sign the essay.

Good thing I didn't say my dad was superman. I mean it's still bad I said he was the designer of the Shenzhou 10, but I think I could trick him into signing it.

I saw Xiao Qin also frowning, so I took a glance at her essay.

Surprisingly, the opening of the essay was:

"My dad is a famous actor&"

Huh, was Xiao Qin's dad an actor? How come I didn't know about it? But I have heard that Auntie Ren only became a martial arts instructor after getting married.

Maybe, unlike me, Xiao Qin's parents still have a good relationship after getting married. But normally, shouldn't she be writing about her life with her mother?

The next line said:

"My mother is a world-famous mangaka. Her penname is Celery sensei&"

Oh, so she wrote it from the perspective of our future child, not herself.

Although I don't have any confidence in becoming a famous actor, but it's still more possible than her becoming a world-famous mangaka. It looks like I would have to work hard or my family of three would starve.

"My father and mother are always very lovey-dovey. Regardless if they are in the kitchen cooking, watching TV on the sofa, or looking at the scenery on the balcony, they would always embrace each other. Then, I would get sent to my room to study, so I don't know what they did next&"

Shit, are you saying I would be in heat 247 after getting married?

"Because I would frequently be sent to my room to study, I was able to finish a lot of books and graduate at 13&"

A child prodigy created due to the parents' lewdness? I'm not sure if I should be proud or ashamed.

"One of my mother's hobbies other than creating manga, is to bring me to the police station to find a woman with long black hair. She would make me call her auntie and ask 'Class leader, when are you planning on getting married?'"

Trying to show off in front of the class leader? Looks like you let your true thoughts slip out in your imaginary world.

"Also, my dad pushed my mother down at the table. I had to go study halfway through the meal and I may end up getting a younger brother or sister&"

Is this how you teach your kids? What if it sets a bad example?

Ahhh, milk powder is already really expensive, it looks I have to work much harder. It was already hard enough raising a dog.

Wait why am I being distracted by her essay?

Old man Zhang's comments were even more eye-catching:

"You need to get checked out."

He's pretty wise since he could instantly tell Xiao Qin is sick. I also support sending her to a research center to get proper treatment.

"Sigh." Xiao Qin sighed, "It looks like I have to put the essay in my drawer time machine and hope my future mother will sign it&"

Do you have a time machine in your drawers. If you do, you should go back in time and tell your younger self to not bully yourself as much. That way, I wouldn't have my current face and you might have a sliver of chance of becoming my wife.

Xiao Qin hung her head down the entire way home. She wasn't sure how she would be scolded after her mom sees the essay.

It was easier for me to get my dad's signature, but either my dad had to come home or I had to visit his hotel.

I decided to visit his hotel without giving him any notice. Firstly, it would be a good surprise. Secondly, it would be a sudden inspection to see if he's been drinking a lot while I wasn't around.

As I went home to grab some things, I noticed the black sunglasses Ai Mi gave me before.

According to Captain Guo SongTao's analysis, the main issue of my scary face lies between my brows. I'm always used to knitting my brows, so it always looks like I'm angry. And my eyes seem to be always saying 'death to those who offend me'.

That's why if I cover my eyes with sunglasses, people might mistake me as a good person.

Since I don't have anything important to do today, I might as well wear sunglasses outdoors and give it a try.

I was wearing my sunglasses, carrying my bag, and about to call a cab when a grandpa swayed towards me.

"Young man, do you know how to get to Pu Tai Nan road."

Some& someone's asking me for direction. A grandpa with a full head of white hair and a weak body didn't avoid me, instead he asked me for directions.

Ever since I got my current appearance, no one has ever asked me for directions.

The only time was when an elementary schooler asked me directions to a net cafe when it was dark out. But he ended up kneeling down and begging for his life when he got a clearer look at my face.

It's been at least two years since someone asked me for directions.

I can't believe my current self would also be able to experience someone asking me for directions. I'm so touched that I started to cry.

The grandpa almost regained his youth as he jumped back when he saw tears streaming down my face.

From then onward, a weird love story about Pu Tai Nan road began to spread around Dong Shan city. It was how a young man would cry tears of sadness every time he hears the words Pu Tai Nan road&

What's there to be sad about? There's nothing on Pu Tai Nan road other than the pet hospital, a cafe, and a hotel.

Am I crying because I didn't take the class leader to the hotel while she still had a favorable impression of me?

If I actually did that, I wouldn't be forgiven if I cry, but I would for sure receive a bullet straight between my eyes.

I decided to head to head to the supermarket to buy some things before I head to my dad's hotel. One reason is because I could show that I'm managing the store properly and have enough profits to buy presents. The second reason is in case my dad refuses to sign my dumb essay, I could use the gifts as a bribe.

I thought as I walked to the Wal-mart near my house. It was close to Qing Zi Academy and it's the same place where I bumped into Ai Mi who had sneaked out to buy chips.

I don't think I would bump into her today. I already called yesterday and it seemed her cold was slightly better. But it seemed the worst part was she still had to act even when she had a cold. It looks like you have no more human rights once you enter show business.

There were a lot of people on Friday night, but luckily I was able to get the last shopping cart. The people behind me gave me dirty looks as they had to take the hand baskets.

But I was happy they weren't afraid of me. It's all thanks to the sunglasses. It was able to transform their treatment towards me from a criminal to a regular student.

I hummed the tune from Jet Li's Fist of Legend as I strolled around the store.

What should I buy for my dad? I can't but smokes or alcohol, so I guess I should buy some high end tea.

I went to take a look at the prices at the tea area, but the prices were outrageous. The tea prices varied from ¥500 per lb to ¥800 per lb. The most outrageous one costed ¥5700 per lb. At that price, you might as well go and rob a bank.

In the end, I decided to go with an oolong tea that costs ¥250 per lb. I bought around 165g for ¥75, just the right amount to put in a small tea box.

After taking the tea, I wandered around into the snacks section.

The chips were now in a lower position, but there were no signs of Ai Mi.

Whatever, chips aren't really healthy, so it's better to have less of it.

I asked myself if I should buy my dad some snacks like beef jerky.

My dad already quit smoking before he got married. He was also afraid of second hand smoke for me after getting divorced, so he didn't smoke again. The reason why I'm buying snacks is not to help him quit smoking.

And if I give him jerky to help him quit drinking, it would probably have the opposite effect since jerky pairs well with alcohol.

Well, it doesn't matter. At least it would be better than him drinking on an empty stomach.

Thus I put four packs of jerky in my shopping cart. The kid next to me sent an envious gaze towards me.

Based on how he was only holding one bag of crackers, it seems his mom only allowed him to choose one bag of snacks. But the jerky isn't even for me, I'm buying it for my dad. But he wouldn't believe me even if I told him.

But now that I think about it, I haven't actually properly eaten snacks since the start of the year.

In order to become the strongest to defeat the Little Tyrant, I was training in every single area, including limiting snacks, but eating more proteins and vegetables. I even forced myself to begin to eat yogurt.

The bright and dazzling snacks section really brings back memories.

But the one think I think about the most aren't the chips, but the animal crackers I ate as a child.

I've known animal characters before I even met Xiao Qin. Every time I eat one I would always check what animal it is. Elephants and whales are always the largest, and it's always a shame when the giraffe's neck snaps off so easily. I would admit animal characters were more of my childhood friend than Xiao Qin.

Also, there are a lot of ways to eat animal crackers, including dipping it into milk. Nowadays, supermarkets don't really sell animal crackers anymore. Goldfish doesn't count since it's only fish, and it doesn't taste as good because of the hollow inside.

I squatted down to see if I could find any animal crackers on the lower shelves.

After looking around, I actually found a large bag with the words animal crackers printed on it. A child usually wouldn't even be able to carry it, is it prepared for people who are reminiscing like me?

But after I took a look in the bag, I realized there weren't any elephants, whales, or giraffes& except a few indistinguishable animals, there were a lot of turtles. Why is it a turtle? Is the owner a turtle lover? Mihgt as well call it turtle crackers instead of animal crackers.

I took a look at the manufacturing location and it was Beijing. The productions company was Green Giant Foods Ltd.

I guess having a bag full of turtles would be considered green enough.

I put down the bag of turtle crackers and went to the stationery section to get a pack of Chinese chess for my dad. That way he can play with uncle He whenever he visits my dad.

I got two bottles of sport drinks from the fridge and began drinking one while walking. I subconsciously arrived at the pet goods section.

This really brings back memories. I'm not reminiscing about the products, but my dog. Back then, most people didn't feed pets actual pet food, but fed them our leftovers from meals. One of the reasons it got sick and passed away could have been because it wasn't food made for dogs.

I stopped in front of the dog food section feeling a bit emotional. I wanted to use a time machine to send this food back into the past.

At this point, I saw a kindergarten girl who skipped towards this area. She stood on her tip toes to reach the dog food, but it's obvious she couldn't reach it.

I think since I was wearing sunglasses and could pass off as a good person, I would soon receive a request for help. I promise this time I won't cry.

Otherwise, there's going to be another weird love story spreading around about dog food.

I was waiting for the little girl to say: "Big brother, can you help me get&", but to my surprise, she said: "Big sister&"

Damn, what's wrong with her eyes? This is why you shouldn't watch so many cartoons, otherwise you would have severe myopia before you even start school. I don't think I would look like a big sister even if I was wearing ten pairs of sunglasses.

When I was still puzzled, I realized the little girl was asking someone else for help. A girl wearing 28 Middle's uniform with long hair took the dog food the little girl pointed at and gently handed it over.

Eh, doesn't this familiar white arm belong to the class leader?

"Than you, sister." The little girl ran back to her mother with the dog food in her arms.

The class leader and I only realized we were standing really close after the little girl left and we both felt a bit awkward.

"Why are you in the pets section?" The class leader blurted, "I thought you didn't have a pet?"

"Sigh, that's unreasonable. Are you saying I can't look at pet goods if I don't have a pet? According to my knowledge, you don't have a pet either, I mean other than Shu Zhe."

"My brother isn't a pet."

Oh right, that's because a pet has more of a conscience than your brother.

By the way, how did the class leader not notice me standing over here?

Was it because she keeps dreaming about having a dog, so she began wandering in the pet goods section?

I mean it's a pretty simple dream to realize. All you have to do is find a newborn puppy, then stay with it every day and it would definitely get accustomed to your hunter's eyes. Or are you afraid to keep it at home because Shu Zhe bullies small animals?

I might be able to persuade the class leader to abandon her worries and just start raising a puppy, but I don't rights to say it to her when I lost the courage to raise another pet after my dog passed away.

It might be a good thing the class leader can't raise a dog. If you never have a dog, then you would never have to experience the pain as it leaves you.

The class leader then began to ignore me after she finished speaking. She stood motionlessly in front of the pet goods as if she was waiting for me to leave first.

What, do you think it's your loss if you leave first? When did we come to the point where we always have to compete in everything?

I noticed the class leader wasn't able to get a hold of a shopping cart. She had around thirty cartons of milk in her hand held basket.

All the cartons of milk and the big discount sticker on it. So she heard there was a milk promotion here and came all the way here to buy it. She must have spent quite a bit of time riding her bike all the way.

It's definitely heavy with all those cartons of milk inside. After holding it for a while, I could see her arms slightly quivering.

I called out to her: "Hey, I still have a lot of space in my cart, you can put your basket inside."

The class leader looked at the empty space with a hint of jealousy, "How did you get a cart?"

"Hahaha, I was fast and got the last one." I boasted.

"Hmph, since you're so strong, you should have left the cart for elderly or people who need it."

"That's not true." I pointed to my sunglasses, "I seem blind with my sunglasses, so everyone left the cart for me. Besides, am I not sharing the cart right now?"

"Who wants to use the same cart as you? I still haven't finished shopping yet."

"I haven't finished either." I persuaded her, "I'm not in a rush anyway, so we can just share the same cart."

The thirty cartons of milk must have been quite a burden on her. She thought about it a bit before putting her basket in the cart. But our stuff was separated clearly with hers in the back and mines in the front.

And at the same time she looked at me angrily. Was she still upset about yesterday when I gave her the bikini?

I pushed the cart as the class leader walked behind me as if she was escorting a criminal. And just like this we began our weird supermarket trip.

At first, the class leader kept her vigilance and didn't want to walk side by side with me. Instead, she chose to walk a meter behind me. And anytime someone looked at us, she would increase the distance between us.

"Class leader, aren't you tired?" I asked, "Are you afraid of people misunderstanding? Do you also do this when you come and shop with Shu Zhe?"

"People can instantly tell we're siblings if it's Xiao Zhe. But if it's you&"

"What about me?" I was curious, "What do you think others will think of us as?"

"Older sister." The little girl who asked the class leader to help us get some dog food passed by us again with her mother. She grabbed onto the sides of the class leader's dress and said playfully: "Your boyfriend's so tall!"

The class leader's face turned red and she quickly denied it.

"He's not my boyfriend. We're just regular classmates."

"Miao Miao, stop messing around." The girl's mother called her to go back, "Let's not interrupt them shopping for their dinner."

Huh, the mother was even worse than the little girl. The little girl at most thought we were dating, but in the mother's eyes, we were already living together. Even my face turned a bit redder.

But I was a bit pleased. I actually dressed up today to visit my dad and used sunglasses to cover my eyes.

Now I can even be mistaken as the class leader's partner.

The class leader got a bit upset after she saw my pleased expression.

"Give my stuff back." The class leader grabbed the cart, "I don't want to share a cart with you anymore."

"Ah~ the young couple is fighting."

The young mother covered her laugh and left with her daughter.

I gripped the cart handles tightly to prevent the class leader from stopping the cart, "Stop messing around. If you make a scene, then everyone would think you have a relationship with me. I'll just keep pushing the cart quietly and you can pretend I'm your brother."

"I don't want a brother who's as out of norm as you."

"Hey, I didn't even say anything yet. I think you're an out of norm sister."

The class leader stopped.

"What, how am I out of the norm?"

She cast an angry look at me.

"Do you think I'm too tall?"

Huh, most people would think it's better taller. And you're already the tallest girl in class 2-3. But you haven't yet reached the status of joining the female basketball team. The main reason is because you have a well-proportioned body, and you don't feel like a giant woman, unlike Yao Ming's wife, Ye Li. The main reason people fear you is due to your Justice Devil aura and not your body size.

"I guess you're considered tall compared with your brother. But you're only average in front of me. But Xiao Qin, on the other hand, only reaches my shoulders and it feels awkward when we walk next to each other."

I then realized I was implying I didn't feel awkward when walking with the class leader and I didn't want to talk anymore.

We then had another hard to bear period of silence.

At this point, we unintentionally passed the female underwear section. Based on the class leader's expression, it seems she's remembering the time I gave the bikini. If I don't give her a convincing reason, she'll think I'm trying to something perverted again.

"Ahem." I cleared my throat, "Actually, yesterday was a misunderstanding."

"What was?" She asked knowingly.

"Uh, how I accidentally put the underwear along with the Qing Zi Academy uniform&"

"&.."

I resolved myself and admitted to the class leader:

"Class leader, there's actually one thing I've been too embarrassed to tell you."

The class leader was scared and moved back a step. She put her hands out in front of her as a defense mechanism.

"What is it? Why do you have to say it in the supermarket&"

"Actually& actually my family runs an online store."

The class leader breathed a sigh of relief, but also seemed a bit disappointed.

"Sigh, I already know your family runs an online store. I heard you guys sell toys for children?"

No, they are all adult toys, not toys for children. It's because those grown ups can't find partners to make babies with, so they can only play with toys all day.

"Actually& it's not toys for children. My dad sells something pretty embarrassing&"

"It's not embarrassing if it's legal work." the class leader said righteously, "You shouldn't look down on your parents' work or it would make them sad."

"Actually, my family sells women's underwear&"

The class leader's face turned red.

Good thing I didn't tell her the whole truth about how my adult goods store is ranked pretty high and even employs her brother as a rope model. But we do indeed sell women's underwear, so it's not a complete lie.

"That bikini underwear was something I was packing for my dad and accidentally dropped in the bag before I left in the morning& it definitely wasn't a gift for you&"

"It's because my mother was an terrible person. She ran away with another dude right when I was born. My dad suffered a large enough shock that he quit his job as a university professor and began holed at home selling women's underwear. He would frequently get dead drunk and I would have to run the business&"

"I originally never liked my dad's store, but I don't really have a choice& I even accidentally showed you one of our store's embarrassing goods yesterday, can you forgive me&"

I followed Shu Zhe's advice of acting more submissive and sneaked glances at her reaction.

Huh, her eyes are filled with empathy. Does she feel empathetic because she's also a left behind child without parents? And my situation is worse than them, because their parents are a loving couple who's working their hardest to bring their kids with them to Shanghai.

"So what you're saying is that you've never had motherly love?" the class leader asked with a bit of hesitation.

It looks like we're completely past the underwear issue. It seems Shu Zhe was right and to deal with his sister, we have to make her empathetic.

"I mean it's not entirely correct." I laughed, "My father acted as both my mom and dad and raised me since a baby& other than the fact his job is a bit embarrassing, he treats me pretty well&"

The class leader held her hand under her nose with slightly red eyes. It was obvious she thought I was forcing myself to smile and be a good person.

"Ye Lin& do you get into fights because your mother abandoned you?"

No, I only trained to become a Spartan to take revenge on Xiao Qin for beating me up every day. It has nothing to do with Ai ShuQiao.

But based on the current situation, the best thing to do is nod.

The class leader sighed after my tacit approval as if my words resolved a lot of her suspicions.

"It's not embarrassing even if Uncle Ye sells women's underwear. It's not like our parents are in complete control of their own jobs&"

She seemed to be a bit sad, maybe she was thinking about her own parents who were currently thousands of miles away.

"But you can't give up on yourself even if you're lacking motherly love. Do you know how scared I was when you almost pulled out their eyes in the fight you had back in the alley."

"Scared?" I was a bit puzzled, "Even if I poked their eyes out, I would be the only one going to a juvenile detention center. It has nothing to do with your or are you afraid of being called as a witness?"

The class leader's right hand twitched as if she wanted to slap me, but she held herself back in the end.

"Anyway& I won't allow anyone from class 2-3 to enter juvy."

"Also, I won't allow you to lose hope in humanity. You may not have received motherly love, but& eventually there will be someone who will treat you well&"

I frowned, "Who's going to treat me well?"

The class leader hesitated a bit, then said after biting her lips:

"Doesn't Xiao Qin like you? She's already told us many times before you're the only person she will marry. Although it's not okay for middle schoolers to date so early, but you guys are childhood friends, so it's not weird to get together&"

What, why do I have to compensate for my lack of motherly love from Xiao Qin? Stop joking, I've never felt inferior for being a child of a single parent family as a child. But I have felt inferior for being beaten up by the Little Tyrant everyday. If I had a time machine, the first thing I do wouldn't be to go back to the time when Ai ShuQiao abandoned me, but find the Little Tyrant and threaten her and say if she keeps bullying me, I would expose the fact she's a girl.

I chuckled and left the class leader baffled.

"Don't believe Xiao Qin's nonsense. I can end up with anyone except Xiao Qin."

"Is it because she lost your little brother?" The class leader still stood on Xiao Qin's side.

"No, didn't I already say I don't have a brother. My mom abandoned us right when I was born, so where would I get a younger brother? Do you think my brother was sent to us in the mail or something? Why would my dad even raise a child of unknown origins?"

"Then& the photo by Xiao Qin's bed&"

"That's not my brother, it's me. If you don't believe me, I can show you old pictures of me and my dad."

"Impossible." The class leader shook her head, "That's a photo of a cute boy&"

So it can't be me because he's cute? It still hurts me even if it's understandable.

"It's me. I looked good when I was a kid, but my face grew deformed, it's as simple as that. If Harry Potter can grow up deformed, then why can't I?"

The class leader analyzed my words and began to think it's possible I didn't have a younger brother.

"Why did Xiao Qin lie?"

"Because she's moronic."

"That means your kids won't be ugly either."

Huh, why are you talking about my kids?

The class leader also realized there was something wrong with her statement, so she changed the topic.

"Since you never had a younger brother, then that means Xiao Qin didn't lose your brother. Then why can't you accept her?"

"There's not really any good reason, it's just& because we're too familiar with each other. We even know how many times we wet the bed as kids. I can't really date her, but only treat her as a sister."

Actually, she's the only one who knew how many times I wet the bed. The Little Tyrant even stuck a note on my back that said 'bet wetter'.

"Then does Xiao Qin know you don't want to progress as lovers?"

The class leader asked cautiously.

"She does." I lied to the class leader, "But what can I do if she's moronic and refuses to give up."

The class leader brushed a loft of hair behind her ear and it seemed she was in deep thought.

"Turn left here."

The class leader, who had been following behind me and going with the flow, gave out her first orders and brought us to the kitchen and bath area she was interested in.

The class leader stopped in the kitchen and baths section for a while. She was mainly interested in looking at dish towels and garbage bags. She also stopped in front of some discounted food containers, but in the end she didn't take any.

Then, her attention was taken away by the half-off oven mitts. She held two pairs in her hand and meticulously inspected the differences.

"I'll be done soon, don't worry."

The class leader said as she inadvertently treated me as her younger brother.

Her face turned red instantly. It wasn't that bad she mistook me as Xiao Zhe, but the tone she used was like a kindergartner trying to amuse a child.

Shu Zhe, do you usually always make your sister worry and always pace back and forth behind her when she's shopping?

But it's true girls take a long time when they are shopping. The only reason I'm so patient today is because I want to increase my popularity with the class leader and because she's wearing a skirt.

I'm definitely not trying to say that every time she bends down, I would always try to sneak a glance to see if I could see underneath.

But the class leader is like a seasoned veteran who's experienced hundreds of wars. She would even inadvertently cover her skirt, so I couldn't see anything.

But it was still pretty exciting looking at her legs while trying not to be caught.

After finally selecting an oven mitt, the class leader put it into the cart. No, after placing it into the basket, she told me she was done shopping and we could checkout after I was done.

I quickly took two boxes of toothpicks of the shelves then pushed the cart towards the checkout counters.

"Is that all?"

Since I waited quite a while for her. The class leader felt bad since she didn't have to wait for me.

"No problem." I said, "Men usually move faster than women. Tens of thousands of years ago, men would be hunting while the women are in charge of gathering. Fruits won't run away if you move slowly, but prey will."

"Oh, is that so, looks like you have a pretty chauvinistic attitude." The class leader's tone was indifferent, "Let's compete at who's better at hunting if we ever get the chance."

Sh& shit. I forgot the class leader's family has a hunting background. Once she picks up a rifle, all prey would fall, even me as her competitior may run into some mishaps.

Why did your forest ranger uncle even teach you how to shoot? Does she want you to be huntress with a sniper when facing your boyfriend who betrays you, instead of an innocent mushroom picking girl?

There were a lot of people at the checkout counters. I swept through aisle 1 to aisle 9 and they were all the same, so I lined up at the end of a random isle.

I got thirsty after shopping, so I took one of the sports drinks from the cart and took a sip, then I passed it towards the class leader and asked:

"Do you want a sip?"

The class leader looked back at me silently as if she was awaiting for me to realize my mistake.

Not& good. Asking the class leader to drink something I already drank is an indirect kiss. Since I always spend too much time with Xiao Qin, I forgot other girls may mind these things.

But the class leader didn't care about the indirect kiss.

"How can you drink it without paying first?"

"Huh, but that's what everyone does. Doesn't everyone eat at a restaurant first before paying? It's not like I'm going to put the bottle back after drinking it&"

"Anyway, the order is incorrect."

Then what would be the correct order? Do you have to get so fussy over a drink?

I pointed at the other bottle of sport drink in the cart.

"If you don't want to have an indirect kiss, then you can drink that new bottle&"

"The problem isn't about the indirect kiss or if it's a new bottle." The class leader continued to lecture me, "The drink belongs to someone else before you pay for it, so you can't infringe on someone else's property."

Stop please, is there a need to make it a serious matter? The aunties behind us in line are all laughing at us.

Also, do you not care about the indirect kiss or if it's a new bottle because we've already kissed? Now that I think about it, your lips were sweeter than this drink.

When it was finally our turn to check out, the class leader rushed first to put her basket onto the counter and said:

"Separate bills, we're not together."

Who said we were together? Why are you being so sensitive? The cashier looked between me and her and thought we were a couple who was in a fight.

After scanning the class leader's goods, the cashier said slowly:

"We have a promotion right now where you can enter the lottery if you buy at least ¥100 of goods, but you're currently short ¥9&"

As the class leader was hesitating, I put my stuff onto the counter, "We'll pay for it together, then we can enter the draw."

The cashier took my money before the class leader could stop him and printed the receipt. The cashier was pretty happy since he didn't have to create a separate order.

As I was waiting in the customer service line with the class leader to enter the draw, the class leader paid me her half of the bill.

Then, to my surprise, she took the unopened bottle of sport drink from my bag and took a sip.

"What are you looking at?" she said confidently, "Count the money again, I already paid you for this bottle, so now it's mine. Why can't I take a sip of my own drink?"

Of course it's fine. I'll let you drink it even if you didn't pay me. If you were thirsty, then you could have taken a drink before we paid for it.

The win rate for this Walmart lottery is pretty high. Usually, you would win a plastic cup or a bottle of green tea. As it was our time to enter the raffle, the uncle in front of us won a handcart. I said to the class leader:

"My luck's not that good, so you can draw it&"

The class leader felt a bit awkward, "My luck's not good either&"

But we're not really expecting a big prize, so she stuck her hands in the raffle box and randomly pulled out a ticket.

We never expected the worker to excitedly call his colleagues after revealing the ticket:

"Ahh, it's the first prize! Our store also won the first prize. We should call Xiao Sun to show off."

When the worker gave the ¥500 gift card to the class leader, she stood still on the spot and wasn't used to the gazes of envy from the surrounding customers.

"I've never even won a balloon before&"

The class leader mumbled in a quiet voice.

I was also a bit shocked, but it was ¥500 not ¥5,000,000, so there's nothing odd about winning once in a while. Once when my second aunt went to a pharmacy, she won a ¥4000 flat screen TV.

"Wow, your luck's pretty good." I applauded to celebrate and she felt a bit embarrassed in front of all the people.

"If I was drawing, I definitely wouldn't win anything. I'm well known for being unlucky. Every time I would draw BOSS for Xiao Ding, I would always pull trash cards."

"Xiao Ding, the university graduate who never talks to me?" The class leader frowned, "Do the two of you always play online games together?"

"No, I just occassionally play for him. Anyway, you have pretty good luck to pull the first prize, you should take the gift card."

"No way." After we left the customer service desk, she said seriously, "We won it together so I shouldn't take it all for myself. And my luck is bad, if I was by myself, I wouldn't even win a bottle of green tea&"

"That's odd." I pushed the shopping cart towards the exit and said, "Does our luck improve when we're together?"

The possibility of my statement caused the class leader to think for a bit before she said:

"We would have to wait until after the basketball and volleyball tournament to see if our luck improves when we're together."

What does those two have to do with each other? We've always been in the third class together. If we could have won by being together, then we wouldn't have lost so miserably in last year's basketball tournament. or are you saying we weren't 'together' since we weren't both working hard?

"Plus, if you're not against it&." the class leader waved the gift card, "If the basketball team and volleyball team reach their goal, I'll use the gift card to buy snacks for everyone as a celebration. But if we don't hit our goals, then I'll return the entire card to you."

Huh, so if we win, you take our money to treat everyone, but if we lose, you will give all the money to me? Isn't the reward and punishment a bit strange?

After leaving the superstore, I volunteered to help carry her stuff to her bike. She laughed but didn't refuse.

I suddenly had a question I've been thinking about for a while and couldn't help but ask:

"Class leader, let me ask you something but don't get mad. Do you not worry about getting exposed when riding a bike with a skirt?"

The class leader pulled out four small clips from her skirt pocket and placed it on her palm to show me.

"What's this for?" I scratched my head.

"As long as you use these clips in the right places, the skirt will turn into shorts. That way you wouldn't expose yourself and perverts like you can't sneek peeks."

Who's a pervert? How am I a pervert for reminding you out of the goodness of my heart?

I looked towards the class leader's familar sky blue bike and noticed a suspicious fatty about to do something to her bike.

Is he a thief? Where are the security guards? But the class leader's bike is already old and there's a brand new mountain bike right next to hers, so why is he stealking the class leader's bike?

Wait, this fatty seems familar. I think he's also from 28 Middle, a third year in the student council called Zuo Xiong or something& Apparently he did wrote the class leader an anonymous confession before, but he foolishly dropped his student ID in the letter. Then the class leader had to return his ID while simultaneously rejecting his confession&

After I took a closer look, his hands weren't even near the locks. It seems he wanted to take off the bike seat. He was even getting closer and sniffing it while removing the seat. Does he want to take the seat home and use it as a pillow?

I got angry, so I rushed towards him and shouted:

"Let go of that bike seat!"

The fatty, Zuo Xiong, was too devoted to stealing the bike. He didn't even notice the class leader and I get closer before I spoke.

Hurry up and stop! If you take the seat and only leave a steel pipe, what if the class leader sat directly on it since it's already dark out (although the chances are slim), what if she gets injured?

His body trembled when he heard my shout, then he looked at me with gloom.

He didn't recognize me at first since I was still wearing my sunglasses. It was the class leader who was standing behind me that made him panic.

Ah, what a familiar sight. The class leader is finally using her special of gaze of looking at someone as if they were trash on someone else other than me.

Zuo Xiong received a large psychological blow when he saw the girl he likes look at him with contempt. He abandoned the bike seat and ran away. He shouted out loud while running away:

"I'm not Zuo Xiong, you got the wrong person!"

No one even said you were Zuo Xiong, why are you revealing it by yourself?

"Should I chase him?" Since I was holding a lot of stuff, I asked the class leader for her opinion.

"No need." The class leader sighed, "It's not like he took the seat off&"

A new situation occurred after she spoke.

Right when Zuo Xiong was escaping with a wrench in his hands, there was coincidentally a traffic police officer dealing with a DUI driver. Zuo Xiong collided right into the officer.

The police officer was a lanky newbie who was getting nervous when the DUI driver threatened him by saying he has connections. It didn't really matter that Zuo Xiong collided into him, but the wrench in his hands scared the officer.

"Ah, assaulting an officer?"

The police officer said as he reached for the baton on his waist.

"It's a misunderstanding, I'm not assaulting an officer!"

Zuo Xiong ran away crying and screaming. The DUI driver took the chance to slam on the gas and escape, but he crashed right into Zui Xiong and sent him flying onto a cart of watermelon. The scattered watermelon dyed his entire body in red juice.

Since Zuo Xiong is a schoolmate and human life is beyond value, the class leader ran ahead first to take a look.

I followed up from behind and saw Zuo Xiong lying on a cart of scattered and broken watermelons. He might have a mild concussion and he thought he was a goner when he saw his body dyed red.

Zuo Xiong reached out one of his trembling hands towards the class leader, but she took one step back in disgust.

"Is this 120 (Ambulance), there's someone here who was hit by a car. The location is&"

The class leader still made a call for the emergency care services.

Seeing as the class leader ignored him, Zuo Xiong turned towards me and said:

"A doctor told me I had high blood sugar during a physical but I didn't believe him, but I never expected my blood was actually sweet&"

That's watermelon juice, not blood. Since the class leader was the one who called the emergency services, the watermelon vendor was currently pestering the class leader hoping she could repay him.

The class leader explained to the watermelon vendor: "In traffic accidents, the culprits are the ones who have to take full responsibility."

After hearing the class leader, the vendor went to pester the DUI truck driver.

"Pay me for the watermelons!" The vendor tried to block off the escaping truck driver while holding a melon knife, "Don't even think about leaving without paying at least a couple thousand."

The driver who was wearing a sweaty shirt filled with the stench of alcohol said: "Do you think you're selling Xinjiang cakes?"

"Put away the knife." the police stepped between the two men, "Let's finish the discussion in the police station."

Zuo Xiong believed he would soon be leaving the world as he lied in the watermelon remains. He continued to speak to me in a dazed state:

"I can't receive Sha Sha's love in this life, but in the next life, I'll definitely become&"

Don't call the class leader with such a corny nickname. According to Shu Zhe, only her parents call her Sha Sha.

"In the next life, I'll definitely become&. Sha Sha's bike seat&"

A bike seat? If you're going to die, at least make a more ambitious dream!

After finishing his sentence, he turned his neck and die&. no, fainted.

I thought since Zuo Xiong's family name was Zuo (TL: Zuo means left), his face should be facing the left, so I helped him correct the mistake.

I turned around and wanted to get credit from the OCD class leader, but she didn't notice my actions.

I then remembered something important. I passed the two bags temporarily to the class leader and retrieved the wrench from Zuo Xiong's hands. I returned to the class leader's bike and tightened the bolts under the bike seat.

"Now it's safe." I patted the bike seat and waited for praise from the class leader.

Huh, it looks like the class leader doesn't really want to praise me. Did it look like I had perverted intentions when I patted the class leader's bike seat?

The class leader coughed quietly and reminded me: "You can return his wrench."

I glanced at the scene of the accident. Since there was a hospital nearby, the ambulance had already arrived and Zuo Xiong was being lifted into the ambulance.

"Why would you return it, so he can come back to remove your seat?" I teased her, "I already did him a big favor by removing the evidence of him assaulting a police officer."

Thus I put the lethal weapon into my shoulder bag.

The class leader didn't say anything else. She put her stuff in the cart on her bike and began riding away.

"It's the weekend tomorrow. Don't only focus on having fun, make sure to finish your homework."

She warned as she rode away.

"Will you let me touch your butt if I finish all my homework?"

I thought in my head as she rode away while nodding my head.

It was already eight when I checked my watch. I quickly called a cab to head to my dad's hotel, otherwise the signature would have to wait until tomorrow.

Since the class leader took the last bottle of sport drink. I was a bit thirsty and sat through the car ride without speaking much to the driver.

We soon arrived in front of the hotel. It was a bit dark inside the car, so I took off my sunglasses to look for money in my bag.

The previously cheerful driver shivered as he saw my appearance through the rear view mirror.

Man, this wrench really gets in the way, I shouldn't have put it in my bag.

I first got the wrench out of my bag.

The driver was already feeling nervous, but he started sweating bullets when he saw the wrench and begged:

"I don't need any money, please forgive me!"

"I have an 80 year old mother and a wife and child who's not even a month old. They would all starve to death if you take my life!"

Why are you treating me as a murderer? In the end, I still gave the money to the driver and also handed him the wrench. I patted his shoulder and said:

"Driver, you can keep the wrench for self-protection."

The driver was moved and said to me with tears:

"I never thought there would be good people in organized crime too."

Damn, give the wrench back. Don't step on the pedal and speed away as if I'm going to fill your car with bullet holes!

Anyway, it was my first time at this hotel. Maybe it's because it's located near the East District University, a lot of university couples would open rooms here.

In order to not be mistaken as a wanted criminal, I wore the sunglasses again.

The front desk was pretty relaxed since they were busy checking in couples. All I told them was that I was looking for my dad and told them his room number and they let me through.

In order to train my body, I took the stairs to the second floor instead of the elevator.

Right as I reached my dad's door and was about to knock, I heard a women's voice.

Ah, so my dad was finally influenced by Director Cao and called a prostitute. Not only did he call a prostitute, he's refusing to pay. Although I have some money in my wallet, it's kind of overboard letting a son pay for his dad's prostitute fees.

But after listening closely, it seems the women was Auntie Ren.

"Return the necklace. It was something my mother left for me and has a lot of sentimental value."

The other yes-man voice was obviously my father.

"I never took your necklace. Maybe you lost it somewhere else?"

"No, I never take it off even when I sleep. It must have been Saturday night& when it got shook off. You must have hid it!"

"I didn't& if it's a silver necklace, it might have been taken by the cleaners&"

"Then go and get the security footage, I want to see who took it."

"Um& I don't think there are cameras in rooms. Otherwise, what we did on Saturday night would have been all recorded&"

"Shut up, didn't I say to not mention it?"

"Yes, yes&"

"Yes, what? Are you having improper thoughts about me? Why did you invite me out for a meal?"

"No reason. I just wanted to get closer since we are old neighbors."

"What old neighbors? There's no relationship between us, do you think I would actually like you?"

"&.."

"Listen closely. Don't you sell adult goods? Last Saturday night, I only treated you as an adult toy and used you once."

My dad feebly reminded her: "It was four times&"

I could even imagine Auntie Ren's face flush red from behind the door.

"So what if it was four times, or are you asking me to pay?"

"No, even if there was a fee, it would be me paying&"

"What did you say?"

"No, nothing, I said I was wrong&"

My dad admitted his mistake again and it really made his Spartan son embarrassed.

I stood outside the door and listened in to the conversation between my dad and Auntie Ren. Not long after, I could feel someone walking quickly towards the door.

I quickly retreated and pretended like I had just arrived. As expected, the door opened and Auntie Ren walked out angrily with my dad following from behind.

"Hong Li, don't panic. You might not have lost it in the hotel&"

Auntie Ren was furious: "Who allowed you to call me by my name? Do you want to die?"

Although I was wearing sunglasses, my dad still recognized me instantly.

He pointed towards my direction, "Not in front of the child&"

He was extremely quiet so Auntie Ren could only hear the word 'child'.

"What?" Auntie Ren's expression changed, "It wasn't enough that you got it easy but now you want a kid? I already took a lot of the Plan B the next day so there's no way I would have your kid."

As I got closer, Auntie Ren realized she let her tongue slip. She stared at my dad and me before walking down the hallway. I'm assuming she went to look for the manager to ask about the necklace.

My dad and I looked at each other with a bitter smile as I walked in.

"Dad, did you really not hide Auntie Ren's necklace?"

"Of course." he spread open his hands, "It's not like I'm the cowherd from the cowherd and the weaving girl."

"That might not be the case." I mumbled, "The cowherd was a lumpenproletariat, and you're an AV reviewer&"

Well, jokes aside, I'm here to do business.

I offered the beef jerky and tea leaves to my dad with a smile. My dad was suspicious before I even brought out the essay:

"You did something bad, didn't you?"

"No, no." I said while passing him my essay, "I may have told a few lies but I hope you won't mind."

My dad glanced through it and said:

"I do indeed have some classmates who took part in Shenzhou 10's design, but it has nothing to do with me!"

"Also, you said America sent a female spy to seduce me, so where is she?"

Wait, that's the line you're unsatisfied with? Then you can temporarily consider Auntie Ren as a spy.

"You even said I have a general rank, and threatened your teacher you would do the same thing as Li Tian if you don't get a good grade&"

"Li Tian had a lawyer, but I can't afford one for you. And I'll be the first one to break your legs."

"Even though I could kind of be considered a general&"

Wait& what did you say? When were you able to become a general without me noticing and why didn't you tell me sooner? If you're a general, then you must have the authority to get an armored vehicle. Lately, my harem doesn't look like it's going well, so hurry up and lend me one so I can hide from the class leader and Xiao Qin.

I grabbed my dad's collar and asked for one, but he changed his words:

"It's not a real general. It's because I purposely complemented North Korea in a recent AV review, so the HHH club president was happy and gave me a general title&"

"Of course, the president didn't speak with me directly, it seems his Mandarin isn't that great. It was actually a representative called General Cui who told me, but his Mandarin is pretty strange too&"

"Besides, Director Cao was also given a rank of general by the president. I'm assuming it's some sort of inside rank for the club."

What's the point of calling yourself a general if you don't have an armored vehicle?

I felt regret that he couldn't move an army, but he still easily signed my essay while complaining:

"Next time don't lie, also this jerky is a bit too hard&"

No problem. The next time I lie, I'll bribe you with softer jerky.

I slept at my dad's room that night since he had two beds anyway.

We chatted late into the night. Other than making fun of my sunglasses, my dad asked about Auntie Ren's interests.

Is he really planning on chasing Auntie Ren? Is he determined to make Xiao Qin my sister?

"Dad, did& you let go?"

I didn't have to state it explicitly, but I was obviously referring to how my dad still didn't let go of the relationship with Ai ShuQiao.

The hesitation in my dad's eyes made my heart sank, but he still said energetically:

"Maybe& it's time to let go&"

Nope, it seems he still hasn't let go. Ai ShuQiao's poison still hasn't fully left his body. Back when I was watching animals on the Discovery channel, I thought platypi were the only mammals with poison, but I was hugely mistaken. It turns out all women on earth has poison, and the prettier they are the deadlier the poison.

But compared to Ai ShuQiao, Auntie Ren's poison is more gentle. I guess you have to fight fire with fire. Compared to letting my dad falling into a deeper abyss of sadness, it's better to help him get Auntie Ren.

What a difficult task. Even if it succeeds, I can't tell if it will be a blessing or a curse.

But I'm really looking forward to the expression on Xiao Qin's face when she becomes my stepsister.

I've already been with Xiao Qin for so long that I would be a bit worried if she's not near me, so might as well make her my sister.

I had a wonderful dream that night. In the dream, I was on a picnic with Xiao Qin after she became my sister and we bumped into the class leader.

The class leader called me over under a tree and told me she had something to tell me with a worried expression.

What's there to be worried about? If you like me just say it outright. Since you're advocate of being frugal, we can just skip the wedding and head straight to bed&

The class leader's words shattered my dreams: "Actually& I'm also your little sister&"

Damn, it woke me right up. A beautiful dream turned into a nightmare.

Also, the class leader's older than me by one day. Even if it was a contrived situation where she became my sister, she would technically be my older sister.

The next day I did a bit of homework because of what the class leader told me on Friday.

I'll do my homework properly, but please don't be blood related, that's my only request.

I suddenly realized that the class leader's poison had unknowingly seeped into my body.

Will the Justice Devil also use poison like other woman? It doesn't really match her nickname.

I shook those thoughts out of my head. I parted ways with my dad after lunch since he still has work to do.

He already wasted a lot of time with the quarantine and the stuff that happened with Auntie Ren. It's a good thing Uncle He is reasonable and didn't pressure him with a deadline.

Don't betray Uncle He's hopes for you. Use the time you would spend reviewing AVs to do your work properly. I mean it's useless to befriend your club's president to receive an empty title.

I gave Xiao Qin a call since I was bored on my way home.

"Ye Lin classmate?"

I could hear the sound of water form the other side.

"I'm currently washing my hair, so I can't open my eyes&"

Don't pick up the phone if you're washing your hair. And you also picked up so fast, do you even carry your phone with you into the washroom?

"If you're washing your hair, then I can call back later&"

"No& it's okay. The washroom is filled with steam, so it's not cold. What did you want to talk about?"

Why would she say she's cold in this weather? Is she&. taking a bath? Did she pick up the phone in the nude?

"Ye Lin classmate, I can take pictures with my phone~"

"I know. It can only take pictures other than looking good, it can't even go on the web. Why did you bring it up?"

"(*^＿^*) Hehe& if you want, I can take a picture of myself right now and text it to you~?"

Who wants to see you covered in bubbles with your eyes closed? If your eyes aren't open, then the picture probably wouldn't be clear. And if you can't see properly you might not even send the picture to the right person. God forbid, what would happen if you accidentally sent the photo to the class leader or Auntie Ren?

After declining Xiao Qin, I asked:

"Xiao Qin, do you know what Auntie Ren usually likes?"

"Huh?" Xiao Qin was baffled but then couldn't hold back her laughter.

"Ye Lin classmate& are you trying to curry favor with your mother-in-law? I never expected you would be so traditional&"

"& you don't have to worry about it. Even if my mom disagrees, I would still force her to let me get married to you."

Stop dreaming, I'm trying to curry favor with my stepmother, not my mother-in-law.

I wasn't able to get information on what Auntie Ren likes, but she did tell me: Auntie Ren hates being controlled, hates despicable behavior, and hates unfaithful men&

My dad isn't the type who would lock their wife at home after getting married. I think one his special trait is to become a henpecked male regardless of who he marries.

Despicable behavior doesn't apply since he can even sell adult goods honestly and righteously.

As for unfaithfulness, he would never be unfaithful. When I was 7 or 8, there would always be a young woman with glasses and braids (I found out later she was my dad's student) who would always come to my house to ask my dad life questions. She would even give me candy to raise my affection level. Now that I think about it, she probably wanted to be in a teacher-student relationship with my dad. My dad was worried about wasting her time, so he purposefully acted rude towards her. He was finally able to send her crying and she never come back again.

But my womanizer plan would incite Auntie Ren's rage. It seems I still need an armored car to protect against the class leader's gun, Xiao Qin's machete, and finally Auntie Ren's flying kick.

A clear crisp sound of a slap on water brought me back to my senses.

"Hehe, Ye Lin classmate, can you guess where I slapped to make that sound?"

Stop making me listen to weird slapping sounds, just tell me what Auntie Ren likes.

"If you have to know what my mom likes, then that would be me&"

"What?"

"Mothers like their daughters best. So as long as you treat me well, my mom will like you&"

I'm not doing this to chase after you, it's so my dad can chase your mom! Or are you telling me my dad should take you to an amusement park to get on your mom's good side?

In the end, I wasn't able to find what Auntie Ren likes (other than Xiao Qin). But it seemed Auntie Ren was anxious over losing the necklace passed down from her mother.

At this time, the taxi had reached my neighborhood. I told Xiao Qin to finish her shower and hung up.

"Ah, how did you know I was taking a shower?" Xiao Qin feigned surprise, "Now you know I was chatting with you while naked& how embarrassing."

My ass! You were the one who said you were going to take a picture and even slapped weird places to purposely make me hear it. Wait until I become your brother, then I'll teach you a lesson.

At night while I was managing the store, Uncle Fireball complained about why the kiss balloons have not yet come out. Right when I was answering a female customer's questions about energy consumption of vibrators, my phone rang.

It was from Xiong YaoYue, but under her intense demand, I changed her contact name to Winnie.

"Winnie, what do you want?"

I spoke on the phone with Xiong YaoYue while using our store's chat to reply to the female customer:

"I recommend Pisen rechargeable batteries. To be honest, I often use these batteries&"

That's right, I was using the account with the Lilac username to pretend to be a female. Otherwise the customer might feel too awkward if she was speaking to a man.

But in order to keep my mind healthy, I decided to gradually transition all the female customer service accounts to Shu Zhe, even if I have to raise his wages.

Ah, but how am I going to explain this to my dad? I mean it's fine I hired a worker, but he's a trap, so my dad might even question my sexual orientation.

"Ye Lin, why are you so absent-minded?" Xiong YaoYue sounded a bit displeased, "Are you jacking off right now?"

"&.."

"If you are, then I'll call back in 5 minutes. 5 minutes should be enough, right?"

You're the one who takes 5 minutes! A Spartan like me needs at least half an hour.

Coincidentally, the female customer asked: "Can you put this model into the ass? I love my wife, but I don't want to injure her&"

Damn, so she's a lesbian! If you love your wife, then stop shoving this stuff down her ass. I mean, it's a Western model! Do you want your wife to get a prolapsed anus?

I quickly typed: "Please don't use this for anal, otherwise your wife would break up with you."

At the same time I muttered: "At least, my ass wouldn't be able to handle it&"

Who would have expected Xiong YaoYue to hear my mutter.

"Ass?" Xiong YaoYue's spirit instantly surged, "Sorry, I forgot you were gay. Of course you wouldn't jacking off, you're probably doing a prostate massage, are you& using a cucumber?"

"Uh Winnie, what did you call me for?"

"It's nothing important. I just wanted you to come with me tomorrow to go to Miss Ai Mi's place to apologize."

"Are you going to apologize because you skipped our meeting to go play games last Sunday? That's your own problem, why do I have to apologize with you?"

"Help me out, aren't we bros?"

Good things she didn't call me a good sister, or I would have hung up.

"Fine, I can accompany you since I was planning on going too. But Ai Mi is pretty busy, are you sure she has time tomorrow?"

"I'm sure, I just gave her a call." Xiong YaoYue said with endless excitement, "I'm a bit nervous since it's my first time visiting a rich household."

It looks like Xiong YaoYue still thinks Ai Mi is simply a rich kid and doesn't yet know her celebrity status.

"Oh right, what should I wear tomorrow? I think shorts would be a bit disrespectful, should I wear a long dress? I think I still have a pair from elementary school&."

Do you think you would still be able to wear a dress from elementary school, do you think you're the hobbit? Besides, you got three bandages on your face during volleyball practice, even if you dress virtuously, the bandages would show your true self.

There's no way she would also have a face full of band-aids on the day she wears her wedding dress, right? If that's the case, relatives would definitely think of domestic violence. He'll be the number one enemy of women and dragged out and fed to the dogs.

"It's 34°C tomorrow." I reminded her, "So whatever you usually wear. You already know Ai Mi is my& one of my relative's kid. I treat her place as my own home, so you can just treat it as visiting my home."

"Uh, that's a good idea&" Xiong YaoYue came to an understanding, "Then can I get some good food if I go there tomorrow without eating breakfast?"

Didn't you just say you were a bit nervous? Just wear whatever you want and eat whatever you want, as long as you don't criticize the French chef's cooking and make him commit suicide.

As I think about the French chef who inherited the tradition of committing suicide, and the prized katana he received from the Japanese chef, I decided to give Xiong YaoYue a heads up:

"You can eat whatever you want, but&"

"What? Do they not give us drinks?" Xiong YaoYue seemed disappointed.

"No, you can drink as much as you want, but you can't bad talk the French chef. It's probably better to praise him or something bad would happen."

"French chef? Does Ai Mi have a French chef? I heard French food is delicious!"

"Hey, did you hear me? You have to praise his food!"

"Relax, as long as someone's treating me to food, I'll definitely praise it unless it tastes as bad as shit. Otherwise they wouldn't treat me to food anymore."

You say it as if you actually tasted shit.

"Oh, I heard miss Ai Mi lives in Qing Zi Academy, why does she live there? The security doesn't even let me in. I'll go look for you first and you can think of a way to get me in."

Really, Ai Mi was the one who invited you but she didn't think of a way to let you in? It's practically the same scenario as when I went there the first time to give her the exercise book.

"No problem. You can come to my place in the morning and I'll think of a way, but do you know where I live?"

"Hehe, I didn't know at first. I wanted to ask you, but your phone was busy. But I just gave the class leader a call and was able to get it."

"Huh, why did you call the class leader?"

"Why not? She's read the student registers and knows where most of our classmates live. Why are you as suspicious like the class leader?"

"Was she?"

"That's right, I asked for your address but she wasn't planning on telling me. She also asked me 'Didn't you say you didn't want anyone interfering with Ye Lin's love'?"

"&."

"The class leader really holds a grudge. If I wasn't a loyal friend, I would have just told her you were gay and your partner was Shen ShaoYi."

Woah, don't say that. I already worked really hard to slightly improve the class leader's impression of me. If the class leader actually believes you, then realizes I gave her brother women's underwear, then she would think my target is her brother. She might even think I've already pushed him down multiple times, then& do you even need to ask, she will pull the trigger without any hesitation!

"Hmph, since the class leader was being petty, I asked her in response: Why do you care if I visit Ye Lin? It's not like I'm going out with him. Are you being so sensitive because you like him?"

"Eh, then how did she respond?" I was quite curious.

"Hahaha& of course she denied it. There's no way someone as strict as the class leader would go against school rules. Besides, it would be a tragedy if she actually likes you since you aren't interested in girls."

Who's not interested in girls, please don't deprive me of one of my hobbies. Even a Spartan like me would occasionally secretly read some H manga.

"Anyway, the class leader didn't hang up after she told me your address as if she was waiting for me to confess my crimes& I didn't know why but I felt kind of bad, so I told her I was going with you to visit your rich mixed-blooded cousin&"

"The class leader also seemed interested when she thought of your doll-like cousin. I asked if she wanted to come, but she sighed and said she wasn't welcomed. Then she told us to have fun and hung up."

Is she referring to how she isn't welcomed by Ai Mi? The reason the class leader likes Ai Mi is the same reason as why the class leaders likes dogs and cats. And the reason why Ai Mi is afraid of the class leader is the same reasons why dogs and cats are afraid of the class leader. What an awkward relationship.

Plus, the class leader was already to brutally pet Ai Mi's pet, Obama, before even meeting Ai Mi. She might be pretty shocked after finding out the dog belongs to Ai Mi.

If I get a chance, I'll defintiely make sure Ai Mi and the class leader get on good terms. After all, the class leader will be her future sister-in-law.

I set a time to meet up with Xiong YaoYue for tomorrow morning and hung up.

I thought about it and didn't want to disturb Ai Mi, so I gave Peng TouSi a call. Other than a walkie talkie, he also carries a cell phone where he has been using the jack D to hookup with men.

"Peng TouSi." I got straight to the point, "Can you come to my house tomorrow morning?"

"Okay." Peng TouSi seemed to be pleased beyond expectation, "Lin, did you hear that I wasn't really successful at getting hookups, so you want to comfort me?"

"No, I want you to pick up me and Winnie. Ai Mi inivited us over, but Winnie doesn't have a uniform, so she can't get in."

Peng TouSi may be built like a tank, but he's really scrupulous. He even remembered Winnie was the nickname Ai Mi gave Xiong YaoYue.

"No problem, I'll pick you guys up at 7, right? Please don't eat breakfast, we will prepare everything."

You don't need to worry since Xiong YaoYue wasn't planning on eating breakfast anyway.

"Plus to make it convenient for the future, I'll also bring a Qing Zi Academy uniform for Miss Winnie. I saw her once before and still remember her size&"

I remembered last time I was really hot when wearing the uniform while fighting young master Xu.

"Peng TouSi, is the Qing Zi Academy uniform the same as 28 Middle where they have summer and winter variants?"

"Nope. There's only one uniform, but there's a removable inner lining. In really cold days, you can also replace it with a wool lining&"

Oh& is that so? That's why the uniform felt more sturdy than normal. It turns out I've been using the winter lining the entire time. Damn, I'm dumb, I almost got a rash the last time I wore it.

After speaking with Peng TouSi, I took out the uniform from my closet and removed the lining that was held up with hidden zippers.

So this is its true form, what a high quality material. It will definitely feel good standing under the AC. Last time I visited Ai Mi, I just put up with the heat since it was for my sister, but it was completely unnecessary.

The next morning, I didn't have to go by the lakeside to train, so I did 100 push-ups after getting up. Then after washing up, I sat quietly in the living room thinking about the meaning of Yin Yang Sanshou while waiting for Xiong YaoYue.

Not soon after, I could hear someone running up the stairs outside. I'm assuming their running shoes was cushioned properly, so it didn't bother the neighbors.

It was needless to say that the energetic Xiong YaoYue had arrived.

I opened the door for Xiong YaoYue before she even knocked.

As we discussed prior, she was wearing an outfit that was suitable for her.

She was wearing a T-shirt with the Superman S symbol in the front and a pair of denim shorts. It really accentuated her proportionate body figure created from long periods of exercise.

"How does it look? Would it be too rude to be dressed like this?"

She breathed a sigh of relief after receiving my approval and began to smile.

I noticed there was only one band aid left on her face compared to the three I saw on Friday. Maybe the other two were taken off because her wounds had already healed.

Why does it feel like her recovery speed is even faster than mines?

Not only is it faster, it's also more effective. Every time she injures herself, it heals within two to three days without even leaving any scars behind.

It's just not the same for me. When I was taking a shower this morning, I realized I had three light scars on my back. I may not have been crushed by the tree that day, but my skin still got cut open.

Of course, I don't mind since scars are medals branded on the flesh. Also, I obtained it by saving my sister, so I would show it proudly to others wherever I go.

I checked my watch and it was 6:40. Peng TouSi should be almost here, so I didn't waste anymore time and headed downstairs with Xiong YaoYue.

After she saw me wearing the elegant uniform with a tidier hairstyle than usual, she said:

"It looks like clothing makes the person! You look much more coquettish than usual."

Coquettish? Would it kill you to call me handsome? Peng TouSi is going to bring you a female Qing Zi Academy uniform for you later and I want to see how you rate yourself.

Since Peng TouSi is very punctual, I brought Xiong YaoYue to wait at the entrance of our neighborhood at 6:50. I didn't worry at all that Peng TouSi wouldn't be here at 7.

"Ah, would we seem to stingy if we go empty-handed?"

Xiong YaoYue suddenly mentioned.

"If I'm going to the class leader's house to get a free meal, I would usually buy some apples or oranges on my way there& but would it seem bad bringing oranges to a rich person's house?"

"You don't have to buy anything." I waved my hands, "Ai Mi doesn't really need anything, but&"

I looked at the nearby convenience store, "If you want to make Ai Mi happy, then but a bottle of cola and a can of chips. Make sure to buy the smallest sizes so you can carry it easily and it won't be found."

"Huh, why those two?" Xiong YaoYue ran towards the convenience store while asking, "What brand should I get?"

"It doesn't matter."

Even if she was full of doubt, she still brought the two items back. I asked her if she could put it into her pant pockets, and it actually just barely fit.

"I'm not really sure what you're planning." Xiong YaoYue complained, "It makes my butt look bigger&"

Peng TouSi drove Ai Mi's black batmobile to pick us up. I was planning on sitting in the back with Xiong YaoYue, but Peng TouSi said to me quietly:

"Lin, you should sit in the front passenger seat. Miss Winnie may be changing on the car later&"

I might feel a bit conflicted sitting next to Peng TouSi, but I can't use it as an excuse to take advantage of Xiong YaoYue, so I sat down on the front passenger seat and buckled in my seat belt.

"Then, Miss Xiong YaoYue, please sit in the back&"

Xiong YaoYue laughed out loud: "I'll get older quicker if you use honorifics, but I'll be grateful if you call me Winnie. Tell me how you want me to call you."

Peng TouSi scratched his bald head with embarrassment, "I like it when others call me Peng Peng."

"Okay, then I'll call you Peng Peng from now on." Xiong YaoYue agreed without hesitation, "Peng Peng, let's go."

After we began driving, Xiong YaoYue glanced left and right and began to relax in her seat.

"The seat is so soft." Xiong YaoYue sighed and praised, "No wonder people say they would rather cry in a BMW than laugh on a bicycle."

You don't have to worry about it, since even if you were in the back of a police car, you would still thoughtlessly joke around with the police officer:

"Teehee, I slipped up."

"Huh, why did the sky suddenly turn dark?" Xiong YaoYue was surprised, then she asked, "Why is the front window still bright?"

"Miss Winnie, the window has the ability to change color." Peng TouSi explained, then said to me:

"Lin, hand the bag under your seat to Miss Winnie."

Xiong YaoYue tooked the bag and found a female Qing Zi Academy uniform inside. At the same time, there were also the linings for the winter lining and the spring linings. There were even stockings and three pairs of matching shoes.

"Huh, are you letting me borrow this?" Xiong YaoYue asked.

"We're not lending it to you, we're giving it to you." Peng TouSi had a slight smile.

"What? Are you giving me these good clothes for free?" Xiong YaoYue was pleased beyond expectations, "Miss Ai Mi is really generous, I didn't even do anything& oh, did Peng Peng darken the windows so I could change?"

"That's right." Peng TouSi answered, "As long as you press the button under your armrest, the entire back section were be sectioned off by plates and you can change at ease."

"I guess I have to wear the uniform in order to get into the academy? Do I have to change right now?"

Xiong YaoYue still couldn't calm down after receiving clothes. She's a girl after all, I would never be this happy receiving clothes.

"Yes, it's best if Miss Winnie could wear it right now." Peng TouSi patiently reminded her, "Don't forget to press the button or you will be exposed."

Then he added on another sentence: "But I'm gay, so I wouldn't get any funny ideas about Miss Winnie&"

"Eh?" Xiong YaoYue exclaimed, "You're also gay?"

"Why did Miss Winnie add 'also'?"

Xiong YaoYue suddenly had a moment where she stayed silent.

"No wonder it looks like you have a pretty intimate relationship with Ye Lin, so you guys are the same!"

Damn, I knew it.

"Lin still might be a bit different than us&."

It's not a bit, it's a huge difference.

Xiong YaoYue laughed and had an interested expression.

"Why do I need the separation if you're both gay? I wouldn't lose out on anything if I change in front of you guys."

Please don't do that. It's fine in front of Peng TouSi, but if it's in front of me, I would start pumping blood towards a certain part of my body.

Xiong YaoYue didn't have a lot of guts as she hid behind Peng TouSi's seat so she wouldn't be seen from outside the car. Then she quickly pulled off her Tshirt by grabbing the collar.

Golden brown skin came into view. Although I didn't turn around, I couldn't help but glance at the rearview mirror. Before I stopped her she had already taken off her shorts and she was left only in her underwear. She really doesn't care about the gazes from the two men in front of her.

"It's the first time taking off clothes in front of men." Xiong YaoYue giggled, "It's pretty exhilarating."

Stop playing around and wear your clothes properly. It's a good thing I was wearing my seat belt, because if we were stopped by the police, Peng TouSi and I would be caught red-handed with a naked female minor.

I sighed when I saw Xiong YaoYue begin to wear the uniform from the rearview mirror.

After struggling for a bit, she was finally able to wear the uniform and she also changed her shoes. She jumped in the middle of the seat and asked excitedly:

"How do I look, would I fit it?"

The girl in the rearview mirror had a carefree and bright smile that was brighter than the sun.

Peng TouSi smiled and said: "Miss Winnie doesn't really look like a student from Qing Zi Academy."

"How come?" Xiong YaoYue was a bit upset and puffed up her cheeks.

"Miss Winnie is too cheerful. At Qing Zi Academy, as long as a girl has a bit of looks, they always think they're superior to others and they are never happy."

Xiong YaoYue didn't really seem that happy when Peng TouSi complemented her.

"I don't really have the right to look down on others. I mean look at the class leader, she's better than me at everything and she never looks down on others. And my skin is as dark as Zhang Fei."

"Miss Winnie has to be more confident. In America, your skin is considered the prettiest and the healthiest."

"Is that right?" Xiong YaoYue cheered up, "Does that mean Peng Peng would like me if you weren't gay?"

"I like you a lot right now." Peng TouSi beamed a smile at Xiong YaoYue through the rearview mirror.

Xiong YaoYue casually patted my shoulders.

"Ye Lin, would you also like me if you weren't gay?"

I had a serious expression: "No comment."

"Tsk, how narrow minded." Xiong YaoYue rolled her eyes, "Why can't you just say something to make me happy?"

We were able to easily get into Qing Zi Academy under the cover of the luxury car and we soon arrived near the VIP building.

004 and 005 were standing guard outside. When they saw me bringing a girl over, the first thing they did was cover their crotch. They wiped away their sweat when they realized it wasn't Xiao Qin.

"Even the gate guards are so muscular!" Xiong YaoYue exclaimed, "Miss Ai Mi probably spends a lot every month on security alone!"

Peng TouSi followed us from behind carrying a bag with Xiong YaoYue's clothes. I assumed the chips and cola were there, so I tapped Xiong YaoYue with my elbow to hint at her to carry the bag herself.

Although she might not have understood I was worried about the chips and cola, she still said to Peng TouSi:

"Peng Peng, I can carry the bag& I have at least enough strength to carry one bag."

Peng TouSi handed the bag over to Xiong YaoYue with a smile.

As usual, 004 and 005 did a quick frisk on me to prevent me from bringing chips and cola to Ai Mi.

"Are you checking for weapons?" Xiong YaoYue widened her eyes, "How strict, I guess I'm next."

Peng TouSi waved his hands, "Miss Winnie doesn't need to be checked, I already did a check in the car earlier."

What check? You mean you watched her change her clothes and felt there was no place for her to hide snacks. Well, you were careless!

Or are you purposely letting us go so Ai Mi could enjoy her forbidden snacks once in a while?

There was a large mirror right as we walked in the VIP building. Xiong YaoYue looked at herself and whistled.

"Private school uniforms look way better than our school's. Look, don't I seem more coquettish than usual? If you were a man, then I bet you would flirt with me."

I am a fucking man! Also, don't use the word coquettish on yourself, it was already shocking enough when you used it to describe me.

"Let's head to the dining room first." Peng TouSi directed us with his hand, "I bet the Miss is getting impatient."

Ai Mi was dressed casually on her hard earned rest day. She had a white night gown with a pair of slippers and she had her hair down. I reckon she just got out of bed.

"You guys are so slow." Ai Mi sat and grumbled at the dining table, "What happens if I starve to death because you came too late."

The dining room wasn't especially large, but the Western decorations were all high quality. The floor, window ledge, and seats, were all made out of solid red wood.

There were also four complex chandeliers hung from the ceilings, the types that would fall down and shatter in Hollywood movies. (Maybe it's because I don't know how to appreciate it, but I feel like it looks like jellyfish)

It was clearly bright outside, but the curtains were drawn shut and the lights were all open. The class leader would be crying inside if she saw this scene.

Xiong YaoYue spoke quietly from behind:

"Hey, hey, if Miss Ai Mi eats here every day, why did you tell me to bring chips and cola& did you trick me on purpose."

"Don't rush. You'll soon understand."

Ai Mi sat at the owner spot at the end of the long table and told us to sit on her left and right side.

The dining table that could seat 8 people only sat the 3 of us. It's a good thing we didn't have OCD.

"Is your cold better?" I asked Ai Mi after wiping my hands with the warm towel provided by Peng TouSi.

Ai Mi snorted, "Why are you only caring now, you could have came to check on me sooner."

I said without confidence: "School's been busy, and don't you rarely get rest days&"

Ai Mi turned around and asked Xiong YaoYue:

"Winnie, I heard you went to play a game last week, what game was that fun?"

Xiong YaoYue answered embarrassed:

"It was League of Legends, aka LOL& my team was lacking people, so I had to go and help&"

"Ah, I think I've heard the manservant mention it before. Isn't it a game for elementary school students, why are you still playing it in middle school&?"

I never said LOL was a game for elementary school students, that's what Xiao Ding from the pet hospital told me. Please don't use my name to attack LOL.

"It's not a game for elementary school students!" Xiong YaoYue retorted, "Even university students play LOL, I've met quite a few of them at internet cafes. There was also a time when two university roommates who got into a fight because of LOL, and it was our team who had to step in and break them apart."

Those universityy are basically as immature as elementary school students. I heard there was an university student who stabbed their roommate to death because of LOL.

"Is it really that interesting?" Ai Mi was skeptical, "My mom only allows me to play dance pad games&"

"It's definitely really fun." Xiong YaoYue strongly reccommended it to Ai Mi, "And you really feel a sense of accomplishment from building a team. Even beginners can rank high if someone carries them."

"Is that right. Is it kind of like of like how Sun Yue has a championship ring, but Yao Ming doesn't? As long as your team is strong, it doesn't matter if you're weak."

"Well, you can't be too weak&" Xiong YaoYue frowned, "But if Miss Ai Mi plays with us, we will all protect you."

Ai Mi leaned her chin and gazed at the ceiling like she was slightly moved.

Damn, don't try to tempt my sister to play internet games. What if she gets addicted and Ai ShuQiao will have to use electric shock therapy to treat her.

Speaking of internet addictions, Xiong YaoYue was opposed:

"It's not easy getting addicted to LOL, for example I'm not addicted. I heard there was a drug addict who gave up his drug addiction to save money for LOL. Look at those positive changes LOL is making on people!"

I think you provided an example of how LOL is even more addicting than drugs.

Ai Mi muttered to herself:

"Anway, I can't go to net cafes because of the foul atmosphere& but I could renovate one of the empty rooms&"

Ai Mi asked Peng TouSi who was standing on guard at the door: "If we want to make a LOL team, do we have a suitable room on the first floor?"

Do you not care about the second floor at all? If you're even afraid of the second floor, then you're acrophobia is even more serious than mines.

Peng TouSi replied immediately: "There is such a room. According to my knowledge, LOL sits in a row of 5. If we want to set up a team, then we need 2 x 5 seats since we also need opponents&"

You don't have to understand it to that extent. Or do you always do a thorough and detailed background check on everyone who gets close to Ai Mi? So when you were investigating Xiong YaoYue, did you also take some time to learn LOL?

"Wait, wait." the shocked Xiong YaoYue blinked rapidly, "Miss Ai Mi, are you saying you want to sponsor the Wasteland Wolves?"

"The team name sounds horrible." Ai Mi fussed, "That mean can at most be our practice partners. Winnie, go and find some actual experts and make a new team with us."

Peng TouSi interrupted: "Miss, even if you have a team, you can only play 40 minutes a day. Otherwise, I can't guarantee that I can keep it a secret from Madam Ai ShuQiao."

"I know, I know." Ai Mi spoke with dissatisfaction, "Peng TouSi, you're so annoying, hurry up and get married."

As Ai Mi said that, Xiong YaoYue covered her mouth and laughed then looked at me.

At this time, the French chef had already served the hot tea, egg sandwiches, and strawberry cheese toast. In the cool room, the heat from the food really stimulated our appetites.

Xiong YaoYue secretly kicked me under the table. Based on her gaze, it seems like she was saying: "It was the right choice to come without eating breakfast."

At this point, I feel like I should talk about the three largest female gluttons in class 2-3.

First is Loud Mouth, her appetite is deserving of being ranked number one. Her only weakness is that she moves around slowly, so she would probably expend all her stamina at a buffet before she even gets full. But if someone was willing to get food for her, she would get her money's worth even if she goes to a really expensive buffet.

The next one is Xiong YaoYue. Her strength is fast movements and speed eating. Her weakness is she talks a lot when eating and she would also spit out all the food in her mouth if she hears a joke when eating.

Finally, you can't forget Xiao Qin. Usually, her appetite is the same as a normal girl's for regular food. But her true strength is revealed when eating seafood. She's the living nightmare of all seafood buffets.

The second ranked glutton was moved to tears as she took a bite of the egg sandwich.

The French chef already had amazing skills. Plus, Xiong YaoYue ran to my house on an empty stomach, so it isn't that weird for someone like her to cry after tasting such delicacies.

"Does it taste good?" Since the French chef was anxiously waiting for her review, I hinted at Xiong YaoYue to give some more compliments.

"It's good, it's delicious." She ate while crying, "It's much better than shit& no, I mean, how could there be such a delicious sandwich?"

Compared to the speechless Xiong YaoYue, Ai Mi threw a piece of bred into her mouth with a lack of interest and she was almost too lazy to chew.

The Frech chef was moved as he saw Xiong YaoYue scarfing down the food. He must have felt his cooking was able to let a girl forget her manners. He returned to the kitchen with tears in his eyes.

Xiong YaoYue really likes talking while eating, so she began discussing the LOL team with Ai Mi and Peng TouSi. I couldn't really say anything for the time being.

"If Miss Ai Mi can only play 40 minutes a day, then I would have to find four other really strong players."

"No way." Ai Mi refused to admit she was awful at games, "I only asked you to find experts so they could match my skill. And they can't have a bad appearance."

"Um&" Xiong YaoYue scratched her face, "I don't really personally think anybody looks bad&."

Then she pointed at me, "What do you think about Ye Lin?"

Ai Mi snorted, "At first I thought he was a criminal, but then it got better as I became more used to him."

We share half our DNA, so don't call me ugly.

Xiong YaoYue sighed in relief, "Then, does that mean it's fine if they look at least better than Ye Lin?"

"I guess." Ai Mi plucked at the food in her plate.

"Hahah, then that's easy. I think everyone in the internet cafe&"

Then, when she saw my expression, she stuck out her tongue and decided not to say anymore.

Ai Mi and Xiong YaoYue were only discussing about the insignificant details, they completely didn't know the important parts about forming a professionally sponsored team.

In the end, it was Peng TouSi who helped them formulate a plan:

Ai Mi gave the new team the name Golden Lightning. It's composed of 10 members split into team 1 and team 2. There had to be at least four good players on call at anytime. When Ai Mi wants to play, the four of them has to carry her without letting her die even once.

What unreasonable requests. With your personality and awful skills, your teammates would always be dead tired.

Since they were a professional team, Peng TouSi suggested to provide free lodging and meals for the players. In addition, they would receive a monthly salary of ¥5000. If they also receive advertisement revenue like other teams, it would be split 30-70 between the team and the players.

"Can we find anyone for ¥5000?" Ai Mi was in doubt, "Should we change it to USD?"

Xiong YaoYue was shocked to the point she stopped eating.

"Please don't." I waved my hands, "It's already enough. If you raise it to 5000 USD, you'll cause a bloodbath in all the internet cafes throughout the city."

Ai Mi, who only ate a bit for breakfast, leaned back on her seat and said:

"Why do we have to split the ad revenue and prize money? Why can't we just give all of it to them?"

Peng TouSi explained:

"Miss, you're always only interested in something for brief periods of time. If one day you disbanded the team, the members might not like the terms of other sponsors because they were treated too well here. So, we're only thinking about their future."

As if it was a joke, the Golden Lightning team was established by Ai Mi.

Even though they planned to have 10 members (not including Ai Mi), at the moment Xiong YaoYue was the only member. And she was even assigned as both a permanent captain and manager. She also has the right to fire any member she deems unsuitable.

"Ah, I& don't have the skills to be the captain." Xiong YaoYue declined, "Besides, I hate firing other people. When I see their pained expression, I would rather fire myself first."

"No problem." Ai Mi said patiently, "If you find any unsuitable members, just tell the manservant and he will fire them. I mean who else would be the bad guy with a face like his."

Is that my only use as your brother? Do you want to spread my bad name into the world of esports too?

Anyway, Xiong YaoYue accepted the task of finding members for the team. By the way, for ¥5000 a month, I would have wanted to join but I don't know how to play at all.

After breakfast, Ai Mi acted as a homeowner for once and brought Xiong YaoYue on a tour of the VIP building. At the same time, she could get her opinions on where to set up the esports room and the member lodging.

When we passed the kitchen, Xiong YaoYue ran to the French chef and bowed. Although they couldn't speak the same language, they were still able to move each other.

After strolling around for a while, Ai Mi said she was tired and wanted to take a bath to recover.

As Ai Mi was soaking in the tub, Xiong YaoYue went to use a different washroom. She impatiently beckoned me from the door right after she flushed like she had something important to show me.

"It's my first time seeing this kind of toilet. It has three rows of buttons on each side and feels really high-end."

"I didn't even need paper, first a rinse, then dry, it felt so good."

"Also the tap over there&" Xiong YaoYue dragged me next to the sink, "Look, this tap is made out of pure good, and this design&"

Damn, it really is pure gold, and it's in the shape of a dragon where the eyes are diamonds. How extravagant, it wasn't here the last time I came.

We back tot he living room after touring the bathroom and waited for Ai Mi while enjoying some tropical fruits Peng TouSi had brought.

There were a few CDs on the coffee table that Ai Mi was using as cup placeholders. Xiong YaoYue suddenly realized Ai Mi was the one who was singing and dancing on the cover.

"What is this?" Like me, Xiong YaoYue couldn't understand the English on the cover.

"It's nothing much. Ai Mi is actually a celebrity with quite a number of fans in America, that's one of her records."

"What?" Xiong YaoYue was surprised, "Are you saying we're in the home of a celebrity?"

"So Miss Ai Mi is actually an American celebrity."

Xiong YaoYue grabbed my collar with excitement.

"Why didn't you tell me earlier? Isn't it rude to not have recognized a famous singer?"

Ai Mi walked out of the bathroom at this time with a towel wrapped around her.

She waked barefooted and left wet footprints behind on the carpet.

"I don't even like being a famous singer."

Ai Mi sat down right down in the middle of the sofa and it seems she was going to use the towel as clothes. Since Peng TouSi left to do some patrolling, only the three of us were left in the room, so no one could really control her.

Ai Mi looked at the CDs on the coffee table as if they were pieces of trash.

"It's not strange for Winnie to not recognize me. Right now the market is segmented pretty diversely. Even if we were in America, only serious lolicons would recognize me."

Ai Mi, you're being a bit too humble. Even lolicons in China pay attention to you. Director Cao spent ¥20,000 to buy your signed underwear, so he's definitely considered a fanatical fan.

"Umm& if Miss Ai Mi is a American celebrity, why did you come to China?"

Xiong YaoYue spoke out her questions.

Thus Ai Mi and I explained the entire situation to her and she had her mouth wide open the entire time.

"The Legend of the Magic Cauldron, an American funded film and even Ye Lin acted in it?"

"No wonder Peng Peng always calls you Miss Ai Mi'er, so that's a stage name."

"Do you live in Qing Zi Academy to learn at the same time? Do you always invite teachers here for one on one lessons and take tests by yourself?"

Ai Mi's gaze drifted towards the ceiling. I suspect her grades aren't that good.

"Let's not mention it anymore." Ai Mi interrupted Xiong YaoYue, "I could tell you more about the lolicon music industry in America if you're interested."

Does that industry even exist? Isn't usually categorized into groups like blues, jazz, country, rap, heavy metal, etc& when was there lolicon music?

"After coming to China, UTA signed a pair of 13 year old twin sisters to compete with my mother's company. Since I haven't shown my face in a while, they have already taken over my place and become the new loli idols."

As for these twin sisters, also know by their group name 'Pisces', Director Cao also mentioned them before.

Compared to Ai Mi, these sisters had a better body and more energy. And their performances are always exceptional. Apparently, in one of their concerts, they purposely imitated Lady Gaga and wore clothing composed of only tape. It drove the crowd crazy to the point where one of the lolicons couldn't hold it in and began to masturbate. He was arrested by the police and sentenced to 72 hours of community service.

Also, the sisters look extremely similar. If the younger sister didn't heterochromia, then even their mother would have difficulties telling them apart.

The two sisters both walked sweetly like Ai Mi and they would often kiss each other and act intimately on stage. Lolicons would often comment 'Double the Pleasure or Double the Sentence'.

They even calculated their prison sentences. If an American teacher was sentenced to 40 years for seducing a 14 year old boy, then are you getting ready to break the world record for the oldest age while sitting in prison?

But at least it's better for them to fantasize about Pisces than my sister. Overall, I'm pretty supportive of the sudden rise of Pisces.

Ai Mi also really loved Pisces.

"I hope they would work a bit harder so all the lolicons would forget about me. Concerts are exhausting and I even have to fake a smile at the pigs underneath the stage& by comparison, acting is easier."

"No matter what, I'll always be a supporter of Miss Ai Mi'er."

That was how Director Cao expressed his determination to me.

"The twin sisters also make many salivate& but they're too mature, they're not as delicate as Miss Ai Mi'er. Plus, they will be 14 years old in a year, which means they will be past their best before date."

Although that's what Director Cao said, I'm willing to bet if he attended the Pisces concert in America, there would have been one extra pervert masturbating in the crowd.

I'm guessing Peng TouSi will be gone for a while, so I nudged Xiong YaoYue to tell her to bring out the chips and cola.

Xiong YaoYue was hesitant and took out the items without confidence.

"Umm& Miss Ai Mi must think I'm joking to use these as gifts&"

Ai Mi's blue eyes widened to its limits and crystal clear saliva began to seep from her mouth. Please don't be so embarrassing. You didn't react at all earlier when Xiong YaoYue was crying over the French chef's food, but now you're acting as if you haven't eaten for days.

"Give it to me."

Ai Mi leaped forward like a wild cat and knocked over the confused Xiong YaoYue.

I left the sofa in a hurry and stood to the side. If Ai Mi was really wearing nothing under her towel, then I would see everything.

But still, the scene of two girls being entangled is still pretty sweet.

Ai Mi did everything she could to try and snatch the treasure in Xiong YaoYue's hands, but Xiong YaoYue could easily overcome her but was shocked Ai Mi would be interested and was afraid of hurting Ai Mi, so she didn't move.

"Miss Ai Mi, don't rush, it's all for you."

"You don't need to add Miss anymore. Since you brought me cola and chips, you can just call me Ai Mi."

"Huh, why? It was really cheap, and it was Ye Lin&"

I tried to silence Xiong YaoYue by placing a finger over my lips, but she still finished her sentence.

"It was Ye Lin who told me to buy it, I didn't even know Miss Ai Mi likes these items."

"Hmph, so it was the manservant?" Ai Mi raised her head and glanced at me, "Even if it was his idea, you were the one who was able to do it. He's already failed several times at trying to sneak in chips."

No shit, I get a body search every single day by your bodyguards. Recently, Peng TouSi increased the security so I can't even enter by the windows anymore. I'm guessing he let us go today, that's why we were able to bring it in.

Ai Mi held her treasures tightly in her lap and glanced around.

"Manservant." Ai Mi pointed towards the door, "Go and distract the bodyguards, especially Peng TouSi. I'm going to enjoy the ~chips and ~cola."

Ai Mi said the words chips and cola extremely quietly like they were drugs.

"Maybe I should go." Xiong YaoYue said as she stood up from the sofa with a messy shirt.

"You don't have to go, stay here with me. Your voice is loud, so it can hide the sound of me eating chips. There might be listening devices hidden in the room."

"Besides, Peng TouSi might not even look at you even if Winnie runs outside naked. To deal with a homo like him, the manservant would be more effective."

"That's true." Xiong YaoYue grinned from ear to ear, "They look like a good fit."

I had no choice but to leave behind Ai Mi and Xiong YaoYue to go and seduce& no, to distract Peng TouSi. I never expected him to be walking straight towards me.

I subconsciously blocked the door, "Winnie's changing so you can't enter."

But it turns out Peng TouSi wasn't intending on entering, he spoke to me seriously: "Follow me, there's something important we have to do."

I followed Peng TouSi and arrived at the top floor of the VIP building.

The VIP building only had two floors and I didn't get really dizzy when peering downstairs, but I still stayed away from the edges due to my acrophobia.

"What's so important?" I had a bad feeling.

Peng TouSi is a receiver, so he doesn't have any reason to find a secluded area to assault my bottom. But if that's not the reason, then what's he looking for?

He pulled out his cellphone, pressed a few buttons, then handed it to me.

"Lin, please remain calm no matter what." Peng TouSi requested sincerely.

I picked up the phone with suspicions, "Hello."

I could hear a woman's laughter on the other side.

Anger quickly rose to my head.

"Ai ShuQiao, it's you."

"Hey, I've worked hard for a whole day and gives my son a call at 11pm, but he won't even call me mom."

"You&"

I wanted to swear at her, but Peng TouSi was in front of me frantically gesturing so I held it back and spoke calmly:

"Call you mom? But you don't even recognize me as your son?"

"Hah, Ye Lin, that's because there's been a slight change to the situation."

"Change? Did you dream of yourself falling into hell?" I said sarcastically.

Ai ShuQiao cleared her throat.

"Listen, don't talk to your mom that way. There's two reasons why my opinion of you changed, but it has nothing to do with your sense of humour."

"First, I heard Peng TouSi say you protected Ai Mi when a tree fell over and the other bodyguards witnessed it. They say you were willing to give your own life to protect her."

"I was afraid they were all lying to me, so I obtained the CCTV recordings. From the recording, it did seem like you were risking your life, so it changed my view on you."

"I've thought about it for a while, but I couldn't understand why? Maybe the rumoured siscons actually exists in reality."

Whether or not I'm a siscon has nothing to do with you. All I know for sure is that you're definitely not a daughtercon or a soncon, the only thing you like is money and power.

"I've also received reports that even though you've stayed close to Ai Mi, you've never revealed your relationship with her& why, are you afraid of my punishment?"

"You&"

I wanted to curse at her, but Peng TouSi shook his head even more frantically, so I swallowed my words.

"I have my own ways of caring for my sister, you don't need to get involved."

I snorted.

Ai ShuQiao was silent for a while, then began to laugh for some reason.

"As for my second point, I noticed a transfer of twenty thousand dollars in my bank that says cutting ties, is that from you?"

"Yeah, that's right, what of it?"

"What I'm curious about is how were you able to earn twenty thousand in such a short period of time?"

I wanted to say I sold her daughter's underwear, but it's too embarrassing.

"Hmph, I can earn it however I want, it's not from my dad."

"That's why I'm curious: A 15 year old child can earn twenty thousand in a month&"

"I'm 14." I corrected the person who wasn't qualified to be a mother.

"It doesn't matter how old you are. Basically, I thought you were a simple minded buffoon who could only say empty words, but I never expected you to actually achieve it at your age&"

"What are you trying to say?"

"Did you do anything illegal to earn it?"

"Uhh&" I was temporarily speechless. Is selling your sister's underwear illegal?

"It might have been unethical, but definitely not illegal. No one will arrest me."

I justified.

"Haha, so you used a legal loophole."

Ai ShuQiao spoke as if she already expected it.

"I won't investigate what methods you used& but you should know that those who has the guts to do illegal acts is worthy to be my son."

What kind of fucking logic is that? You planned a murder that involved Ai Mi and complimented my potentially illegal actions. Are you planning to make a happy crime family or something?

"Look, a person who would risk his life for his sister, one who can earn large sums of money, and is apparently very muscular, is only 15 years old&."

I'm 14, do you not listen at all?

"A child with this much potential may be able to become my assistant with the right training."

She spoke with an enticing voice like something reaching out from the depths of hell:

"I'm giving you a chance& Ye Lin, do you want to return to being my son?"

I could only sneer at Ai ShuQiao's proposal.

"Do you think&. I want to be your son again?"

It was almost as if I could see the Ai ShuQiao lift up the corners of her mouth through the phone.

"Why not. If you do become my son, you'll become ultra-wealthy& I can make all of your dreams come true&"

"Is that so?" I wasn't really interested, "I only want my dad to go back to teaching at the university, can you achieve that?"

"What?" Ai ShuQiao did not expect my request, "As long as you recognize me as your mother, you won't have to worry about clothing or food at all. Why would you care about what Ye YuanFeng does?"

I repeated my statement without emotions: "I want my dad to go back to teaching at the university."

Ai ShuQiao got a bit upset, "Listen, I'm interested in you, not your father. Ye YuanFeng is basically useless, I won't do anything for him. As long as you follow me, you'll have an endless amount of wealth. As for how much you give your father, that has nothing to do with me. Due to the nature of the business, you may regularly appear next to me, but Ye YuanFeng can't come. Just let that pitiful hindrance settle down somewhere and retire."

I already expected Ai ShuQiao's answer. My dad doesn't actually need any help, because the biggest hindrance preventing him from returning to teach is his heart. If Ai ShuQiao was willing to say to my dad 'I want you to go back to teaching', then he will definitely do it. I don't want to admit it, but Ai ShuQiao still has a large influence on my dad even when they have been separated for a long time.

What a dreadful poison.

"Ye Lin, I don't like being forced to do something that I don't want to do, so you have to change your conditions."

I didn't express my thoughts and waited for her to continue.

"A kid like you who grew up from the bottom probably doesn't understand the difference power makes. Let me tell you what you can do after becoming my son."

It seems our relationship of mother and son isn't decided biologically, but only for people she approves.

"For a 15 year old like you, you're probably in constant turmoil because of your hormones."

I already stopped trying to correct her that I was 14 years old.

"According to my knowledge, your school& no, your class has quite a few beautiful girls."

So, what? Did you get that information from that private detective, it's not that impressive.

Ai ShuQiao continued to speak calmly:

"You can rape whoever you want."

What& is that something a mother should say to her son?

"There's no limit, you can rape as many as you want."

"If you have special hobbies, you can even call your friends over and gang rape them."

"It would be the best if you leave them alive, but it's fine if you accidentally kill one or two& I'll make sure your friends are the ones who take the rap, I mean that's what friends are for."

"If your classmates aren't enough to satisfy you, then you can increase the range to the entire school. It doesn't matter how many girls you rape or how many gets pregnant or dies& I'll take care of the aftermath."

"I'll prove it to you that your mother has power. Even if I'm abroad, I still have influence on the Chinese judicial system."

"Of course, if someone dies, make sure to bring at least one scapegoat. You're smart so you should know what to do without teaching you."

Didn't you already teach me enough? You're even worse than Li TianYi's mother. All she did was raise her son poorly and continue to cover up for him, but you straight up instigated me to commit gang rape.

Is it true that humans have an 'evil' side? I'm not saying I'm interested in Ai ShuQiao's outrageous proposal, but there was an instant where I imagined 28 Middle turning into a dedicated harem just for me.

But it's more accurate to say the 'good' blood running in my veins from my father wouldn't agree. Even if I'm not punished by the law after I rape a girl, the class leader's gun will still enact justice.

Of course, if I go along with Ai ShuQiao's plan, then the first one I rape would be the class leader and break her index finger she shoots with in the process. Maybe Ai ShuQiao's son can do it, but I can't, so I have proven that I am not Ai ShuQiao's son.

"Do you find joy in hurting others?" I replied to Ai ShuQiao, "Even if I feel happy in the moment, my conscience hasn't been rounded yet and I'll regret it."

My dad mentioned once before that everyone's conscience is like a triangle resting in their chest. If you do something bad, the triangle will spin and cause you pain, so a lot of people try not to do bad deeds. However, some people who persists in doing bad deeds will eventually have their triangle grounded down into a circle and they will no longer feel uncomfortable.

I remember a specialist once said on social media: A conscience is a weakness, you have to get rid of it if you want to get successful.

A weakness is fine, since I would only feel human if I feel pain in my chest. If the cost of becoming successful is to become apathetic, then I would rather go do physical labor. At least I would be able to keep my real emotions.

Going back to my previous example, if I raped the class leader and broke her index finger, even if Ai ShuQiao helps me out, my conscience wouldn't be able to support it.

So instead of saying I have a lot of integrity and never thought of having girls under me, it's better to say I don't want my conscience to be tormented. On this point alone, I don't have the ability to rape a girl.

Seeing as I haven't spoken for a while, Ai ShuQiao thought I was tempted and kept speaking:

"Believe me, once you get a taste of power, you can't live without it."

When did raping girls become 'power'?

I guess anything that disturbs someone else's lives is considered a form of power in your eyes.

"Ai ShuQiao." I steeled my resolve and didn't call her mom, "Do you think I'm the same as you?"

"Hahaha, a lot of times blood runs thicker than you imagine."

"My dad's blood is stronger than yours."

Ai ShuQiao stayed silent for a while.

"Funny that you would even compare me to Ye YuanFeng. He's a loser for falling to his current state with his talents."

I got too emotional, "Who do you think made him like that?"

Ai ShuQiao remained unmoved, "Don't push your own problems onto others. Whether you admit it or not, you're much closer to me than Ye YuanFeng."

"Bullshit."

"As for the conscience you mentioned and the loser ideologies that Ye YuanFeng taught you, I will help you get rid of them as your mother. I'll do my duty and give my all to turn you into someone like me."

I wanted to immediately hang up, but Peng TouSi was dissuading me with his eyes, so I could only keep on listening.

"I won't rape anyone no matter what, so give up."

"Based on my knowledge, you should still be a virgin, right?"

Why do you have to investigate that?

"A virgin at 15 years old. It's a bit sad from an American perspective, no wonder you're still immature."

"In order to express my sincerity, I'll introduce a good partner for you to say goodbye to your virginity. And you wouldn't get a guilty conscience when you're with her."

What, are you referring to Xiao Qin? I definitely wouldn't feel guilty if I stripped her, but isn't that exactly what she wants?

"Do you still remember Su Qiao?" Ai ShuQiao suddenly said.

She was the one who left home because she didn't like acrobatics and was finally able to become a fulltime actor. Recently, she signed a contract with Tian Mu Xing Guang Limited Media Company. She's the girl who's older than me by three years and has long braided hair.

"She's mine."

"What?" I didn't understand Ai ShuQiao's words.

"I'm saying she's one of my chess pieces. I was the one who gave her the role of Blood Prince's maid, do you get it now?"

Her words cleared up a lot of my doubts. No wonder Ai Mi never admitted to helping Su Qiao, and Auntie Ren was also puzzled on how she was able to get a role with her mediocre English skills. So, it was because Ai ShuQiao had a chat with the director.

But what benefits would Ai ShuQiao get in return?

Ai ShuQiao said in a loathsome tone:

"Su Qiao didn't have a brain or any connections, it made me mad when I saw her trying to get into the acting world."

"It was actually her idea to go to your hotel room that night. I still haven't contacted her yet and wanted to test her reactions."

"Seeing her childish actions, I thought what a 'foolish girl' and I may be able to use her to deal with you&"

"But she was dumber than I imagined and couldn't even properly put weed in your bag."

I was stunned and finally realized why Su Qiao was acting so strangely. The weed had nothing to do with Kyle the fool and it was actually done by Su Qiao. Was she the one who almost made me into a drug trafficker?

"Are you getting mad at her now?" Ai ShuQiao added some more oil to the flames, "When she was a background actor, you made sure Ai Mi didn't pick on her or fire her, but she immediately bites your hand once she receives a tiny benefit from me& that was a drug and it almost sent you to juvy."

I was a bit upset. She kept calling me Mr. Ye, but was harming me behind my back.

"How about it? I don't think you're conscience would be affected much to use someone who betrayed you."

"Use? What do you mean?"

"What else could it mean?" Ai ShuQiao laughed, "Do her."

"What?"

"What's so strange about it? She got an important role from me, but she didn't complete my tasks properly. She can't even be used as a chess piece, but she has to at least pay the price somehow."

"So, I'm wrapping her up and giving it to my son as a gift. You can punish her to your heart's content while also losing your virginity. You don't have to feel any psychological pressure since she owes us."

"You&"

"Oh, and it's not the gift that counts, but the thought behind it. I think we still need a contract to signify you becoming my son again. Why not use Su Qiao's body as the contract."

Are you using a person as a product? Su Qiao probably doesn't know she's already been sold out.

"Ye Lin, there's a saying that goes: In this world, some people let things happen, some people watch it happen, and some don't even know what happened."

"Su Qiao is the person who doesn't know what happened. The last order I gave her was to get into an intimate relationship with you, and she couldn't back down even if it meant a physical relationship. It should be easy to get with her as long as you're willing."

"Don't you kind of feel like the emperor when you can go play with an ignorant person after finding out the truth."

"If you accept her, you can use her like a dirty rag or stay as a couple for a while, it's up to you."

"She won't cause you any trouble on the legal side. To be honest, I'm the boss of Tian Mu Xing Guang Limited Media Company."

"She basically signed her rights away with the contract and I control the next ten years of her life& she should be proud if the boss' son is willing to use her."

"You made a mistake." I declined Ai ShuQiao's proposal, "I'm not interested in older women."

That was actually a lie, the class leader is older than me by a day.

Su Qiao may be older than me by three years, but she's frail and lacks confidence. She's also not as tall as the class leader and appears younger than her actual age.

It seems there aren't many tall acrobats. I don't know if it's because shorter people have more stability or if it's because the intense training at a young age affected their growth.

No, now's not the time to look at Su Qiao as the opposite sex. The problem is that Ai ShuQiao's proposal is insane, who gives their 15 year& no, 14 year old son a mistress?

"Really." Ai ShuQiao wasn't very surprised about my decision, "Well, that's a shame. Since you don't like Su Qiao, and I never have losses in a business, I could only make her drink with clients or provide bed service to corrupt officials&"

"You& dare." I blurted.

Why am I protecting a girl who set me up? It might be because Su Qiao's tears moved me. On the other hand, Ai ShuQiao ordered Su Qiao to plant the weed on me and didn't go easy on me. But the final result was some of the weed spilled out and Constable Ma couldn't punish me with the full extent of the law.

Even with Auntie Ren's connections, if I was carrying over 50 grams of weed, Constable Ma would not have let it go. I should be glad Su Qiao had some doubts when planting some weed and spilled some.

Afterwards, when Su Qiao was scolded and crying in the bamboo forest proved she reduced the amount of weed on purpose and didn't follow Ai ShuQiao's plans.

Now that I think about it, the one who notified Auntie Ren that I was in trouble was probably Su Qiao.

In short, even though Su Qiao played a large part in the weed incident, she was coerced by Ai ShuQiao the entire time. But she still notified Auntie Ren to save me, so I can't really judge her too harshly.

The one who took away brother Optimus Prime is the one I vowed to enact revenge upon.

As for Su Qiao, she's merely a 17 year old girl who ran away from home because she dreams of becoming a celebrity. Because she got involved in the fight between Ai ShuQiao and me, does she now have to service those corrupt politicians for the next ten years?

And what kind of media company is Ai ShuQiao running? You don't have to learn from Korea and make your artists also act as escorts!

"You're a dishonest child." Ai ShuQiao laughed, "If you're not planning on using her, why do you care if someone else uses her."

"& you can't be so cruel to her."

"Ha, only those with power can decide if someone is treated nicely or poorly. I'll pass over the rights to decide Su Qiao's fate to you and you can have a taste of power."

"I'll take the twenty thousand you gave me and convert it into stock in the Tian Mu Xing Guang Limited Media company. Although your shares are nothing compared to me, but you would still be the second stockholder of the company. As a stockholder and my representative, you have the right to make changes to the company's plans and employees&"

"Who wants to be your representative, I&"

"Don't interrupt me. I'm going to let you know that manager Fu, the person I assigned to be in charge of Su Qiao, is a well known pervert who lived in Korea for pretty long time. If it wasn't for my orders, he would have already laid his hands on Su Qiao. How would you compete with him if you weren't a stockholder and my representative?"

"Why would I compete with him? Isn't it your company?"

Ai ShuQiao chuckled, "I firmly believe that competition leads to success. You can really ascertain a person's qualities through competition. Just view it as one of the tests for becoming my assistant."

Ai ShuQiao continued to speak while ignoring my wishes:

"Anyway, if you're not going to use Su Qiao, then give her to someone else. If you don't manage her as a stockholder, she will have a hard time at the company. I'll let you decide her fate."

Then she hung up the phone without waiting for a response.

I threw the phone in a fit of anger on the ground, but instead of breaking, it bounced back up and almost hit my nose. As expected of a rugged military phone.

Peng TouSi, who heard the entire conversation, quietly picked up the phone and persuaded me:

"Lin, keep calm, this is a once in a lifetime opportunity."

"An opportunity?"

"Because of the tree and returning money incidents, Madam Ai ShuQiao has changed her hostile attitude towards you. Which means you would have less of a psychological burden in everyday life."

"Tsk, so, I ain't afraid of her."

Although I may have said that, but Ai ShuQiao only thinks of me as a housefly. She will try to hit me if she sees me, but she doesn't take the effort to use pesticide. If that was the case, I would have been long dead.

"Lin, based on my many years of observation, Madam Ai ShuQiao loves it when people get caught up between two difficult choices. Since her interests are currently focused on you, you can try to get to know that girl and the company more and maybe even cause a ruckus."

It would be hard for me to screw up a company as an outsider. The problem is what should I do with Su Qiao?

"Do you hate her because she betrayed you once?" Peng TouSi got straight to the point.

"Maybe& a bit."

"Then get your revenge."

"Huh?"

"If you can't get rid of the hatred, release it instead of hiding it deep inside of you."

"Teach Su Qiao a lesson in a manner you find fair. Afterwards, whether it's helping her escape the company or leaving her alone, just listen to your heart."

I haven't really thought of a lesson for her. She already has the face of a tragic heroine that makes you feel guilty if you punish her, but I'm not kind enough to help her out while feeling resent towards her.

I guess we could make an equal exchange. The cost of her betraying me plus my future help will be paid with me bullying her a bit.

I was thinking as the online store grows, I would need to hire another worker. It's not a good long term plan to let Shu Zhe keep acting as a trap. Firstly, it would be dangerous if the class leader found out. Secondly, I wouldn't be able to keep taking pictures of Shu Zhe in those outfits once my dad comes home.

The thought of making Su Qiao become the rope model instead of Shu Zhe flashed through my mind. Even though she has a good body from acrobatics, I feel it would be a bit bad to ask an aspriring celebrity to be a rope model.

I'm actually looking forward to her cooking skills. If she can cook for me for half a month until I win the basketball tournament, then I could begin to head to the class leader's house for free meals and I could generously forgive Su Qiao for her crimes.

Look, I'm perfectly content with only 15 meals. If it was Shu Zhe, then Su Qiao would definitely tortured and put through hardships.

I came to a compromise with Peng TouSi that I would continue to attract Ai ShuQiao's attention while John and him continue to look for incriminating evidence.

I stuck my hands in my pockets and asked Peng TouSi:

"Even though you said you want to save Ai ShuQiao's soul, it really just looks like you're betraying her, so why does she trust you so much?"

Peng TouSi smiled mysteriously and began taking off the top of his suit.

Peng TouSi pointed to his left ribs.

"What do you see?"

"Abs."

"Is there nothing strange other than abs?"

"Which part is strange?"

"Peng TouSi shook his head and explained:"

"Last time I visited Ai ShuQiao, my left ribs were broken."

Ah, did Ai ShuQiao break it with her heels? In old photos, Ai ShuQiao gave off an image of Femme Fatales, but is she more like a female Tyson?

"The reason I was called back to America was partly because I let you get near the Misses, but the other reason was because one of our singers got into an argument with the Sicilian Mafia. It seems that male singer laid his hands on the daughter of the godfather&"

"Damn, that's fucking bold. What else is there to say, just cut off his third leg."

"But this singer is currently ascending in popularity, so Madam Ai ShuQiao wants to protect him. The godfather didn't agree with receiving money, so he suggested: each side send out three people to fight a metal cage deathmatch. He'll admit defeat if he loses, but we have to hand over the singer if he wins."

I could kind of already guess how he was injured.

"Madam Ai ShuQiao sent me alone against three people to completely dominate them."

"Steelcage deathmatches are my speciality. I shouldn't have made mistakes, but I was still a bit jetlagged and didn't want to kill the opponent, so I accidentally recevied a knee strike. Fortunately, I was still able to win and didn't embarrass Madam Ai ShuQiao."

"Because I was willing to put my life on the line for Madam Ai ShuQiao, and she doesn't know anything that's more precious than life, so she believes I'm the most devoted person to her& which is correct, I am indeed willing to use my life to pay back her grace."

"You're full of contradictions." I smiled bitterly and told him to get dressed.

"Thanks." Peng TouSi received his jacket I passed to him and appeared shy, "Lin, you're too kind."

Shit, don't give me those flirty eyes, do you want me to break your right ribs too?

When I returned to room 101, Ai Mi had already finished all the chips and cola. The two of them even destroyed all the evidence.

But wait, what's the scene I see? Why is Xiong YaoYue letting Ai Mi ride her like a horse? I only left for a bit and the capitalist Ai Mi is already beginning to enslave the working class.

I mean it's fine for Ai Mi to look proud, but why does Xiong YaoYue look so happy while being ridden?

The worst part is Ai Mi became excited to the point where she began to spank Xiong YaoYue's butt to make her faster. Xiong YaoYue, you're wearing a skirt, are you not afraid of being exposed?

I said loudly for them to stop and grabbed Ai Mi by the waist to take her off Xiong YaoYue's back.

Xiong YaoYue stood up indifferently and began to speak in defense of Ai Mi:

"We were bored, so we began playing rock paper scissors. We said if Miss Ai Mi loses, she would run a lap around the living room, and if I lost, I would draw on my face&"

"But Miss Ai Mi lost ten times in a row. She only ran the first lap, the remaining nine laps were resolved with Chairman Maos&"

A hundred dollar bills? So you would rather give away 900 instead of exercising?

"Hehe, I lost the eleventh time. I was worried I wouldn't be able to wash marker off my face, so I was willing to act as a horse. It was pretty fun for both of us, so we played longer than we planned."

"Ye Lin, don't worry. It was actually good I got some exercise. Isn't it almost time for lunch, now I can eat more."

The French chef lived up to Xiong YaoYue's expectations and brought us salmon caviar, seared foie gras, and black truffle with sea bass for lunch.

The caviar was large and plump akin to red pearls. The spoon was made from a shell because metallic spoons would ruin the caviar's taste. Black truffles doesn't look aesthetically pleasing, but apparently it's worth its weight in gold.

"What? Then doesn't that mean we're eating gold?" Xiong YaoYue said wide-eyed.

"Don't listen to the manservant's nonsense." Ai Mi had no interest in the table of luxurious cuisine after enjoying her chips and cola, "Only Italian white truffles are worth its weight in gold. French black truffles are only at most one tenth of its price."

"That's still insane. That would mean I ate 1 gram of gold for every 10 grams of truffles."

Ai Mi sent a nasty look towards me:

"Does the manservant feel bad that it's not white truffles? I heard white truffles are great for boosting a man's sex drive."

I ignored the joke that shouldn't be told by my sister and continued to eat the foie gras.

Peng TouSi who was standing guard at the door advised Ai Mi to eat more caviar:

"Miss, caviar is good for the brain. Please eat some more, maybe your grades&"

"Don't mention my grades."

Ai Mi slammed her hands on the table and Peng TouSi went silent.

Xiong YaoYue acted as if she heard a good tip, "Can you become smart after eating this?"

She rapidly shoveled multiple scoops of caviar in her mouth without even tasting it.

After eating 5 scoops, she stopped and grumbled:

"It feels fishy after eating too much and I don't think I became any smarter&"

I don't know if you became smarter, but you look kind of dumb after stuffing your face and staining your face red.

After trying the trying the caviar, she went for the expensive truffles. This time she's a bit smarter (perhaps it was because of the caviar), she didn't stuff herself but instead slowly savored the flavors in her mouth.

I was different than her. I prefer eating meat rather than the fishy caviar and strange fungus, so I focused more onto the foie gras. I was too busy too even try the dessert and soup the French chef brought later on.

Every time I ate here, I would always feel there's a dog under the table, so I asked:

"Where's Obama?"

"In America?" Xiong YaoYue answered with a bit of confusion.

"Not the president. Ai Mi's dog is also called Obama."

"Oh." Xiong YaoYue lowered her head to continue to exercise her jaw muscles. It seems she doesn't like dogs as much as the class leader.

"Obama went to get some oral care." Ai Mi replied, "He's been eating random stuff lately so his mouth stinks. He should be back soon."

I remember when I was younger, my dad told me the best way of finding truffles was using a dog's nose. There would be truffle hunters in France and Italy who take their hunting dogs to forests to find truffles.

Since I liked to 'teach others', I told them the story of dogs finding truffles. Ai Mi already knew about it so she showed zero interest.

Xiong YaoYue was surprised and asked with caviar stuck on the corners of her lips:

"Can you use dogs to find something so precious? Does Miss Ai Mi's dog, Obama, also have this ability? If so, please let me borrow him. I'll bring him to the forest everyday to gather truffles and I can earn the price of a golden necklace in a single day!"

Stop dreaming, gathering truffles is a very technical job. All the hunting dogs need special training, a dumb dog like Obama wouldn't find anything. At most, he would only piss everywhere to mark his territory and confuse the other hunting dogs.

Though I heard from my dad that it's actually the best to use female pigs to look for truffles as they a contain a compound that excites them. But because pigs love truffles, they might accidentally eat them. So hunters who use pigs to hunt for truffles have to learn how to snatch food from a pig's mouth.

One of the reasons I don't want to try truffles is because it may have been snatched from a pig's mouth. I mean it may have even been the pig's leftovers. I lost all of my appetite once I think of that possibility.

After the sumptuous meal, Xiong YaoYue wiped her mouth clean and held her hands in a prayer.

What religion do you practice? Christians pray before the meal, why are you praying after the meal? Were you too excited before the meal and forgot to do it?

Xiong YaoYue looked towards the empty space in front of her like she was the most devout follower:

"It was worth living."

Do you already have no more regrets in life after only one luxurious Western meal? How come you're so easily satisfied?

A short while later, Obama was led back from the salon with shining teeth.

"So it's a Husky." Xiong YaoYue beckoned Obama over, but he only went over to get food without letting her pet his head.

So is his only remaining resolution to allow only me and Ai Mi to pet his head?

After playing outdoors with Obama for a while, Ai Mi began complaining about the sunlight and we all returned back to room 101 with Obama.

"I want to take a bath." Ai Mi announced, "Winnie, I have a really large whirlpool tub, do you want to bath with me?"

Xiong YaoYue was moved by her invitation and was just itching to strip her clothes off immediately.

"Ye Lin." She spoke to me with tears in her eyes, "You can kill me after I finish my bath."

What a strange request. Guys will imagine a lot of things after a girl gets out of a bath, but killing them is definitely not one of those things.

"What are you talking about?" Ai Mi pouted, "Winnie, as long as you remain loyal to me, I will give you benefits. But if you betray me, I'll ask Peng TouSi to kill you."

Xiong YaoYue was moved again: "I won't betray Miss Ai Mi. I still have to become your future bodyguard."

"You?" Ai Mi was skeptical, "It might be easier in certain aspects, but can you pass the strict requirements to pass the bodyguard test?"

"No problem." Xiong YaoYue vowed, "I'm confident in my physical abilities, and Peng Peng can train me."

Ai Mi sent a mischievous look at me.

"Manservant, look at Winnie's diligence. You've never said you want to be my bodyguard."

But I'm already protecting you, do you have to make me wear a suit?

"You can leave."

Ah, are you going to kick me out because I'm not going to be your bodyguard? What a heartless sister.

Ai Mi frowned.

"What are you standing there for, I told you to leave the room. Do you want to stay here and bath with us?"

"If it's Ye Lin, then it's fine&" Xiong YaoYue said but then shut her mouth because she felt something was off.

Thus the dog was left in the living room while I was kicked out.

Ai Mi's decision was right. If I stayed behind, I would have nothing to. Plus when two girls bathe, they may talk about more private topics. It would feel awkward for me when they start saying things like "Winnie, why is this part whiter than the rest of your body?".

I walked outside to the flower gardens and saw Peng TouSi watering the flowers. The flower garden under his care were filled with blooming sunflowers.

When he saw me walk out by myself, he asked me quietly:

"Lin, I'm a bit curious. How were you able to earn the twenty thousand you gave Madam Ai ShuQiao."

I definitely can't say I made it selling my sister's underwear. I will be despised for sure if I told Ai Mi's protector.

"That's& a business secret. If I told you, you would go do that business instead of being a bodyguard."

Peng TouSi nodded in understanding, but I had a guilty conscience. It's a good thing he didn't ask me in front of Ai Mi.

At this time, Obama diligently came over while holding something white in his mouth.

He scratched my leg with his front paws hoping to get my attention.

I looked down and it was another pair of underwear. Did he bring her underwear looking for a reward again?

After a closer inspection, it wasn't Ai Mi's underwear. Ai Mi doesn't have a lot of plain and simple underwear. That plain white underwear belongs to Xiong YaoYue, I saw it when she was changing on the car.

Since Obama wasn't able to get any food from me last time with Ai Mi's underwear, does he now want to try someone else's underwear? Why does he think he can use a girl's underwear to exchange something with me?

I pulled the underwear from his mouth, but it was stained with saliva and couldn't be used anymore.

Peng TouSi sighed, "Obama still can't get rid of his weird habit."

I held Xiong YaoYue's contaminated underwear and hesitated a bit before tossing it into the flower pots.

"Peng TouSi, bury it."

"Okay." He readily agreed, "Come and check it out in autumn and see if it grows more underwear&"

Please don't say unscientific things. Even if you used Jinkela, you can't grow a panty tree.

I left behind the underwear Peng TouSi buried. To change my mood, I took a stroll around the outside of VIP building.

I suddenly felt an indescribable feeling of familiarity.

Not the intimate type, but the type that makes your blood run cold.

I followed the familiar feeling and noticed a girl wearing a floral dress instead of the Qing Zi Academy uniform.

I could tell it's Xiao Qin from the side profile. Why is she at Qing Zi Academy and how did she get in without an uniform?

Although her specialty is climbing walls, it doesn't look like she sneaked inside. She was walking around outside even more confidently than the other students.

She was walking with a middle aged man over fifty years old. He had white hairs on the sides of his head but was full of energy. He had a dignified aura and was wearing a full suit.

Am I mistaken. Why would Xiao Qin be with an unknown man on a Sunday instead of being with Auntie Ren?

The second reason why I had doubts if she was Xiao Qin was because she didn't seem to be acting dumb. She was attentively listening to the man's words and quietly nodding along.

I'm definitely mistaken, she even seems to be prettier than Xiao Qin.

The girl who looks like Xiao Qin brushed her bangs and that familiar action made my heart tremble.

Was Xiao Qin pretending to be virtuous in front of the middle aged man? Or& was Xiao Qin always acting in front of me to make me like her?

As she was walking with the middle aged man, the girl's body suddenly trembled and she turned around. It was like a hunting dog who had discovered truffles and she cast her burning gaze towards me.

I'm not mistaken. The thirst in her eyes coupled with her slight predatory smile makes me confident that she is Xiao Qin.

Fortunately, there was a street between us and a car happened to drive by and blocked Xiao Qin's line of sight.

What a scare. Even though I never anything to wrong her, my heart's still beating frantically when she sternly looked over at me.

Is it because of the Little Tyrant? Is my heart beating faster due to the threatening aura that Xiao Qin is unintentionally leaking?

I quickly hid around the corner of the VIP building under the cover of the passing vehicle.

Xiao Qin stopped and looked towards my direction a couple times until the middle aged man called her and she began to walk further away.

As I was finally able to calm down, I felt some changes to my nether region like something was vibrating. It feels like my eggs are about to burst.

It took me a moment to realize it was the cell phone in my pocket. My phone would move a lot when it vibrates and usually always gives me a scare every time.

I took a look and it was a call from Xiao Qin.

Did she call me to check if she can hear a ringtone when she saw someone who looks like me?

How sly, but luckily I always keep my phone on vibrate. If I was caught, then the girls hidden in the room&.

Wait, I don't have any girls hidden in the room, but Xiao Qin should already know my sister lives inside. Even if Xiong YaoYue is naked right now, she's not a part of my harem! At least there's no indicators to show she could be a part of my harem. It's more likely that she would become a part of my sister's harem.

While Xiao Qin may already be far away, but her five senses are amazing. If I picked up the phone right now, I can't guarantee she won't discover any traces.

Thus I rejected the call. Xiao Qin may have been afraid I would get upset, so she didn't call me a second time.

I leaned against the outer walls of the VIP building and sighed in relief.

What a close call.

But the hiding actions really make me remember the times I played thriller games with the Little Tyrant.

The name was called 'Hide and Seek and Get Beat Up if Caught'! The Little Tyrant would order her lackeys to block the door to my house while they gave me ten minutes to hide in the alley. Then they would grin while looking for me and give me a good beating if they found me.

She's scared me a lot in the past, but now she's acting if she's the woman of the house and checking up on me. Who gave her the right to do that?

I suddenly had a bright idea. I'm about to make a break through in my womanizer plan in order to chase Xiao Qin away! I could make Su Qiao come over to my house to make me dinner, then purposely let Xiao Qin see. Then I would tell her that Su Qiao is& my maid, and we've already done 'that'. I have to make Xiao Qin say she hates me and make her run away in tears.

Ahahahahaha, I'm a genius. I'm definitely my dad's son!

I thought of an another interesting topic: I could classify all the girls around me as an animal based on their traits.

As a metal blooded lone wolf, I would obviously be a wolf, an Artic Wolf.

Ai Mi would be a small wildcat and Xiong YaoYue would be a panther.

Gong CaiCai would be a rabbit& the type that wouldn't run away even as you prepare a pot next to it to cook her.

Of course, I can't forget Xiao Qin.

Xiao Qin would be a sabre-toothed tiger. A sabre-toothed tiger who pretends to be a cat in daily life. But if she gets serious, she can easily devour all of the previous animals.

Finally, the class leader& would the class leader be a lion, a blank panther, or a eagle.

All the answers above are incorrect, the class leader is a hunter not an animal! The type of hunter who carries around a double barreled shotgun! Other than the cute animals like rabbits and cats who could be taken home as pets, the class leader would instantly shoot to kill any other animals who show any intentions of harming a person. Even an Artic Wolf like me would have to rely on ambushes to secure victory.

My phone vibrated again as I was imagining my own Animal Kingdom.

Was it Xiao Qin again? I looked at the screen and it was a call from Xing Xing.

After I picked up the phone, I could tell Xing Xing was sobbing a bit.

"Brother Ye! We got beat up!"

Huh, when did my phone get hi fi speakers? Why does it feel like Xing Xing's sound is also coming from another direction?

Did you even need to call me? I looked around and saw the Five Tiger Punishment Squat on a nearby bench. Each of them had a badly battered face and looked even worse than the soldiers in the Dunkirk evacuation!

Xing Xing who was on the phone with me also spotted me and began to limp towards me. I signaled to him he should wait there and I walked towards the bench.

At the same, I couldn't help look towards the direction where Xiao Qin headed towards. Xing Xing looked towards the same direction and asked curiously:

"Brother Ye, why are you looking at our principal?"

Huh, from this distance, I could only see Xiao Qin walking with the middle aged man, so he's the principal? Is he the principal of Qing Zi Academy? Is he in the process of discussing exchanging schools with Xiao Qin. Is she finally tired of me giving her the cold shoulder, so she wants to change to Qing Zi Academy? I mean, she's almost about to become my sister, so she might as well come here and join my other sister.

But I heard the principal of Qing Zi Academy in Dong Shan city is also the chairman of the Qing Zi education group. It's a conglomerate with over 36 branches across the country. The middle aged man appeared reserved, you can't even tell he owns that much property.

Why would an education magnate like him personally attend to Xiao Qin? Does Auntie Ren's previous world champion titles have that much weight?

"Brother Ye, brother Ye."

I was brought back to reality with Xing Xing's words. I didn't know whether I should laugh or cry when I saw the sorry states of the four of them sitting on the bench.

"Why did you guys get beat up?"

"They were super unreasonable." Xing Xing complained, "We only strolling around when we accidentally bumped into them and they beat us up."

"Are you sure you didn't curse at them first?"

"We didn't." The other four of them said in unison.

"We listened to you and didn't go around causing trouble. We actually tried to control ourselves, but those guys kept cursing and eventually started using their fists."

"They were high school students?"

"No." Xing Xing shifted his gaze away, "They should be middle school students, no& they're definitely high school students."

"How many people did they have?"

"Th& thirty." The second tiger rushed in to answer.

I snorted, "Don't lie, it was probably only three. It only took three people to reduce you to this state."

The five tigers lowered their heads in shame.

It was actually within my expectations. Even Loud Mouth, Little Smart, and Xiong YaoYue could beat up the five tigers without Little Smart even moving a finger.

"You guys are awful, did you guys mention my name?"

I'm not bragging, but I'm pretty infamous. My name is already a deterrence to those under 16.

"We did. We clearly mentioned your name and were still beat up."

The four of them started speaking at the same time.

"Not only did they beat us until we couldn't get up, they did it while saying that they hated people called Ye. It was better that we didn't mention it, but once we mentioned we were Ye Lin's little brothers, they beat us even harder."

What, what do they have against the Ye surname, if they hate people called Ye, wouldn't they hate my dad as well. What if he was drunk, met them and got beaten up?

No, the five tigers is still a minor issue. They may be wailing right now, but they didn't get any serious injuries. The main problem is I have to fully understand who these people are otherwise I would be at a disadvantage.

Thus I told the five of them to describe the fight in detail to get a gauge of the opponent's strength.

"I'll go first." Xing Xing raised his hands and leaped up, "The first thing they did was kick tiger two down the gutter&."

"Nonsense." Tiger two retorted, "Weren't you the one who was kicked into the gutter?"

Xing Xing coughed awkwardly, "Anyway, one of us was kicked into the gutter, then they took out a blade&"

"Isn't it just a sheet of metal? They would be fugitives if they brought out a knife."

"No, it was a blade." Xing Xing said, "It was a razor blade. It was pretty intimidating in his hands, so we couldn't get closer&"

Huh, those guys are so weird? I've been in so many fights, but it's the first one where a hoodlum would use a razor blade.

"The next person also wasn't careless and picked up a nearby brick&"

How dumb. If there were bricks nearby, why weren't you guys the first ones to get them in your hands?

"We couldn't get closer to the ones holding the razor or the brick, so we chose the empty handed one who seemed like their leader, who would have thought&"

"That person was also the tallest and was wearing a mask." One of them chimed in.

"Anyway, it turns out the masked person was even more brutal than the other two. All of us dropped like flies with a single punch."

Xing Xing always likes to use exaggerated metaphors, but now I have a better understanding of their strength.

"Only fists?" I asked, "Do they use legs?"

"Also& used legs too." Xing Xing added in haste, "When she wanted to kick us, she would lift up her skirt&"

Wait& wait, what? Did you say skirt? The tall and masked leader is a girl?

Xing Xing nodded in shock:

"Didn't I mention that they were all girls? It was a group of vicious female hoodlums."

"You guys&"

I'm pissed. You guys said you were related to me but were beaten up by three girls? Don't tell me it was actually Loud Mout, Little Smart, and Xiong YaoYue.

"Um, brother Ye, don't listen to him. I think they go to an all-girls school&"

"That's right. Dong Shan city only has one all-girls school. I looked it up online and realized they were wearing uniforms from that school."

"I think it was called Thousand Crane Girls School, it's on the border between the east and west districts&"

That has to be the school He Ling attends. The only person I could think of who attends an all-girls school and hates the Ye name is He Ling. Does she pretend to be virtuous in front of others but is actually a female delinquent?

Becuase He Ling has freckles, I asked if any of the three had freckles.

"She did have them." Tiger two said, "The one holding the brick was fat and had a lot of freckles. Also, one of her eyes was larger than the other."

No, that's not He Ling. Plus, her freckles might not even be obvious under the sunlight.

Since their injuries weren't serious, and I had two girls who just bathed waiting for me in room 101, I told them to go back and rest first. I could use the time to look up information on those female delinquents. I usually don't hit woman, but if they came looking for me, I can't have second thoughts.

As I walked backed to the room and was about to knock, I could hear Xiong YaoYue scream:

"Why's my underwear missing?"

"Underwear must have been taken by Obama."

"Why does your dog steal underwear?"

"Who knows. I'm assuming it was the stalker who trained Obama back when I was in America."

"Why doesn't he become an animal trainer instead of being a stalker with his skills!"

"Winnie, if you steal the manservant's line, he wouldn't have anything to do&"

I wasn't trying to eavesdrop on their conversation, but I couldn't find the right time to enter.

"Winnie, I have a lot of new underwear here, so just pick any one of them."

"Eh, I would feel bad&"

Is this the right time to be polite? Then you wouldn't feel bad returning home with no underwear?

"What about this pair? It's pretty elastic, so you should be able to fit in it too."

"Why are you saying it like I have a large butt&"

"It is larger than mines by a lot, but try it on."

"Ah, it's too tight, it's strangling me."

"It can't be helped, that's the largest pair I have. Just put up with it for a while."

"Aah, why did I wear the Qing Zi Academy uniform again? I should have worn my t-shirt and shorts, that way it would be fine even if I wasn't wearing any underwear."

"You'll be questioned if you walk around the academy without an uniform. Don't you think it would be awful if you get taken in for questioning while not wearing underwear?"

"That's true& but the underwear is too tight&"

"If you can't bear with it, I'll tell the manservant to take his off and give it to you&"

What a rotten idea. It sounds like they were both changing, so I entered the room. I could see Xong YaoYue standing with her legs pressed together with an uncomfortable expression while Ai Mi was sitting on the sofa drinking a can of sugar free iced coffee.

"How did you get in?" Xiong YaoYue asked, "I clearly locked the door."

Ai Mi looked up and said calmly:

"Obama opened the door after stealing your underwear. He can open most simple door locks."

Ai Mi realized both me and Xiong YaoYue were looking at her with a strange expression.

"Why are you looking at me like that?"

Why else? It's because of crafty and sly dog.

Xiong YaoYue wanted to stay for dinner before the underwear incident, but she changed her mind and said farewell to Ai Mi.

"Miss Ai Mi. Tomorrow is Monday and I realized I have a lot of unfinished homework. May I head home first?"

"Alright." Although she seemed indifferent, you could hear slight disappointment in her voice, "I'm also getting tired& I'll let Peng TouSi drive you home."

"No need." Xiong YaoYue frantically waved her hands, "My home's not far, so I'll walk back by myself. I ate too much for lunch and I'll get fat if I don't get some exercise."

"It's fine since you only gain weight on your breasts and butt&" Ai Mi grumbled.

"Miss Ai Mi, I have another& how do I say it& presumptuous request."

"Go ahead, I'll give you a lot of benefits as long as you stay loyal to me."

"Um& can you let Ye Lin accompany me?"

"Why?"

"I have some stuff I want to discuss with him. But if you're unwilling to let, then I could head home my self since it's not that important."

"Tsk, I could get a thousand menservants like him at the subway station, why would I be unwilling. You can take him with you and discuss about our Dota team."

"Ah? Isn't it LOL, I don't know how to play Dota!"

"Whatever." Ai Mi said, "Anyway, you have to make sure to build a team that would carry& no, a team I could lead to victory. Then, that would be a great merit and I'll raise you to a level 7 follower and you can experience better treatment."

I was curious, so I pointed to myself and asked me: "What level am I?"

Ai Mi twisted her head to one side and snorted.

"You're at level -1000. You only raise one level for every year you're loyal to me."

So I would have to wait 1000 years to even get into the positives? Do you think I'm a thousand year old tortoise?

Thus I accompanied my level 1007 senior filled with gloom and walked out towards Qing Zi Academy's gates.

As we passed by the gate, the security guard glanced at them, but I was already a familiar face since I've been coming a lot. Xiong YaoYue was also wearing a uniform, so we didn't get exposed.

"Ye Lin." We walked to a secluded alley across the road and Xiong YaoYue said with a poor expression, "I think I'm out of luck."

"What, why?"

"Didn't you hear the phrase joy and sorrow go hand in hand? Wasn't there someone in England who won the lottery but was then sued, so in the end he actually owed tens of millions of dollars?"

"How is that related to you?"

"How is it not? Too many good things happened today, so I knew I would get retribution. Look, my underwear was stolen by Clinton."

It's Obama, not Clinton, thought Clinton may actually have a hobby of stealing underwear (maybe those that belong to White House interns).

"If I stayed for dinner, I may encounter even worse misfortune like being flattened by a road roller when I leave."

Does a normal car not satisfy you? Do you have to be flattened into a sheet of paper?

"Ye Lin, why aren't you scared? Haven't you heard that the amount of happiness you have in life is finite? If you use it all early on in life, then the only thing waiting for you is misfortune."

Who told you those unscientific claims. If you even believe those outrageous lies, be careful so you won't be tricked into joining a MLM.

"I have to take steps to change my fate."

Xiong YaoYue pulled out the ¥900 she won from Ai Mi.

"It must have been because this was earned too easily, so I have to donate it."

I held back my laugh, "Who are you going to donate it to?"

Xiong YaoYue scrunched her brows and began to think:

"Well, the red cross wouldn't work, since I would rather just spend it myself than give it to Guo MeiMei& do you know any reliable charity foundations?"

"If it was me, I would donate it to Jet Li's One Foundation. At least they make their financials public every year and Jet Li has a well-known reputation. If something does go wrong, then we all know who to blame."

"Huh, it sounds like you've donated to One Foundation before?"

Actually, I've never donated, but my dad has donated during the 2013 Lushan earthquake. At the time, they even posted on their website what they lacked most were supplies like tents, sleeping bags, and comforters, and hoped people would donate them.

Our shop had a number of supplies, but none of them can be used in a disaster&

"Alright, since you have experience, I'll let you donate this money to the One Foundation." Xiong YaoYue said as she stuffed the money in my hands.

Her fingers trembled slightly as she parted reluctantly with the money.

I noticed and laughed: "You earned it by letting Ai Mi ride you like a horse, so you should at least keep ¥100."

"Is that alright?" It was as if she was awaiting permission.

"Why not? Haven't you seen All for the Winner where they would donate 95% of their winnings from gambling so that they would keep winning? You won't lose moral character as long as you donate a large portion of it."

"That makes sense, but what's 95% of 900&" Xiong YaoYue counted her fingers.

"You don't have to calculate it, it's fine if you donate ¥800. When I get home, I'll use online banking to&"

I suddenly remembered that Jet Li talked about how getting donations was difficult, but spending donations was even more difficult. It seems they also have certain costs when they legally spend donation money.

If that's the case, why give the One Foundation so much trouble? Isn't there a perfect place nearby? It's the school for handicapped students that Peng TouSi brought me to before.

The handicapped school was established by Ai ShuQiao's husband, John. But Ai ShuQiao has always wanted to dissolve it, that's why the school's been running into financial troubles lately. Some of the teachers even took the initiative and deferred their own paycheques.

I could connect with Peng TouSi and ask him to donate this money to the school. Even though it's not a lot, it would still add up over time. Then if Xiong YaoYue wants to donate again, I can even take her to the school to check it out.

But I won't play Go anymore with Xiao Yu, the kid with cerebral palsy, because it's too embarrassing to lose every time.

I told Xiong YaoYue about the handicapped school in the Yi Ning district and asked her if she would allow me to donate it to the school instead.

I heard there are a lot of children there who suffer from various handicaps, but even if the teachers are loving, some students may have to leave due to the financial situation of the school. Xiong YaoYue couldn't help but be moved and it seemed she was about to cry at any minute.

She gave the remaining ¥100 back to me and said:

"Give it all to them. I'm happy enough that I have all four limbs."

"If you're trying to save your character, then 95% is enough&"

"I'll do 95% next time, they are living difficult lives& but I was enjoying my luxurious meal& sob sob&."

Don't wipe your tears with your sleeves, passersby would think I'm bullying you!

Since Xiong YaoYue was wearing tight underwear, she had to keep her legs together when walking and it made her seem more virtuous.

"Winnie, you'll definitely be more popular with the boys if you want like this." I'm not sure why I told her that.

"Well, if I walk too fast, my underwear will explode."

"Explode?"

"Even if it doesn't explode, it would still tear! That's why you should walk slower!"

She reached out and held onto my arm.

"What are you doing!" I was shocked.

"What else." Xiong YaoYue leaned half her body on me and rolled her eyes, "To make you walk slower while borrowing your body to prevent the underwear from tearing."

"If you're that worried, you should have let Peng TouSi drive you home."

"But that would drop my character, I didn't even stay for dinner."

Xiong YaoYue's ample bosom rubbed against my arm and made me feel weird.

"Please stop& I can't walk properly, can I call a cab for you?"

"You want to take a cab when you have four functioning limbs? How can you face those handicapped kids?"

Huh, why are you trying to educate me? I was only worried about your underwear& tearing.

"It's fine for us to link arms since you're gay."

"Haven't I already told you a hundred times that I'm not gay."

"Okay, okay, I'll make sure to keep it a secret in public&"

Since we were both wearing Qing Zi Academy uniforms and acting intimately, most other passersby would mistake us for a couple.

"Hehe, it's pretty fun&"

"How?"

"Everyone passing by thinks you're my boyfriend, but they don't know you're ga&"

I stared at her fiercely and she swallowed her words.

But she was discontent, so she turned around and spoke to an elementary school girl who was returning home from class.

"Make sure to never find a boyfriend with a bad temper."

She said as she pointed to the bandaid on her face.

"That's domestic violence, and my legs were almost crippled."

The little girl glanced at us and quickly ran away with a pale face.

"What are you saying?" I wanted to hit her on her head, but she caught my fist.

Then she began to shout: "Hitting me in public? Someone come and help! My life is so cruel!"

"Stop talking, I'm begging you." I admitted defeat before a crowd gathered.

"Ah!" Xiong YaoYue suddenly screamed and her face flushed red.

"What?"

"My underwear& ripped."

Since Qing Zi Academy was a private school, the female skirts are shorter than 28 Middle's skirts.

It's short to the point where it only barely covers the knees. It's still pretty avant-garde even though it's not a miniskirt, to the point where they were assigned stockings with their skirts. The absolute territory would definitely be revealed when walking around in this outfit against the wind.

But as for Xiong YaoYue, it wasn't as simple as absolute territory. How torn was her underwear? Would she be completely exposed if the wind came by and flipped up her skirt?

"Is it really torn?" I asked for confirmation.

Xiong YaoYue dragged her feet and turned into a nearby narrow alleyway. Based on the garbage placed at the entrance, this alley should be a dead end.

Using me as cover, right in front of me, she stuck her hand under her skirt and felt inside. It only took a fraction of a second, but for me, it felt like an eternity.

Xiong YaoYue scrunched her face and said with a frown:

"It really tore, it's a crotch-less underwear now."

You don't really have tell me those details, or are you really treating me like one of your female best friends?

"It's like I'm not wearing anything. It feels like the underwear you can buy on those online adult shops."

Please don't say anymore. My store sells these types of underwear and Shu Zhe even wore them once.

"Ye Lin, help me keep watch, I'll head deeper into the alley to take off my underwear."

Don't& take them off! A torn pair of underwear is still better than wearing nothing! Do you really plan on walking home while not wearing underwear? If that's the case, I'm afraid my blood will all fill up one of my body parts. It's a good way to prove I'm not gay, but the price to pay is a bit high.

I realized I was wrong when I saw the bag on her shoulders.

Xiong YaoYue was wearing a Tshirt and shorts in the morning. As long as she wears the shorts underneath her skirt, then it's sufficient to act as safety pants. I mean there's no way she would have walked home without wearing underwear and do some outdoor play.

I stood on my tip toes and peered deeper inside the alley, it turns out there is a dead end. It made me remember the fight I had with Xia B, Li LaoEr, and Zhao GuangTou in the alleyway to protect the class leader's chastity.

"Are you sure an alley is fine?" I asked, "There's an ice cream shop 50m from here, you can use their washroom to change."

Following my finger towards the direction I pointed, Xiong YaoYue saw the ice cream shop's white sign and showed a bitter expression.

"I don't want to go to that store, their goods are too expensive. And the employees all have a bad expression if you order too less, so forget about using their washroom without ordering anything."

"Don't worry." I said, "It's hot today, so I'll treat you to some ice cream. Then, you can use the washroom openly."

"Stop teasing me, do you acutely think you're my boyfriend? If you were actually my boyfriend, I would make you treat me to ice cream everyday until you were out of money!"

After refusing my proposal of going to the ice cream shop, she took out her shorts from her bag. Then, she passed me her bag and told me again to keep watch and she entered alone deeper into the alley.

Before Xiong YaoYue disappeared after moving behind a bend in the alley, it seems she had to take off her underwear first instead of just wearing the shorts over the torn underwear.

In order to free her hands, she used her mouth to hold her skirt, and clutched her shorts under her arms.

There must be a pretty alluring show going on behind me, but how can I peek at a girl changing as a newly-appointed philanthropist? I have to properly stay on the lookout.

Right when I was holding Xiong YaoYue's bag with nothing to do, I saw a familiar figure come out of the ice cream shop.

Speak of the devil, it was Shen ShaoYi. He asked me to relay his love to Xiong YaoYue a few days ago and was rejected.

I quickly tried to cover my face with the bag, but I was too late.

"Ye Lin." Shen ShaoYi walked over astonished, "Why are you wearing Qing Zi Academy's uniform? I almost didn't recognize you."

Shen YaoYi wasn't dressed up as he only had a white shirt and trousers, but he was still exceptionally handsome. But he seemed to be a bit down in spirits.

"I& you& well, what a coincidence." I responded awkwardly, "Why did you come so far away from you home to eat ice cream alone?"

Shen ShaoYi sighed, "Today's Sunday and I was planning on bringing Winnie to this ice cream shop and confessing to her, but it failed. I was feeling a bit depressed and somehow ended walking near here, so I went to the shop and rested there for a while."

I think the best option is to tell him to scram, but he just got his heart broken, so I can't really chase him away without comforting him.

"Um& there's plenty of fish in the sea, don't be too heart-broken."

"I'm not." Shen ShaoYi said, "Winnie only misunderstood that I was gay, but it's not like she has someone else she likes, so that means I still have a chance."

"That's true." I responded while racking my brains to think of a way to get him to leave.

"By the way, are you here with your girlfriend?"

Shen ShaoYi suddenly asked.

"Huh, why do you say that?"

Shen ShaoYi smiled, "You're standing here and it seems like you're waiting for someone while carry a girl's bag."

I looked at the bag in my hands in a fluster: it was pink. It doesn't matter if Peng TouSi prepare it specifically for Xiong YaoYue or it was his own tastes, but this would look like a girl's bag to anybody!

"No&." I didn't know what to say.

"You don't have to be embarrassed." Shen ShaoYi said, "I heard there's a girl called Ren XiaoQin who's always been glued to you recently. It also seems the class leader of class 2-3 also has a slightly ambiguous relationship with you, you have quite the luck with the ladies!"

Shen ShaoYi patted me on the shoulder and it only made me more embarrassed.

"If someone likes you, cherish it." Shen ShaoYi waved at me with bleak eyes, "I'm going to continue with my walk, but whoever your girlfriend is, make sure to spend time with her."

I don't think you have the rights to say those words to me. I think there's enough girls who like you in 28 Middle to form an union. I heard even the prettiest girl in school is interested in you! Why do you only like Xiong YaoYue the tomboy.

I heard a scream from deep in the alley not even three minutes after Shen ShaoYin said farewell.

"Aiiyaaaa"

I was already in a nervous state due to my conversation with Shen ShaoYi, so I subconsciously tuned and ran deeper into the alley.

"What happened, are you okay?"

"It's nothing, I just tripped on a brick&" Xiong YaoYue faced me and maintained a legs apart posture to prevent her from falling. She was holding her shorts in one hand, and a warm pair of freshly removed underwear in her other hand.

Did you take that long to remove the underwear? If you're actually nude under your skirt, then stop staying in this current posture.

I was intending on heading back to stay on the lookout, but Xiong YaoYue said:

"Don't leave yet, take back your cousin's underwear first so I can free up one hand."

She's not a cousin, but my actual sister. Besides, since she already gave it to you, it already belongs to you. Do you really have no qualms about handing over your worn panties to a man?

"Stop dillydallying and take it." Xiong YaoYue urged, "My butt's feeling chilly."

The Qing Zi Academy uniform might have a lot of fake pockets, but the pockets on the skirt are real! Did you forget skirts have pockets because you don't wear them often? You could have just put the underwear into the pockets.

And I can't touch my sister's underwear anymore. Director Cao isn't satisfied with his pair of signed underwear. He reached out to me recently and gave me a new purchase order. He wants at least three pairs, one for collection, one for preaching, and one for daily use. What the hell is daily use? What are you going to do with my sister's underwear everyday? And what do you mean by preaching? Is it not enough to be a pervert by yourself, so you want to share with others?

The worst part is that Director Cao is willing to pay big bucks. Even if it was an unworn pair, he's willing to pay a minimum of ¥10,000. It's even fine if it's dirty or damaged and the underwear Xiong YaoYue is trying to pass to me fits all those conditions.

Before I could reject, Xiong YaoYue actually threw the pair of underwear towards my face.

"Catch."

Damn, I have to catch it or it's going to hit my face! I bitterly held the warm pair of underwear as I retreated from the alley.

Eh, one trouble follows another. I accidentally stepped on a broken brick and lost my balance. But I can't fall in front of Xiong YaoYue. She didn't fall earlier, but if I fall now, then I'll actually be a manservant who's 1007 levels lower than Xiong YaoYue.

I tried to use my left foot that was in contact with the ground to perform a Yin Yang Sanshou move to pull my tilted body back forcefully.

It should have had a one hundred percent chance of success and would have looked cool and received Xiong YaoYue's admiration. Who knew when Xiong YaoYue saw I was about to fall, she pulled me back in the same direction I was also applying force towards. This time I really fell and no one could stop it.

Xiong YaoYue wasn't standing steadily either, so in this process, she also fell down with me. Now we're about to fall onto a ground filled with broken bricks.

The best I could do is grab Xiong YaoYue's waist and flip her on top of me, so I could act as a meat cushion.

It hurt a lot& I had muscles on my back, so it was only minor injuries, but it hurt like hell when my tailbone was pricked with small stones. It would have been a disaster if the stone hit an inch lower.

The final result was me lying on the ground with Xiong YaoYue sitting on top of me like a cushion.

"Huh, how did I get on top of you?"

She couldn't understand my Yin Yang Sanshou moves I used to swap our positions.

"Anyway, hurry up and get off, my back hurts."

I wanted to push her up, but accidentally laid hands on a smooth and elastic part of her body.

Xiong YaoYue shrieked, then began giggle to the point she lost her strength. It didn't even hurt when slapped my hands.

"Ye Lin, don't be a pervert and touch my ass. Even good female friends don't joke around like this."

Then she tried to stand up but shook her head:

"Not good, I laughed too much, and I think I sprained my ankle earlier&"

If that's the case, then stop moving around! If you keep rubbing your bottom area on me, it's making my body feel hot. If I wasn't purposefully diverting my attention, then we would no longer be good female friends.

I screamed out Sparta in my mind and clenched my teeth. I used one hand to hold the ground and the other hand to support Xiong YaoYue's waist, then I pushed myself to stand up along with Xiong YaoYue in my arms.

Xiong YaoYue supported herself with the walls and rested for a bit, but I still didn't let go of her waist to prevent her from falling again.

In the process of standing up, Xiong YaoYue's skirt lifted up slightly and revealed a bit of light skin.

Xiong YaoYue's light skin are all in private areas! We're in a bad position right now and if someone sees&

Huh, why do I feel someone looking at me with killing intent? Was it Xiao Qin who caught us red-handed?

Oh, he scared me, it was only Shen ShaoYi, not Xiao Qin. Did he hear someone shriek, so he came here to check it out? What a good handsome young man who loves to help others.

But his eyes seem a bit red like they are about to spit out fire. He wasn't like this earlier, is he getting a heatstroke?

As expected of a brother from the basketball team. He came over to help once he heard abnormalities, but don't worry, the situation is already under control.

It looks like Shen ShaoYi is about to explode. From his perspective, it looks like Xiong YaoYue is being pressed against an alley wall by me. Her skirt was also raised up to a dangerous degree and it made it seem I was raping her in broad daylight.

Please don't misunderstand. The reason she has a pained expression is because she sprained her foot. We were just both laughing earlier when we fell down, do you think someone being raped would be laughing?

Eh, he originally clenched his fist and wanted to punch, but when he saw the smile on her face, he held his chest and staggered backward.

Did Shen ShaoYi think Xiong YaoYue was cooperating willingly and not being forced?

Please don't misunderstand, I haven't even taken my pants off.

To prove my innocence, I spread my hands out and stepped away from Xiong YaoYue.

"Shen ShaoYi, it's not what you think, let me explain&"

Shen ShaoYi's sights was locked onto my right wrist.

Huh, what are you looking at? I have a watch on my left wrist, but there's nothing on my right wrist.

I took a look, shit, it was the torn underwear Xiong YaoYue had just taken off.

This once again confirmed his suspicions: Xiong YaoYue wasn't wearing any underwear because I had taken them off.

I'm innocent. Even though she's not wearing anything underneath, I wasn't the one who removed it!

"How& long have the two of you been together?"

Shen ShaoYi clenched his teeth and squeezed out those words.

"It's an accident." I said in a hurry, "Believe me, I won't do anything to wrong a brother."

Shen ShaoYi completely didn't hear my words. His voice got deeper and he was like a volcano that was about to erupt.

"I'm not angry because you're with Winnie, but because you didn't tell me you two were already together."

"Was it fun watching me be distressed over someone you already obtained?"

"You even lied to me and said Winnie rejected me because she thought I was gay&"

"You still say you won't do anything to wrong a brother& but this level of betrayal&."

"Alright, alright, are you done?"

Xiong YaoYue interrupted Shen ShaoYi's tearful complaints.

"What right do you have to get mad at Ye Lin?" Xiong YaoYue seemed to be even angrier than Shen ShaoYi and it made him flabbergasted.

"You say Ye Lin betrayed you& but weren't you the one who betrayed him first?"

"What?"

"Don't act dumb. Weren't you the one who told Ye Lin to tell everyone you wanted to go on a date with me? If you want to dump Ye Lin, just tell him straight out instead of using these low-life tactics."

Shen ShaoYi was pissed speechless.

"I& I'm not gay. Besides, in the rumors it was supposed to be me and captain Guo SongTao& no, it has nothing to do with the captain or Ye Lin."

Xiong YaoYue had a look of disdain.

"Hah, looks like you're denying it pretty well. But why can't you admit the truth since you've already been with Ye Lin for a while. In order to please you, Ye Lin was even willing to wear black lace panties&"

Shen ShaoYi looked at me in shock and I quickly shook my head in denial.

Xiong YaoYue continued to say:

"Well, you were the one who dumped him first, so don't blame him when he doesn't want you anymore. And don't worry about what the two of us do together because it has nothing to do with you. Ye Lin isn't wrong, so if you have dissatisfaction, come to me."

As Xiong YaoYue lectured Shen ShaoYi, she sent me a meaningful glance as if to say: "How's that? I'm helping you out."

I'm not an abandoned wife who needs your sympathy. Shen ShaoYi felt like I stole his woman, but you feel like you stole Shen ShaoYi's man. Other than the victim always being Shen ShaoYi, the misunderstandings only keep increasing.

After being scolded by Xiong YaoYue, Shen Shao Yi closed his eyes, then opened it and asked with hesitation:

"When& did you get together with Ye Lin."

"Does it have anything to do with you?" Xiong YaoYue slapped her own chest, "Hit me if you're mad!"

The situation was extremely weird like I was the wife who had an illicit lover.

Shen ShaoYi sighed with incomparable sadness, "Winnie, I don't have the right to prevent the two of you being together, but& you should take care of yourself and don't& with Ye Lin in this kind of place&"

"What's wrong with this place? It just suits my tastes." Xiong YaoYue purposely wanted to make him mad.

"Perhaps, did Ye Lin force you&"

Shen ShaoYi might be better than me at basketball, but he's light-years behind in a fight. He calmed down a bit and abandoned the idea of fighting me, but only kept glaring at me.

"Ye Lin didn't force me." Xiong YaoYue pushed the blame on herself, "I watched too many AVs in internet cafes and wanted to try some outdoor play with Y Lin. We already took a bath together in the morning, if you're jealous, you should hit me!"

Who took a bath with you, that was my sister! And the person he really wants to hit is me.

As expected, Shen ShaoYi actually believed Xiong YaoYue's nonsense. He staggered back and looked at me while tightening and loosening his fists. He finally yelled out angrily:

"Ye Lin, you& for making fun of me, don't call me your bro anymore."

He turned around and ran away after a tear appeared in the corner of his eyes.

"Just you wait. In this year's basketball tournament, I'll make class 2-3 lose even more miserably than last year."

After laying down his threat, the most handsome boy in school ran away with tears in his eyes.

Xiong YaoYue punched my chest lightly while pleased with herself.

"How about it, I'm pretty great, right?"

It's pretty great you were able to help while ignoring your reputations, but you caused more trouble instead and made him pissed.

"But it seems Shen ShaoYi still cares since he shed tears for you. There's hope of the two of you getting back together&"

Shen ShaoYi was crying because of you! It's because the girl he likes doesn't have any self-respect and was fooling around with another guy in an alley! I promised the class leader I would take number one in the basketball competition and Shen ShaoYi was the biggest obstacle to our class. Now because of Xiong YaoYue, he's going to try his hardest. I can kiss my dreams of getting free meals at the class leader's house goodbye.

The only comforting fact is that Shen ShaoYi isn't one to gossip, so he wouldn't make today's events well-known. He wouldn't do anything to damage Xiong YaoYue's reputation nor would he make all the members of the basketball team think I'm a bad person. He would only silently keep it in his heart and try his hardest against me in the competition. Even, Liu HuaiShui, the rear guard in his class would wonder about why he tries so hard.

Xiong YaoYue rubber feet, then you could hear a startling crack. She then announced she fixed her sprained foot.

How did you even recover that quickly? The last time I was injured by Xiao Qin, I had the cast around my arm for two weeks!

After putting on the shorts under her skirt, she returned back to a sports girl. She said her farewell and began running back home.

Because her skirt fluttered in the wind, a lot of males would do a side glance but be disappointed when they see the safety pants under her skirt.

I went to the rec center after simple dinner and played some basketball with a stranger.

I can't neglect my basketball skills. If we can't take the championship and I also score fewer points than Niu ShiLi, then I won't be able to get free meals and I would also have to drink Fu Yan Jie.

Due to the amount of psychological pressure I felt, my performance was average and I returned home dejected.

The next day was Monday. As I sat in my seat trying to copy homework, Xiao Qin closed her eyes and began to sniff me from afar.

"Ye Lin classmate had physical contact with a girl yesterday, right? I could smell it."

Hey, who gave you permission to speak as if you're my wife. Besides, it's normal to have a woman's scent since I visited my sister yesterday.

"There's something wrong with your nose." I denied it with an unnatural expression, "The whole street is filled with women who use perfume, so it's not strange to get a bit of their smell on me."

"But&" Xiao Qin furrowed her brows and said quietly, "10% is an unknown smell, 20% is from Ai Mi, and 80% belongs to the our PE committee member&"

That's already over 100%, no wonder you failed the sciences. But your sense of smell is incredible.

I haven't done anything wrong, so there's nothing to be afraid of. But even if she does suspect me, that's exactly what I want to happen.

"Tsk, none of your business of who I hang out with. But I saw&. no, someone saw you with the principal of Qing Zi Academy&"

"So, it was Ye Lin classmate at Qing Zi Academy yesterday?" Xiao Qin asked with a red face, "Did the dress look good on me?"

"Don't change the topic." I said seriously, "What were you doing with the principal? Are you planning to transfer, if so, that's a huge reli&."

"How would I be willing to part with Ye Lin classmate?" Xiao Qin exclaimed, "Even if it's someone who only wanted to change seats with me, I would kill& no, I would persuade her to give up."

So you would kill her if she doesn't give up? What a cruel and merciless childhood friend.

"If you're not transferring, why were you with the principal&"

"Do you really want to know?"

"What, are you trying to keep it a secret from me?"

"No, no, no&" Xiao Qin replied in haste, "The only thing that's a secret is my weight. Even if you wanted to know my breast size, even if it's a bit embarrassing, I would still tell you. I just measured it yesterday and it was&"

"Don't start talking about breasts, I was asking what you were doing with the principal, was it something unspeakable?"

Xiao Qin swallowed and replied:

"What unspeakble things can I do with my uncle?"

"What, who's your uncle?"

"The principal! He wanted me to visit their new swimming pool. I didn't want to go, but my mom made me go."

"Lies. The principal already has half a head of white hair, but Auntie Ren looks really young. How could your uncle be that old?"

"It's not a lie, my uncle is older than my mom by 20 years! He adores my mother, but my mom feels a generation gap with him, so their relationship is a bit strange."

"Why is there such a large gap? Does Auntie Ren have a lot of siblings?"

"Nope, it's only the two of them."

"Then why is there a 20 year age difference? What did Auntie Ren's dad go to do for twenty years?"

"I asked my grandfather and it seems he went to compete in martial arts. He disappeared for 20 years, so everyone thought he was dead, but he gave brith to my mom after coming back&"

Wait& wait, why does this sound so familiar? If I think about it, didn't gramps also leave for 20 years after his son was born to train his martial arts, then also had a daughter when he returned?

I already knew the martial arts circle was small, but not to this extent! Gramps is actually Xiao Qin's grandfather and Auntie Ren's father!

No wonder Xiao Qin showed a lot of Hua Jin when I went to her house to save brother Optimus Prime. So the genius granddaughter gramps was talking about was Xiao Qin!

That's also why Auntie Ren asked me who taught me when I was fighting He Ling at the taekwondo dojang, becuase it was her own family's fighting style!

But why didn't Xiao Qin use Yin Yang Sanshou in the fight in the construction yard?

Is it because she had already lost her sense of reasoning when she went into dark mode? That means she didn't even use her full strength during that fight!

Gramps already told me before that his granddaugher was more skilled than me, and Xiao Qin must have already learned Fa Jin too.

I originally thought I was on a level playing ground, but I would still be too weak if she fought with her full strenght?

Why? Why is stronger than me even after staying at home for three years? I hate these genius types.

I originally wanted to tell Xiao Qin I was learning from her grandfather, but I thought it would be too embarrassing to let her know I still couldn't beat her with her family's skills.

So I changed the topic towards her uncle who was both the principal and chairman of the Qing Zi education conglomerate.

"Wait, if your uncle is so successful, why were you living in those compounds with Auntie Ren when you were younger? Can't Auntie Ren find a good place to live just by acting cute towards her brother?"

"Oh that& my mom had a falling out with my grandfather and my uncle stood on his side, so my mom hated them both&"

So, Auntie Ren was living in an old house in a compound because she was having a fit? If she accepted her brother's help, then the Little Tyrant would have never become my neighbor! I hate Xiao Qin's uncle so much. If you're going to be a siscon, then do your job properly! How could you let Auntie Ren live in that old house for so many years!

I think the reason Auntie Ren and gramps had a falling out was because Auntie Ren got married in Hong Kong without the approval of her parents. I think Xiao Qin's father had the surname of Huo. No wonder gramps hates people named Huo. There was an article in a film magazine that described Auntie Ren's story. Apparently, Huo still couldn't change his philanderous ways after being married to Auntie Ren and he ended up being caught in the act. Auntie Ren didn't give him a chance to explain and beat them silly and ran back to mainland China with her child.

I also hate Xiao Qin's father. If he didn't betray Auntie Ren, then I wouldn't have been bullied by the Little Tyrant for so many years!

It's been so many years, but Auntie Ren and the gramps' relationship still haven't recovered. You can tell their relationship has improved a bit since Xiao Qin has learned Yin Yang Sanshou from gramps, but with his strange temper, he definitely would have said this to Auntie Ren:

"Didn't I tell you he wasn't trustworthy, why didn't you listen to your elders&."

Auntie Ren, who has an explosive temper, would have instantly erupted and split apart Xiao Qin and her father. Xiao Qin's uncle would have tried his best to console both sides.

I suddenly thought of something.

"Xiao Qin, if you're uncle is both the chairman and the principal, it should be pretty easy for you to get your hands on a set of their uniform, right?"

"That's right. I have a few sets of the female uniforms at home, I even have versions that are no longer used. Plus& I also asked my uncle for a few male outfits based on your body size, so we can use them as matching couples outfits&"

Screw that, if you had uniforms, then why didn't you give them to me earlier when I asked you to help me sew the buttons? So, you didn't forcefully take those buttons, but instead took brand new ones off a brand new uniform and sewed it back onto an old uniform. I have no words to describe your stupidity.

"About, about the button&" Xiao Qin stammered, "It's a rare chance to be able to sew clothes for you and to fulfill one of my top ten greatest wishes, so I couldn't give it up. That uniform who was picked clean of its buttons will also forgive me."

Hell no it won't forgive you. It's going to fly out of the closet tonight and smother you to death in your sleep!

I returned Gong CaiCai's language homework after I finished copying it, and she spoke feebly:

"Um& Ye Lin classmate, it's better to do homework on your own&."

Gong CaiCai's homework didn't stay in her hands for more than a second before if was snatched by Xiong YaoYue.

"Is Ye Lin done, then let me copy it."

Gong CaiCai could only turn to Xiong YaoYue and say: "Xiao Xiong, it's better to do the homework on your own&"

"I know, I know." Xiong YaoYue said while copying, "I'll do tomorrow's by myself. And lately I like the name Winnie, so call me Winnie instead of Xiao Xiong."

"But& Winnie the Pooh is male&" Gong CaiCai said.

"How do you know he's male? Winnie the Pooh never wears pants, but I never see a dick between his leg."

Gong CaiCai's face turned red and became silent when the topic of dicks were brought up.

It seems Xiong YaoYue had already forgotten that in the alley yesterday she was also not wearing any pants like Winnie the Pooh.

By the way, in order to avoid conjectures, I have to make something clear: I didn't sell the underwear that Ai Mi gave to Xiong YaoYue to Director Cao.

It was& cremated! In order to stop its temptations, I burned it on the gas stove.

The flames shot up really high and it almost hit the kitchen hood and caused a fire! A man like me almost died to a pair of underwear!

After wrapping up with the underwear issue, I called Peng TouSi and asked about donating to the special needs school.

I only then found out that Peng TouSi donates half of his monthly income to that school. The school could only barely hold on with his generous contributions.

"Huh, Peng TouSi, you're a selfless model citizen. It's certain you're going to heaven if you've done this many good deeds."

"I can only hope. I've taken many lives before, so I'm doing as much as I can right now to make up for it. If I can't go to heaven, then I can't meet the enchanting God."

Are you still thinking of hooking up with God. Have you already resolved yourself to be the mistress between God and Mother Mary? If you succeed, then you'll become Jesus' stepmother. Should I try to get into a good relationship with you while you're still a mortal, so I would have someone covering for me after you become a god?

Finally, I transferred the ¥900 from Xiong YaoYue through online banking and asked Peng TouSi to donate it to the school.

In my eyes, Peng TouSi is even more reliable than the Red Cross.

Now, it's time to go back to Monday after recounting the underwear and donation events.

Every time before gym class, the girls would have to change, so all the boys would be chased out the classroom. Today was no exception.

Xiao Qin who still wasn't participating in gym class, came next to me while I was practicing basketball and whispered:

"(*^＿^*) Hehe& I found a secret. Someone as perverted as you would for sure be interested, do you want to know?"

Don't use the perverted adjective to describe me, at least use words like outstanding, or great, or divine.

"When everyone was changing in the classroom, I realized a lot of girls aren't wearing bras because it's too hot."

"No way. Usually we sweat more when it's hot out, so wouldn't that mean it's more likely for them to expose themselves."

"It's true." Xiao Qin vowed, "The ones who were afraid of it sticking out used pasties, and they even compared whose pasties looked better!"

It's definitely a lie, but it's a scene to yearn for&. a class full of nude girls huddling around and discussing pasties&

Xiao Qin exclaimed and seemed to have remembered something.

"The class leader wasn't wearing a bra and her pasty was in the shape of a shell."

I am now positive you're lying. There's no way she would come to school without underwear, and she would never use a pasty.

"It's your choice if you want to believe me." Xiao Qin pouted, "It's getting hot, so the class leader's becoming more fickle. All secondary female characters have those personality traits."

"The class leader must think she's like a mermaid with those shell pasties. You can go take a look if you don't believe me."

Xiao Qin said as she pointed towards the volleyball court where the class leader was practicing.

I ignored Xiao Qin and played a bit more basketball.

As class was almost over, I strolled over by the volleyball courts due to boredom and watched the class leader and Xiong YaoYue play.

Xiong YaoYue's foot had already fully healed. What an extraordinary healing ability, is she an earthworm? Would she become two of her if I split her in half?

Xiong YaoYue moved nimbly on the court and didn't hesitate when it came to hitting the ball and was especially fierce during spikes. A perfect example of a tomboy.

As for the class leader's volleyball skills, I could only see:

The class leader's breasts, the class leader's breasts, the class leader's breasts, the class leader's breasts, the class leader's breasts, the class leader's breasts&.

What's going on, Xiao Qin's words left a strong impression on me. I kept staring at the class leader's breast trying to figure out if she was going no bra and wearing a pasty.

Eunuch Cao came up from behind and offered a tissue to me with both his hands.

"Master, please use this."

"Huh, why are you giving me a tissue?"

"Master, you're drooling&"

As I was wiping up my drool, the bell rang and for some reason Eunuch Cao ran away. In an instant, the class leader had already walked up to me while holding a volleyball.

Although I knew it was a bad situation, I couldn't control my eyes, and the only thing I was thinking was:

The class leader's breasts, the class leader's breasts, the class leader's breasts&

Huh, there doesn't seem to be a shell-shaped pasty.

"Did you know girls can feel a perverts gaze?"

"I'm not a pervert." I denied it while hiding the drool covered tissue behind my back.

"Then why are you staring at my breasts?"

"I'm only curious&"

"Do you also stare at other people like this on the streets?"

"No, other people don't have shell-shaped breasts&."

Ah, the class leader struck me square on the face with the volleyball, then she turned around with a flick of her hair. In the time she turned, I could see the slight outline of bra straps under her sportswear.

She's clearly wearing a bra. I fell for Xiao Qin's tricks again and lowered the class leader's impression of me again.

I tried to correct myself to the class leader:

"It's all Xiao Qin's fault. I thought you weren't wearing a bra&"

The second consecutive volleyball strike and this time I got a nosebleed. I was able to personally experience the might of the class leader's spikes. It looks like there's a high chance of class 2-3 taking home the win.

I went to the infirmary to ask Chen YingRan for some cotton swabs and found Xiao Qin was already there having a delightful conversation with Chen YingRan.

"Ah, why's Ye Lin classmate's nose bleeding?" Xiao Qin jumped up and came closer to take a look, "I already told you to not be so perverted or it will be dangerous!"

I glared at her.

I got nosebleed because I listened to your lies! Did you want the class leader to get mad at me on purpose? I'm never going to believe your words from now on.

After plugging my nose with cotton swabs, I noticed Chen YingRan was reading a newspaper with shocking headlines: "Fu Jian women molests 4 year old boy and kissed his dick until swollen".

"Kissing a 4 year old, how inhumane." Chen YingRan criticized with self-righteousness.

So is it considered human when you kiss a 14 year old?

When I returned to the classroom, someone had slipped a note in my desk: "I'm returning the gift card, don't think you can take advantage of me by giving me benefits."

Next to the slip was the ¥500 gift card I won last Friday with the class leader. It was sitting there quietly as if it was ridiculing me.

I looked at the class leader and she was studying intently and didn't even look at me.

Xiao Qin, on the other hand, was abnormally happy.

"Ah, where did you get that gift card? How about I go shopping with you tonight?"

Xiao Qin purposely made the class leader believe that I'm a pervert and wanted to bait me in going shopping with her.

Of course I would reject her unreasonable request.

"Since you made up lies to trick me, your favorability with me has dropped."

I said to her clearly.

Xiao Qin made a wail like an injured animal to get my attention, but I ignored her.

During physics class, Xiao Qin who couldn't understand anything kept fiddling with her pencil case and began to chat with me.

"Ye Lin classmate, recently I've been reading Adachi romance manga&"

"Oh, the author who has identical protagonists in all his books?"

I already knew all the stuff being taught, so there was no need for me to listen attentively in class.

"I saw a boy in the manga who loves girls' underwear&"

"Hey, don't bring the conversation in a strange direction! I guess Adachi is a pervert for making these manga."

"No, you can't bad mouth Adachi-sensei. His manga are perfectly healthy and very romantic."

It could be because Japan has way too many serious perverts, so Adachi seems healthy and normal in comparison.

"I heard Li Ao's first love also removed her underwear and gave it to him& is giving a boy your underwear some sort of romantic etiquette I haven't heard about?"

"No such perverted etiquette exists and what are you trying to say?"

"Uh&. do you want mines?"

"What."

"I've only been saying it, but haven't actually given you my underwear. I've been disrespectful. The reason why you don't really like me is probably because of my lack of manners."

Manners from which planet? And why are you certain I like underwear?

"The fairy godmother told me in a dream last night that Ye Lin classmate is suffering from a lack of underwear. He would get sick if he doesn't come into contact with a girl's underwear for a prolonged period of time, and it's true because you got a nosebleed today&"

Xiao Qin grabbed the hems of her skirt and said with embarrassment:

"Since Ye Lin classmate said you would help me with my androphobia, then I should help with your lack of underwear& It's my responsibility as the girlfriend&"

You don't have to take responsibility, I don't want you to take responsibility.

"That's why&" Xiao Qin closed her eyes and said with determination, "If Ye Lin classmate wants underwear, I can take it off for you anytime, even now."

Now&? Our class is filled with 40 students and the teacher is currently teaching a class and you want to do a live strip show? Which AV has this plot?

Even if you don't get noticed when removing your underwear, what would you do afterwards? Would you return home wearing nothing underneath? Did you already forget about the pervert you met on the subway?

"Um& does Ye Lin classmate not want it?"

She looked at me with abashedly and with a hint of bitterness.

I don't have a bad hobby of asking my female classmates for their underwear and forcing them to wear nothing for the rest of the day. If the class leader found out, she would greet me with her gun.

"Ye Lin." the physics teacher suddenly called my name, "Come up and answer this question."

The physics teacher always calls on me in class to answer questions because I have a good physics grade.

As I walked towards the front of the classroom, Xiao Qin looked as if she was a wife sending her husband off to the front lines.

"Ye Lin classmate, you have to return alive. I'll be waiting for you at home."

Can you even consider your desk as home? Maybe you consider answering a physics question as the front lines, but for me it's as easy as eating a meal.

I quickly answered the question and the teacher nodded proudly and let me return to my seat.

It seems like the physics teacher believes the only reason a bad student like me has good physics grades is because of his unique teaching style.

It actually has nothing to do with him. My dad was a space physics professor before he opened up an adults goods store, and even now he can still create teaching materials for university students.

It was unexpected as Xiao Qin was silent when I returned to my seat, but her face was flushed red.

I knew something was wrong and realized there was something extra placed in my desk.

Damn, it was a perfectly folded pair of underwear. It was still warm to the touch, so it was just taken off!

Did you do it? Did you really do it? I never expected you to actually take off your underwear during class! Is this because of that H manga you read two months ago?

Dang, it's a red and white striped cartoon underwear with a picture of angry birds on the back.

I wanted to toss it back to her and tell her to wear it, but wearing underwear in class may be even harder than taking it off. It's not worth it if she gets discovered.

So I kept it in my pockets, and I was planning on forcing her to wear it in the washroom after class.

"It looks like you're getting more guts!" I looked at her with contempt.

"Hehe, I'll get embarrassed if you compliment me (????) ~~~"

Who's complimenting you? Most girls wouldn't even be able to sit down on their bare bottoms.

"Put it back on after class." I ordered her.

"But it took a while for me to make up my mind and take it off for Ye Lin classmate."

"Then put it back on for me."

"I'm not wearing it. If you want to know why, it's because I'm very comfortable right now."

Com& comfortable? Does it really feel that good wearing nothing underneath your skirt? I'm disappointed, I never expected her to be a licentious girl. No wonder she goes and chats with Chen YingRan everyday. She's walking on the path of becoming a huge female pervert.

After the bell rang, Xiao Qin jumped out of her seat and it almost gave me a heart attack as I was afraid she would have exposed herself.

"Try to move less&." Xiao Qin went to look for loud mouth before I even finished speaking. She had no intention of worrying over the fact she was wearing nothing underneath.

"For some reason I feel like playing Jianzi and skipping rope today."

"Can your body handle it?" Loud Mouth expressed her concerns.

Her body is fine, but her clothes aren't. There's a high chance of being exposed playing either of those two games while wearing a skirt! And in your case, if you're exposed, everything will be revealed!

Little Smart joined the conversation, "Nobody skips rope anymore, although some people do play Jianzi, it's too tiring& I could recommend a book to pass the time. 'Rebirth of Son and Father' is pretty good, even if it has a crappy ending&"

What kind of crap are you recommending! But at this time, reading any kind of book would be better than playing Jianzi or skipping rope.

The class leader was passing through during their conversation, and when Xiao Qin went to make way, she actually tripped on the leg of a table and fell.

It was definitely on purpose. Her lower body was as strong as steel when she was the Little Tyrant.

I started to sweat bullets as her waist began to bend up as she fell.

Good thing the class leader caught her.

"Did I bump you, sorry." The class leader apologized.

"It's okay." Xiao Qin revealed her natural ditzy smile, "It was my own fault. By the way, can you play Jianzi with me later?"

"Jianzi?" The class leader was curious, "Did you suddenly take a liking to sports? But the teacher was looking for me, I won't make it for this class, but what about lunch break&."

"Oh, then you can go ahead, I'll look for you at lunch." Xiao Qin waved at the class leader.

Xiao Qin then went to the washroom with Little Smart and Loud Mouth without giving me any time to make my move.

I couldn't hand her underwear back in front of other people, so I tried to call her out alone. But Xiao Qin held her stomach and pleaded:

"Ye Lin classmate, can we talk later? I& I can't hold it&"

Loud Mouth stared at me coldy, "Do you have any sympathy? Girls already have to wait a long to time to use the washroom, what if she can't hold it in?"

Little Smart muttered like she was chanting a curse: "Shen ShaoYi belongs to captain Guo SongTao, the person's who's trying to interfere won't meet a good end&"

Damn it, Xiao Qin's clearly faking! And Xong YaoYue was the one who made Shen ShaoYi have a change of heart, so go look for her!

I stood about 10m away from the entrance to the girl's washroom and watched Xiao Qin and the others chat among themselves.

"Where's Zhuang Ni, the arts committee member, is she still on sick leave&.?" Little Smart sighed, "I was hoping she could draw some pictures for my novel."

Novels like 'Rebirth of Father and Son'? Unspeakable pictures such as a father pushing down his son?

"I don't think Zhuang Ni's sick, I think she just doesn't want to come to school." Loud Mouth said, "It was her birthday a few days ago, so I gave her a call, but the first thing she asked me was: 'Are you still fat?', it seems like she really wants a beating."

"That's just her personality, she always hits other people's sore spots. But her reason was actually pretty frightening. She took a three month leave since new years and said she had leukemia, and now she hasn't come at all for this semester because she said her leukemia turned into Ebola&"

"The worst part is they actually accepted her reasoning. I also want to laze around at home and not come to school."

"It won't work for you. The only reason they accepted Zhuang Ni's excuse was because she cut her own wrists in class in her first year and scared the school. The school must have thought it's better for her to die at home than at school."

"The school really has no conscience&"

Xiao Qin couldn't join in their conversation, then she suddenly lifted up Loud Mouth's skirt from behind.

What thick tree trunk legs. A lot of nearby girls laughed. Loud Mouth was both embarrassed and angry and glared at Xiao Qin and said:

"Okay, so you want to play? I'll get you back."

She said as she reached for Xiao Qin's skirt.

St& stop! Although I'm the only boy around, there's a lot of girls here from other classes! If they realized Xiao Qin was naked under her skirt, she would get a reputation of not wearing underwear!

Xiao Qin placed her hands in a defensive manner in front of her chest, she had no intention of protecting her skirt.

Did she life Loud Mouth's skirt because she wanted to get her to lift her own skirt? Is she not satisfied until she shows the entire school her naked butt?

In the worst possible timing, the class leader had just finished her conversation with teacher Yu and began walking towards the girl's washroom.

She saw me and said: "Did you come to take advantage of girls, even if it's the girl's washroom&."

Before she finished, Loud Mouth used all her strength and pulled up Xiao Qin's skirt.

Xiao Qin twisted like a petal floating in the sky and yelled: "Nooo~~~~~"

I widened my eyes in despair.

White skin, white skin, white skin& we passed the absolute territory and was about to head towards the forbidden territory.

Xiao Qin, the days of you being a nobody is over. You will now become a famous person in 28 Middle and be known as the perverted girl who doesn't wear underwear.

Right when I was upset, there was a piece of triangle fabric between her legs. She was wearing underwear! It was a pure white underwear with a picture of Hello Kitty!

What's going on? The pair she gave to me in class was still warm, unless& she wore two pairs to school today? Did she purposely make me feel alarmed to play with me?

The class leader looked at me scornfully.

"So you were waiting for something like this? Your eyes widened to that extent& how vulgar."

"Don't play around in hallways anymore." The class leader scolded Loud Mouth, "Do you not see the pervert standing on the side?"

Xiao Qin happily waved at me and went in the washroom.

I returned to the classroom seething with anger and stuffed the underwear back into Xiao Qin's bag.

In the end, my actions were spotted by Gong CaiCai who was carrying a stack of homework.

"YeYeYeYeYe Lin classmate, if I'm not mistake, you just stuffed& a pair of girl's underwear into Xiao Qin classmate's bag&"

"That's right." I openly admitted. I would have had a heart attack if it was the class leader questioning me.

"Why does Ye Lin classmate have female underwear?"

Ever since I saved Gong CaiCai from the rabbit incident and also borrowed her homework to copy from, she seemed to be no longer afraid of me and even questioned me continuously.

"It was during class when Xiao Qin&. no, she gave it to me last night, but I'm returning it to her now."

Gong CaiCai showed a frightened expression and the homework she collected slowly fell one by one to the ground, and I could only help her pickt them up.

"Thank you for your help& but why did Xiao Qin classmate remove her underwear and give it to you, it's so embarrassing&."

"It's because I'm perverted and love forcing girls to do embarrassing things. Didn't I tell you to keep your distance from me?"

"I& I'm not afraid of Ye Lin classmate."

Gong CaiCai lowered her head and mumbled.

"What?" Someone like Gong CaiCai who cries when a beetle lands on her head can claim she's not afraid of me? Is she implying I'm inferior to a beetle?

"I've read that the ones who say they are bad are never really bad&"

"Don't believe everything you read! When I was in elementary school, I read in a book that eating sweet potatoes can increase Neigong, so I ate it for a whole week but only got diarrhea as a result."

Gong CaiCai pursed her lips and laughed a bit after hearing my childhood story.

"Ye Lin classmate really knows how to joke around, why would you need neigong as a kid?"

It's not a joke, it's a true story. I needed neigong to defeat the Little Tyrant. There were no travelling masters nearby to pass me their skills, so I could only eat sweet potatoes on my own!

"Ye Lin classmate must have picked up Xiao Qin's underwear by chance and wanted to return it to her without embarrassing her."

Gong CaiCai gave a benevolent conjecture on what had happedned.

"No, even if I did pick up a pair of underwear, how would I know it belongs to Xiao Qin? Listen, Xiao Qin took a nap at my home yesterday and I took off her underwear while she was sleeping."

"Uh&. that&."

"I'm shameless and I already said I'm an incorrigible pervert. Don't come into contact with me other than lending me your homework for me to copy."

"Ye Lin classmate, the class leader will be sad&"

Do you still think the class leader and I are a couple? Do you still firmly believe it because you witnessed us kissing first?

"And it's not good to play around with Xiao Qin classmate's feelings& if Ye Lin classmate can't endure it, I&."

You& will do what? Are you going to act as a substitue for Xiao Qin?

"I could let you borrow two year's worth of FHM magazines. You can use them to alleviate your lust&"

Isn't FHM essentially a Chinese playboy magazine targeted towards males? I heard it's filled with female celebrities wearing revealing clothing. Why would you have two years worth of that magazine? If your father ordered it, he should do a better job of hiding it from his daughter!

"Actually& my dad didn't order it, I did&"

"Why would you order that?"

"Because& when I was home alone, a salesman came to our house and I couldn't refuse him, so I could only place a order&"

Forcing a sale and making a middle school girl buy FHM. That salesman has no morals.

"I also ordered 'Modern Weapons', 'World Military Affairs', 'Navy Warships"&. and 120 cases of makeup and gave it all to my mother&."

You're basically the savior of all salesman. You will definitely have to pay bitterly later in life if you don't learn how to reject people.

"If Ye Lin classmate needs it&"

Xiao Qin and Loud Mouth and the others came back before we finished speaking. When she saw me speaking with Gong CaiCai, she frowned and said while grabbing Gong CaiCai's collar:

"Give my breasts back to me."

Gong CaiCai trembled and escaped back to her own seat. She was close to falling flat on the ground while running with the stack of homework.

Xiao Qin mumbled: "Trying to show off to Ye Lin classmate because you have large breasts& I'm working really hard and will have bigger ones than you one day."

It's not something you can get with hard work. I remember when we lived in the compound there was a kid who worked hard to try and become ultraman. But even if his wish came true, your wish wouldn't come true.

"Hmph, if you're still larger than me in ten years, then I'll cut&"

Seeing me glower at her, Xiao Qin quickly picked up a history textbook and said to me with a smile:

"Which year did Colombus discover the Americas?"

Well, it's defintiely not the year when you cut off someone else's breasts, or are you actually thinking& of doing a transplant? Will your hate disspate after you switch out your flat breasts?

I spent the entire history class managing the online store on my phone. Lately, business has been going pretty well. We've even been able to sell two blow-up dolls that hasn't been selling well before.

The perverts Uncle Fireball, Cilantro Buns, and Popeye still fight over 'Southland Red Berries' underwear. Especially Cilantro Buns who always chats with her and got entranced by Shu Zhe's sweet words. He would always message me about one thing: how can he make Southland Red Berries agree to open a room with him.

Uncle Fireball also criticized our store for a lack of new products. Even the lipstick balloons he suggested aren't available for sale. I could only tell him it's being prepared and will be sold within the next couple of days.

During lunch break, the class leader fulfilled her promise and brought Xiao Qin to play Jianzi on the sports fields, but Xiao Qin had terrible performance and couldn't catch nine out of ten hits. Later, she even pretended to faint from lack of stamina, so the class leader could only stop and buy some sports drinks for Xiao Qin.

Xiao Qin drank the sport drink the class leader gave her while mumbling:

"Although I let the class leader take the first sip, I still can't guarantee she didn't poison it. If I die, then it would be a while before I'm able to see Ye Lin classmate again&"

Are you not going to give up even after you die? Are you going to be waiting in the nether world?

And isn't it an indirect kiss if you drank it right after the class leader? But I guess it's harmless since you're both girls. But why am I feeling a bit jealous of Xiao Qin?

I continued to do customer service during the afternoon's chemistry class. I strained my eyes too much when class ended, so I laid on my desk to rest for a while.

"Ye Lin classmate, you'll damage your eyes if you keep playing with your phone." Xiao Qin said with worry, "You should let me hold onto your phone next class."

"Give it to you?" I lifted my head, "Then you will look through my SMS and chat histories again."

"I won't this time." Xiao Qin promised, "I only want to play Angry Grandma."

So in the end, it's you who wants to play? I guess you still have traces of a boy's personality left inside of you. Now I know why I was feeling jealous earlier, it's because the one who indeirectly kissed the class leader was the Little Tyrant!

I opened the Angry Grandma app and coincidentally Xiong YaoYue passed by at the same time. She saw the colorful screen on my phone and exclaimed:

"Oh, you can play this game on your phone! My phone's CPU is really bad, so I can't play any games on it, you should let me borrow your phone some time."

"I was the one who asked for it first." Xiao Qin protested.

"Ah, sorry. Then, I'll be after Xiao Qin."

I rolled my eyes and passed my phone to Xiong YaoYue: "You can use it first. Xiao Qin sits right next to me, so she will have plenty of chances in the future."

"No~~~~ (gt;__lt;) ~~~ I want to play it now." Xiao Qin pouted.

"Then I'll give it to you if you call me sister Winnie." Xiong YaoYue said.

"Ye Lin classmate is bullying me." Xiao Qin ignored Xiong YaoYue's request, laid down on her desk and began to fake cry.

Xiong YaoYue patted Xiao Qin's head, "Don't cry, I'll give it to you. It's only a game, we shouldn't let it affect our relationships."

I waved at Xiong YaoYue to tell her to ignore her, "She's faking. If you don't believe me, you can tickle her."

Xiong YaoYue curiously reached into Xiao Qin's armpits. As expected, Xiao Qin bounced up and began laughing uncontrollably.

"Hahahahah, hurry, and, stop."

"So you were that sly." Xiong YaoYue puffed up her cheeks, "Then I'll use Ye Lin's phone first. You can use it next class."

"Remember to delete Xiao Qin's save file." I heartlessly reminded Xiong YaoYue.

"Don't worry, I'll make sure to keep an eye out." I'm guessing Xiong YaoYue didn't hear me clearly and thought I told her to make sure she doesn't delete Xiao Qin's save file.

Xiao Qin once again laid on her desk to cry: "I already spent 5 hours on that file!"

I asked her out of curiosity: "What's your record on Plants Vs Zombies: Endless?"

Xiao Qin stopped crying and wiped out the tears she got earlier from being tickled: "177 rounds, why?"

177 rounds. My record is only 28 rounds, where do you get so much time to play games? Normal girls wouldn't even like to play games that much.

"It's because Ye Lin classmate helped me install it the last time you came to fix my computer. Every time I play Plants Vs Zombies, I could always feel Ye Lin classmate's love."

"In order to remember Ye Lin classmate's childhood. In survival, I would always fill the firont row with shrooms and use coffee beans to wake them up&"

How do you even get to round 177 with such a poor tactic? And why does puff shrooms make you think of my childhood?

"I would try my hardest to prevent the puff shrooms from being eaten by the zombies, but if they were eaten, I could only place a doom-shroom in that spot& since Ye Lin classmate is odler now too&"

So it's still that vulgar comparison of a puff shroom growing into a doom shroom? I don't really care, just tell me how you got to round 177!

When the class bell rang, I realized I made a mistake.

This class was language, it was the annoying old man Zhang's language class.

Xiong YaoYue recklessly kept the phone between her legs and was playing with her head lowered. We were too far apart, so I couldn't warn her.

"Quick." I said to Xiao Qin, "Use your phone and send a text to my phone and tell Xiong YaoYue to play after class. It will be too late if old man Zhang catches her."

Xiao Qin slowly took out her phone and pouted: "Why are you so concerned about Xiong Ni?"

Who's Xiong Ni? Did you combine Xiong YaoYue's name and Zhuang Ni's name? I can't use your phone because your keyboard is too strange, hurry up and send her a text to tell her to put away her phone!

"But wouldn't it be worse if your phone rings during class?"

"I always set it to vibrate, so hurry up and send it!"

As Xiao Qin was dillydallying, old man Zhang stepped down from the lectern and walked aggressively towards Xiong YaoYue.

One of the class leader's loyal dogs was sitting to the right of Xiong YaoYue. He patted Xiong YaoYue's arm to let her know the teacher was coming towards her.

Xiong YaoYue broke out in cold sweat. Although our school does permit cellphones, it would still be confiscated if you're caught using it in class. The only way to get it back would be for your parents to come and pick it up.

It would be fine if it was her cellphone, but it just had to be mines. She felt it would be bad if I had to invite my parents to school because she was caught playing games in class. So, in a panic, she made an absurd decision.

Xiong YaoYue put my phone into her underwear without hesitation.

I can't see anything from my angle, but based on her movements, she had definitely stuffed it into her underwear. If she only put it down her shorts, then the phone would slide out when the teacher tells her to stand up.

There was a third year senior girl who used to cheat with her phone and this was how she got past the male exam proctors. In the end, she was actually able to pass safely and the incident spread through the school. Xiong YaoYue must have been influenced by her.

It's the only way to prevent the phone from being confiscated.

Both the loyal dog and the teacher were dumbfounded.

"Xiong YaoYue, stand up." old man Zhang wasn't going to easily let the matter drop. Even if he couldn't make her take out the phone, he still could force her to read aloud a passage of text before making her sit down.

With help from the loyal dog, Xiong YaoYue began to unnaturally read aloud a passage from 'The Song of the Stormy Petrel' by Maxim Gorky.

"High above the silvery ocean winds are gathering the storm-clouds, and between the clouds and ocean proudly wheels the Stormy Petrel, like a streak of sable lightning&."

Xiao Qin then suddenly said to me: "Haha, I finally finished writing that text& I'll send it now."

Ignoring my words of obstruction, she happily pressed the send key.

I've mentioned before that my phone has really strong vibrations and that it also has a built-in 'female entertainment app' which has three different modes of 'heart beating', 'flushing', and 'fainting'. It's clear that it's supposed to be used as a vibrator for females.

If it actually became a vibrator, then Xiong YaoYue would be the unlucky first user. It would happen right in the middle of class as everyone is watching her&

Xiong YaoYue was already reading 'Song of the Stormy Petrel' in an odd tone, but she suddenly felt the phone vibrate in her underwear.

It caused her raise her voice by eight pitches.

"The gulls are moaning in their terror-moaning, ————darting o'er the waters, and would gladly hide their horror in the inky depths of ocean."

Old man Zhang frowned, "That's a comma, not an exclamation mark. It's not the correct time to add an exclamation."

Xiong YaoYue's face turned crimson red, "But&" she wanted to explain, but couldn't really say anything.

Thus she continued to read while trembling.

"And the foolish penguins cower in the crevices of rocks&. while alone the Stormy Petrel proudly wheels above the ocean&"

Since it was only a text, the vibration quickly ended. Right when I wanted to heave a sigh of relief, who knew Xiao Qin began to call the phone after she sent the text.

"Why is no one picking up?" Xiao Qin said.

How would she answer in that situation? Xiong YaoYue wanted too keep reading, but she froze at a certain point.

My phone actually vibrates twice as hard when receiving a call compared to receiving a text. As long as Xiao Qin doesn't hang up, it would keep on vibrating.

Even from this distance, I could hear the faint buzzing coming from Xiong YaoYue's body.

In order to hide the noise, Xiong YaoYue could only read louder.

"Strikes the thunder&. Now the waters fiercely battle with the winds&."

"with the winds&."

She can barely even properly hold the textbook in her hands! She arched her body forwards to prevent the vibration sounds from leaking out and it kind of looks the same as when guys randomly pop a boner and then try to hide it.

Because of the heavy vibrations, Xiong YaoYue was afraid it would fall out of her underwear. Then, all of her efforts would be in vain, so she clenched the phone between her legs.

It was a beginner mistake as she felt the intensity even more closely. Her entire body shuddered and almost began tearing up.

As expected of an energetic girl who would never admit defeat. She managed to finish reading another passage in her current situation.

But old man Zhang was baffled. He was probably wondering why she was trembling so much while reading a passage of text.

"Did the PE committee member catch a cold?" A few students began to discuss.

"Stop joking around, when has Xiao Xiong ever caught a cold? She's even more robust than a bear!"

"Hey, hey, Xiao Xiong doesn't like other people calling her a bear. Lately, she wants everyone to call her Winnie."

"But Winnie is still a bear! Winnie the Pooh&"

I snatched away Xiao Qin's phone and stopped her malicious actions.

It was like Xiong YaoYue had just finished running in a marathon as she breathed out weak sighs.

In order to hide the previous awkwardness, she continued to read:

"In the crashing of the thunder the wise Demon hears a murmur of exhaustion. And he is knows the storm will die and the sun will be triumphant; the sun will always be triumphant!"

But her crimson red cheeks and still yet to recover to normal.

Xiao Qin suddenly said to me: "Ye Lin classmate, my phone has a persistent dialing feature. If you stay on the dial screen, it will redial after 3 minutes."

What? Why does your phone have such an annoying feature but it can't even go on the web? Then, I have to quickly exit out of the dial screen.

Since Xiao Qin's buttons were really small and in different spots compared to a regular keyboard, I accidentally pressed the redial button in a panic with my fat fingers.

Xiong YaoYue had thought the marathon was over, but with the unexpected vibrations again, she could only read the text as:

"It's the storm& the storm& The&. storm&. is breaking!"

The people who didn't know what was going on would actually think she had caught a cold based on her red face and trembles.

Even though she didn't finish reading the entire passage, old man Zhang had a daughter himself, so he couldn't keep watching and said:

"Okay, you can sit down. Next time pay attention in class."

Xiong YaoYue slumped down on her desk after old man Zhang left. You would usually never see her in this near exhausted state.

What left me bewildered was that she didn't take the phone out of her underwear. If she doesn't take the phone out, then I can't return Xiao Qin's phone.

After about ten minutes, Xiong YaoYue got up from her desk. She turned around and looked at me while full of grievances.

She made a face of realization after she saw me holding a phone at staring at her direction, then she resentfully stuck out her middle finger at me.

It's a misunderstanding! Xiao Qin was the one who purposely called you and made you embarrass yourself in front of the class!

Although the last hit was because of me, it was done out of good intentions! I fell for Xiao Qin's tricks again! It's all because she's an amazing liar and I can't tell if she's telling the truth or not!

After class, Xiong YaoYue borrowed something from the class leader before going to the washroom and taking out the phone.

Of course, I was still holding Xiao Qin's phone. I have to give her a scolding before I will return her phone.

"Are you even a girl? How could you torment your fellow female classmates?"

Xiao Qin pouted and it was clear she didn't learn her lesson, "It was her fault for making moves on you. I saw you guys leaving& no, smelled you guys leaving Qing Zi Academy together&"

So I was seen on Sunday? No wonder, there's no way Xiao Qin could actually get that much information on scent alone. So, you saw us together while you were with your uncles, so you couldn't chase after us?

"It's a misunderstanding." I said, "I went to Qing Zi Academy to go see Ai Mi. You already know she's my sister, right? It's because Ai Mi and Winnie gets along well, so I'm glad they could play together&"

"I'm not listening, I'm not listening, I'm not listening." Xiao Qin covered her own ears, "Ye Lin classmate already has a girlfriend, but he was wearing matching outfits with another girl. I'm going to drown myself in the river tonight after dinner."

Why do you have to do it after dinner? Is it because you don't want to die on an empty stomach? Besides, don't you have amazing swimming skills, can you even drown to death?

"Hey, we were wearing Qing Zi Academy uniforms, not matching outfits."

"You even intimately called her with an intimate nickname."

"It's not a lover's name, it's a nickname Ai Mi gave her."

"I also want an intimate nickname. You only call me Xiao Qin, which is no different than the treatment you give to the class leader, so I want an intimate nickname."

"Then what should I call you?" I asked.

Xiao Qin began counting her fingers, "You can pick one of the following: dear beloved, sweetheart, darling, or mother of my child&"

Are those nicknames your family would use? Those are clearly lover's nicknames used between couples.

Suddenly, I could feel somebody grab my back collar. I took a look and it was Xiong YaoYue. I was dragged into the hallway.

Xiao Qin said, "Not good, the black bear's coming to steal men!", but she didn't stop Xiong YaoYue.

After she dragged me near a window without anybody around, she returned my phone to me. But before she returned it, she wiped it down again and again with a moist towelette. I suspect she had already wiped it before too.

"Ye Lin, you're awful."

"Huh?"

"I did my best to prevent you're phone from being confiscated and that's how you repay me?"

"Although it was my fault for not being on guard against old man Zhang, you didn't have to go that far!"

"I had to ask the class leader to borrow a pa& anyway, you went too far."

You had to ask the class leader for a pad, right? I've already heard about the class leader always carrying extra pads in her bag for the girls in our class, but why do you need a pad if you're not on your menstrual period?

"Why are you not saying anything?" Xiong YaoYue punched me on the chest and it actually hurt quite a bit.

"It wasn't me." I raised my right hand and vowed, "It was Xiao Qin's retaliation for not being able to play Angry Grandma. I was holding her phone because I was trying to stop her!"

"Believe me, I'm telling the truth. If I'm lying, I'll be a sanitary pad in my next life!"

Xiong YaoYue blinked vacantly after hearing my vows, "Oh&"

Her expression turned better,

"So it was Xiao Qin. She may seem frail, but she's ruthless. It looks like she's a game addict, does she play LOL?"

"Huh?"

"Huh what? Miss Ai Mi wanted me to create a team, so I'm looking for members. If Xiao Qin is good at LOL, we can try to recruit her. Then once she's a member, I can slowly get my revenge."

"Hmph, I have to give her a taste of her own medicine. I'll make it vibrate once she's playing ranked."

Please, you're pretty much the only girl in our class who can play LOL. So, are you already going to forgive her for humiliating you in front of the class?

My phone vibrated at this moment and it felt a bit awkward holding the phone up to my face in front of Xiong YaoYue.

She wasn't really comfortable either and said farewell and headed to the courts to practice volleyball.

The phone call was from Xing Xing. He told me he was able to get more detailed information on the deliquent girls who beat them up.

As expected, they were leaders of the girls school, the regional boss of the 'Thousand Crane Girl's School'. Other than the three who beat up the Five Tigers, they still have twenty something other members, all female. They copied Japan's 'Yamaguchi-gumi' naming sense and called themselves the Rose Group.

What a chuuni name.

Chunni refers to a condition that originated from Japan, also known as middle schooler syndrome.

I have to make it clear that although I'm in middle school, I do not suffer from this syndrome.

The first time I encountered that word was when someone was watching the anime 'Chuunibyou demo Koi ga Shitai!' at a net cafe. The main character Rikka always wore an eye patch even though she did not have any eye issues, but it was pretty cute.

"Rose Group." I couldn't help but laugh, "Don't they frequent the west district, but I rarely hear about them."

"Brother Ye, they actually mainly focus in the east district, but recently they've been expanding into the west."

"What can they do? Girls can't fight as well as boys. Some small hoodlums can find dumb girls to be their girlfriends when they fight, but what benefits do they get when they fight as girls?"

Xing Xing spoke with a trembling voice:

"Brother Ye, the times are changing and we can't keep up. Did you know that Rose Group's main goal is to expand their influence under the leadership of their masked boss&."

"But what would they get for expanding their territory?"

"They get first picks on all the handsome men in their territory! If a girl dares to fight them for a man, then they would be abused!"

I was momentarily speechless after I heard the main reason Rose Group wanted to increase their influence was to take control over all the handsome men.

Xing Xing asked anxiously:

"Brother Ye, iff they took over the west district, what should I do if they took a fancy to me and forced me to be their boyfriend?"

Relax, it will never be your turn. The amount of acne on your face is enough to make up the star charts of the northern hemisphere. But the most handsome boy in our school, Shen ShaoYi, is in imminent danger.

Shen ShaoYi already said we weren't friends anymore because of the misunderstanding with Xiong YaoYue, but I can't just stand idly on the sidelines and watch him fall into the hands of the Rose Group.

I first comforted Xing Xing: The Rose Group wouldn't fall for you with your looks. But since the masked leader said they hate people with the Ye surname, it's best to follow their movements and try to figure out what grudges they have with the Ye family.

And I told him to notify me immediately if there's any signs of them progressing to 28 Middle.

Xing Xing grumbled: "I actually looked good when I was younger&"

What good is it even if you looked as good as me when you were younger? I mean, you still ended up with your current appearance, so you should face reality like a man.

The class leader came to look for me during the afternoon break. She wanted me to go with her to the clothing factory at our school to test the clothing.

I was a bit curious and asked: "Why pick me?"

"I wanted to go with Xiao Xiong." the class leader said with regret, "But she suddenly got her period, so it's not convenient for her."

It was hard for the class leader to break her habits as she still called Xiong YaoYue as Xiao Xiong, unlike other classmates who have gradually begun calling her Winnie.

Actually, Winnie wasn't on her period, but something worse happened partly because of me. If the class leader knew the truth, she might have already picked up her gun and sent me on my way.

Currently, there were only two samples of clothing made. The largest size available for men and women, respectively. Our main goal is to feel the quality and check any errors on the design.

In terms of height, the class leader is first among the girls. I'm on par with Niu ShiLi (he might actually be a few centimeters taller if he didn't slouch). So, it's reasonable the class leader came to ask me to try on the clothes.

But there's a problem if I take a closer look. If you have to try on both the clothes for both men and women, why did you arrange for Winnie to accompany you? Or were you planning on inviting both Winnie and Niu ShiLi, but since Winnie wasn't feeling well, you got rid of both of them?

I feel better the more I think about it.

After entering the clothing factory filled with loud machines, a skinny male worker wearing a blue uniform, a blue hat, and a pair of white gloves was explaining the benefits of ordering from this factory to another student.

He might seem like a regular worker, but he's actually the vice-director of this factory and also the husband of the director. There's a weird phenomenon in the factory where all the male workers look okay, but all the female workers look appalling. Apparently, the hiring was all based on the director's decisions.

The factory is hotter than ever in the summer and the large overhead ceiling fan doesn't really help. The vice-director got cotton mouth explaining their products:

"We use a different method from traditional screen printing. Images printed with the traditional method easily cracks and leaves sticky residue. Ours feel great, the image is clear, and the materials are soft and breathable!"

"Can you make it a bit cheaper." He seemed to be a male class leader for one of the third year classes. He looks educated but gives off an air of being a profiteer. The mole on his forehead just makes people even more uncomfortable.

"We really can't make it any cheaper." The vice-director said, "¥35 a unit is already the lowest margin we accept. If I reduce it by even a dollar, my wife wouldn't forgive me& and you really get what you pay for&"

The mole boy interrupted the vice-director and said, "Okay, then sell it to e for ¥40 a piece."

"What?" The vice-director thought he misheard.

The mole boy lowered his voice, thinking he wouldn't be overheard as he was surrounded by the rumbling of the machines.

"You write ¥40 a piece on the receipt, but still only charge me ¥35 a piece, so I'll receive a kickback of ¥5 per piece. Do you understand?"

How immoral. How can you betray your classmate's trust as the class leader? I mean even if your class had 50 students, you would only earn at most 5 x 50 = ¥250. If you even have to embezzle ¥250, then if you become a politician later on, you would definitely be a greedy and corrupt one.

If you're wondering why the class leader and I could hear his whispers, it's because I already developed greater than average hearing trying to hide from the Little Tyrant as a kid. As for the class leader, her hearing and vision are both better than mines as she inherited the genetics of superior hunters.

Although his words makes you mad, it's still an outside matter that doesn't have anything to do with us. It's not like he's the class leader of class 3-2 where brother Tao attends, so I was really to lazy to get involved.

But the class leader was furious and walked behind the mole boy without any hesitation. She glared daggers at him and questioned him in a loud voice:

"Is a person like you even worthy of being a class leader?"

The mole boy quivered and turned around. He didn't know how to respond when he saw a slender beauty with long black hair down to her waist.

The vice-director quickly tried to resolve the conflict: "It's all a misunderstanding, classmates shouldn't fight!"

"What misunderstanding? We all heard it loud and clear." The class leader glared at the vice-director, "Have you even given any other students kickbacks before?"

The vice-director, who was afraid of conflict and his wife, appeared to be half a head shorter as he trembled in front of Shu Sha:

"No, no, I've never done it before. He's the first one to make that request!"

He was quick to betray the mole boy.

The mole boy was enraged and pointed at Shu Sha and asked: "Which class are you from? You're not a third year, right? Why are you interfering with your senior?"

The class leader looked at the mole boy with despise. Since he was taller than her, she had to purposely raise her head to stare at him like he was a pile of trash.

"I'm class 2-3's class leader, Shu Sha. A degenerate like you doesn't even deserve to hear my introduction, so the introduction was actually for the vice-director. It can't be helped if you overhead it."

The vice-director rubbed his hands together in an untimely manner, "Nice to meet you."

Nice to meet you my ass, it's not like this is the first time you've met the class leader! It's only because the last time she came to place the order, she was acting reasonably without emitting her Justice Devil aura.

"So, it's you." the mole boy grimaced, "I heard there was a second year female class leader who likes to stick her nose in other people's business, but I never expected to meet her. What benefit do you obtain from interfering in our class' business?"

"Do you always need benefits to do something?" Shu Sha asked in response.

"No shit. Who wants to work for free in today's society? Don't think you have the right to criticize others simply because your hands are clean. You had your own selfish reasons for becoming the class leader."

"Huh, that's the first time I've heard that. Then please enlighten me on the reasons I don't even know myself."

"You& only want to be popular with the boys?"

"What?"

"Isn't it obvious? Your looks are on par with the prettiest girl in school, you're also impartial and just. Such a perfect person wouldn't exist in this world, so you must be pretending."

Even though the class leader does spoil her brother, she has OCD, and she's hated by animals, the mole guy is still partially correct as she's the closest girl to being perfect at 28 Middle.

"There's been a ton of girls like you in history who pretend to be pure and different than the others, because they wanted men to adore them and worship them."

Shu Sha sighed with ridicule, "I've met too many petty and vulgar people, so I can't be pure anymore. Gong CaiCai from our class is someone who's actually pure& but I guess I still learned a bit from you."

The mole guy realized his attacks weren't effective, but didn't give up:

"You're acting as a lovable and respectable class leader so you can attract attention and hook in a wealthy husband."

Shu Sha laughed out loud, "Gong CaiCai is probably the one with the best family background at 28 Middle, so am I going to marry one of her cousins?"

"Well, you're definitely different than how you appear on the outside. Oh right, I remember how you once tortured cats in the cat society when you were still a first year. This proves you have a twisted mind, and you probably even posted videos online of you killing cats by stepping on them with high heels."

"Non&sense. I've never tortured or kileld cats."

"Then tell me why you were kicked out of the cat club?" The mole guy became more giddy.

"I know." the vice-director suddenly interrupted, "Before the cat club was disbanded, they used to host club activities at our factory."

"At that time, when this girl walked in, the cats would all run away when she didn't even do anything as if they've seen a ghost&"

So you've already seen the class leader last year!

"That proves it." the mole guy was relentless, "Your hands must have been covered with the fresh blood of cats, so they all ran away."

"That's not why they ran away."

"Then why?"

"It's because&" the class leader seemed embarrassed to say she had hunter's eyes that disperses animals.

"No words left, you cat torturer?" the mole guy got back his feeling of superiority, "I'm only a bit greedy, but someone wicked like you will pretend to be innocent and marry into a rich family and maybe even kill your own kid to keep all the money to yourself!"

The class leader bit her lips, but when she was about to rebuke him, I walked out of the shadows of one of the machines.

Right when mole guy met my gaze, he went limp and retreated two steps and bumped into the vice-director.

"Please be careful, there's a cutting machine here&"

Mole guy trembled as if something on his body was 'cut', then he darted forward right into a position where he was surrounded by me and the class leader.

"Aren't& you Ye Lin? What are you doing with the class leader from class 2-3?"

"Did you forget I'm also from class 2-3? I've recently also become the PE committee member for our class."

I pretended to smile amicably, but since I actually look scarier when I smile, the mole guy backed up and crashed into the vice-director once again.

"Shit. Since you're always with Guo SongTao, I almost forgot you weren't a third year."

"It's fine if you forgot." I spoke amicably while cracking my knuckles, "Senior, our class leader is young and doesn't know any better. If she offended you in any way please don't be upset. I'll give you a beating as an apology, okay?"

The mole guy went deathly pale. He suddenly moved his feet and wanted to escape. I could have easily caught him and gave him a beating, but the vice-director got between us and waved his arms: "Don't fight, don't fight."

The class leader also blocked me with one arm: "I asked you to be the PE committee member, not a hired thug."

In the end, the mole guy got away. But before he left out the factory doors, he turned around and said nastily:

"Don't look down on third years! There will eventually be people in the school who disapproves of you and then you'll be taught a lesson!"

"Senior, why are you running?" I ridiculed from behind, "If you're a man, then I'll see you today at 6 by the school's back gate!"

"I stoop to the level of a crazy person." His voice gradually disappeared along with his figure.

Shu Sha went to the vice-director and asked for mole guys contact info. He had just taken down his number so he gave it to her.

Shu Sha immediately called the mole guy's cell phone.

"Hello, who is it?" the mole guy's tone was really unfriendly.

"Shu Sha, the one who was just arguing with you." Shu Sha replied calmly.

"You& why did you call me?"

"I wanted to warn you to not proceed with your plan of taking a cut of the profits."

"I just want to do it. If this factory doesn't cooperate, then I'll just go to another one."

"Actually, my phone has a recording feature and I've recorded our entire previous conversation including our current one."

"What?"

"It should be easy to find out which third year class you're from? Then, I'll find the proper prices based on the clothes you bought. If I find you took a cut, I will play your 'brilliant ideas' for your classmates to hear, do you not care? "

The mole guy was still reluctant to admit his mistakes, but since Shu Sha had a voice recording, he eventually still admitted defeat.

"Don't& let my classmates hear the voice recording, I won't try to take a profit on the uniforms&"

"I'll still be keeping an eye on you." Shu Sha coldly ended their conversation.

After the matter with the senior student was completed, Shu Sha began discussing about our uniform with the vice-director.

The vice-director of the factory still had some lingering fears due to the fact we almost began a fight earlier, so he desperately advertised his product to shift our attention.

"Class 2-3, I've already prepared the samples last night. Look, the male version is loose and relaxed while the female version is a slim fit around the waist. It uses the most modern printing process, guaranteed the colors will last and won't&"

"Uncle." I said impatiently, "You can just let us try it on."

"That's true." the vice-director smiled and brought us to the employee change rooms since they didn't have dedicated rooms for clients.

I took of my shirt and looked at the pattern on the tshirt for a bit. It was the number 3 with a crown, then I put it on over my head.

The quality was better than I imagined for only ¥35 a piece. I also smelled the design and it didn't have any strange smells.

The male change room was right across from the female change room. I had to wait 8 minutes after exiting the change room until Shu Sha came out from the female change room.

How slow. The guys and girls pretty much have the same school uniform for the summer. I only took two minutes to change, why did it take her ten minutes?

But after I saw the slim fit Tshirt and the curves on her upper body, it would still be worth it even if I had to wait another ten minutes.

Good job Tshirt! Shu Sha usually intentionally hides her breasts, but now they're off the charts!

Did she take so long because she was embarrassed about being wrapped so tightly?

"It looks good, right?" the vice-director stuck up his thumb in praise.

Shu Sha frowned while inspecting the cuffs and said:

"I don't think I've specified that the girl's shirt have to be a slim fit? It would be nice if it was loose like the boys&."

I'm against it! If the girl's shirts were also loose, where would I go to find this stunning scenery? It would also raise the morale of our class when you wear the shirt!

"But girls these days all want to look good. I thought you guys would be happy with slim fits&" the vice-director said anxiously, "Would I have to change them&"

The clothing plant who rents the building in our school has always had bleak business and was barely holding on. They had to make 28 Middle's summer and winter uniforms for free because they owe the school rent (but of course the school still charged the students for the uniforms). Although the materials might be plain compared to Qing Zi Academy uniforms, ours are exceptionally sturdy. I once got hit three times with a brick while wearing the winter uniform and it still didn't rip.

This business is one of the few remaining businesses who actually have a good conscience. Other than the female workers looking appalling, there are no other areas to criticize. They also used to let the cat society use a corner of their storeroom, so it shows both the factory director and vice-director are loving people.

Although she was critical about the fact the uniform tightens around her breast, she didn't want them to bear the cost of redoing the shirt, so she nodded:

"It's fine, I've tried it a bit in the change room and it doesn't inhibit my movements. If I could comfortably move my body, then our classmates should&"

She stopped halfway through her sentence with a slightly blushed face.

She was basically admitting herself that among the girls in class 2-3, not only is she number one in height, she also places in the top ranks for breast size.

"It's good we don't have to change it." the vice-director breathed a sigh in relief, "My wife wouldn't forgive me if she found out I wasted materials."

"When can you finish the 45 uniforms for our class?" Shu Sha asked.

"If we work through the night, we can deliver them the day after tomorrow."

"Okay, then I'll pay you then."

I suddenly had a question, "Class leader, are we ordering 45 uniforms? Are you ordering one for Zhuang Ni even if she never comes to class?"

"She's still one of us." Shu Sha sighed, "I'll ask Geng YuHong to deliver the uniform for me."

Geng YuHong is Loud Mouth. Shu Sha never calls people by their nicknames, unless it's someone like Xiong YaoYue who clearly expresses they hate it when people call her by her real name.

"Did you help pay for Zhuang Ni's uniform?"

Shu Sha didn't answer, but her expression confirmed it.

"I don't think you have a good relationship with Zhuang Ni, right?" I said, "I remember the time when she wanted to draw portrait of you in first year. She drew everything perfectly but left your eyes completely blank, I think you even had nightmares because of it."

Shu Sha's face turned as white as the T-shirt as she recollected the strange picture.

"Zhuang Ni& is a little strange, but I have nothing against her personally." Shu Sha pulled herself together and said, "I'm buying her a shirt so she can quickly become a part of the group again, besides you can't buy a lot with ¥35&"

Liar, the last time we were at the supermarket, you hesitated whether you should buy the discoutned containers and they were only ¥25 each!

And Zhuang Ni isn't a little strange, she's super strange. Which normal person would slit their wrists in art class with an utility knife, then proceed to paint a maple tree with their own blood? Teacher Yu has vasovagal syncope and was the first to faint when he saw blood.

"You guys can also take a look at the design on the back of the shirt." The vice-director reminded us.

There's actually no design on the back, but only words, it wrote: "We were together that year". I turned around to let Shu Sha take a look and she said the words were still pretty clear. But when she turned around, I could only see a waterfall of long black hair.

"Class leader, your hair is blocking the words."

"How about now?" Shu Sha tilted her head to the left and her hair flowed towards a different direction.

"I could only see the words 'that year'."

"How about now?" Shu Sha tilted her head even more.

"Still can't see 'We were'."

"Forget it." the class leader returned to her normal posture, "I'll just pretend those words don't exist for me."

The vice-director brought us two bags, "If it's a good fit, you can take these shirts first and show them to your classmates."

The class leader took the bags, passed me one, and headed back into the female change room.

"We don't need to change." I suggested, "We can go back and show how it looks on us."

"You can wear it back yourself." The class leader's voice came from inside the change room, "I'm used to washing new clothes before wearing them. And it feels a bit weird if we're the only two wearing the class uniform&"

How is it weird? Is it because it would seem like a matching couples outfit? When did you start caring about what others think?

After we returned to class, the class leader too the shirt out of the bag and laid it on the table for everyone to see.

"Hey, it's a slim fit. The class leader is pretty fashionable, I thought she would get those rectangular straight cuts."

"Class leader, have you worn it, how does it feel on the skin?"

Shu Sha patiently responded to everyone's questions.

"Good thing it's a slim fit." Little Smart commented, "Our class uniform only has a T-shirt and no bottom, so if we were wearing skirts, it would look awful with those rectangular shirts."

As for me who wore the shirt back for display, none of the boys crowded around but remained in their seats and whispered to each other.

"It doesn't seem bad, it looks better than what you could buy at night markets."

"It shows off your figure quite well. That vice-director who's afraid of his wife has some good skills!"

"It shows off the figure because Ye Lin has muscles. You wouldn't look good wearing anything with that gut of yours."

Xiao Qin looked at me from the side.

"Ye Lin classmate looks good wearing clothes too."

It sounds as if you've seen me without clothes&

Wait, I think she has seen me nude before. Once when she lied about brother Optimus Prime being stolen by triads, and she kept teasing me as I had a towel wrapped around me. I got worked up and dropped the towel and revealed everything to Xiao Qin.

It seems dirty when I think back on it, no wonder she ran away screaming.

"There's no use trying to kiss up to me. I'm already disfigured because of your fists, so I wouldn't look good no matter what I wear."

"Ye Lin classmate will always be the most handsome in my eyes." Xiao Qin clenched her two fists and said, "If other girls can't discover Ye Lin classmate's inner beauty, then they have no right to fight for you."

"Ha, then tell me what inner beauty do I have?"

"&. your muscles are beautiful."

"Are muscles considered inner beauty? Other girls can also find my muscles beautiful if I take off my clothes."

"Ahhhhhhhh, Ye Lin classmate is going to undress in front of other girls. I'm the only one who can admire what's on the inside."

So whatever is on the inside is considered inner beauty for you? If that's the case, I also really admire the class leader's inner beauty.

Eunuch Cao walked towards me without me noticing.

He walked towards me as if he was a minister meeting the emperor, then he knelt down in front of me without any warning.

"Long live master, may he conquer the world!" Eunuch Cao cheered, "The emperor's robe is really fitting on you, master."

All the classmates, including me, all looked at him with disdain. Only Xiao Qin had a look of approval.

"It's only a class uniform, how is it anything similar to an emperor's robe?"

"You can't say it like that. The first one to wear the class uniform is the king of class 2-3!"

"What kind of king? The type who's king when the tiger isn't home?"

"Master, don't undervalue yourself. Although we do have tigers in our class, it doesn't mean you can't outdo them! Look, the picture on the front is a 3 with a crown which means the first one to wear this is the king of class 2-3!"

Although he was spewing nonsense, it was still enjoyable.

"Ummm& actually my dad wanted to ask master for help&"

So, you had a request? Is Director Cao willing to let his son beg me simply to achieve his goals? But since they have no morals, they can't be asking me for anything decent.

The bell to get prepared for the next class rang. I told Eunuch Cao to head back to his seat and we can talk about his dad's request later.

Before we left school, Xiao Qin mentioned she wanted to borrow my phone for the night to play games. In return, she would leave her phone with me.

"Why are you so addicted to games?" I mocked, "Didn't you say you want to focus on being a girl? Have you seen a shojou protagonist that's addicted to games?"

Xiao Qin pouted, "It's because I have a file that's I've only played halfway through. I have OCD, so I don't feel good if I don't complete the game&"

"You don't have OCD, the class leader does."

"Stop~ it. In order to make Ye Lin classmate, I'm trying to give myself an OCD personality trait. Why did you have to expose me so soon?"

"Do you think you're playing a game where you can give your own character any trait you want?"

"Anyway, I hope you could lend me your phone. It's best if you can give me a call at night to remind me to not play too long&"

It was a normal conversation but Xiao Qin was embarrassed and twiddled her thumbs together.

"It's best if you can call me at 8:20 at night. Please don't get mad if might be busy and don't pick up right away&"

Who are trying to trick by telling me to call at a specific time but saying you might be busy? Your expression has already sold you out!

Since Xiong YaoYue got vibrated by my phone today, you probably felt jealous because even if it's my cellphone, you don't want anyone else having intimate contact with it.

So if I lend you my phone, you'll definitely put it somewhere bad at 8:20 and wait for you to call me.

I would be screwed if Auntie Ren hears strange sounds from your room and finds my phone.

After rejecting Xiao Qin's request of exchanging phones, I went to the school's back gate first before heading home. It was just in case there was something wrong with mole guy's brain and he was actually waiting there for a fight. It would be humiliating if I missed an appointment I set myself.

As expected, there were only a couple of students at the back gate and mole guy wasn't one of them.

As I was planning to buy some food from the food street for dinner, I received a call from Su Qiao.

"Xiao Ye&" Su Qiao's voice was a bit hesitant and a bit hoarse.

"Did you drink?" I was vigilant.

"I drank a little." Su Qiao admitted, "Lately& I've been a bit unhappy and there's no one around I can talk to. If possible, can I go to your place and chat with you?"

"&.."

"I& won't disturb your personal rest time. Aren't you living by yourself right now? I can help you tidy up, wash your clothes, and cook& I've been suffering from insomnia for the last couple of nights, I don't want to go back to that rental house. I would rather film for 24 hours straight&"

As Ai ShuQiao's pawn, Su Qiao still doesn't know she's already been abandoned. The last order she received was still to maintain an intimate relationship with me. But I haven't even been going to the film grounds, so she can't see me, so it makes sense to get anxious.

"Okay." I agreed, "It feels bad getting insomnia. Maybe you have too much pressure because you signed too many movie contracts?"

"There haven't been any movie contracts&" Su Qiao murmured, "I've been thinking if I've been tricked by Tian Mu Xing Guang&"

Of course you've been tricked! Ai ShuQiao's business in America always resolves around organized crime, so in China where they don't have an as good legal system, her actions would be even more unbridled. She definitely colludes with the government and criminals to use girls like you with dreams of becoming a celebrity as cattle.

Since film city was somewhat far from my house, Su Qiao would arrive after 7:30, but I'm not afraid of waiting for a good meal. I secretly prayed Su Qiao's wouldn't cook something dark and mysterious as I slowly walked home as I ignored the food street vendors trying to sell me food.

Suddenly someone patted me from behind. I turned around and it was Shu Zhe.

He had an unsatisfied expression while chewing gum.

"Bro Ye Lin, let's not exhange the goods at school anymore. It's too dangerous and you keep forgetting to bring the new goods."

If Constable Ma heard his words, he would definitely think Shu Zhe and I were exchanging drugs. He would excited and cuff my both my arms and legs.

Shu Zhe was actually only talking about our online store's underwear business. He was able to pull in a lot of business as Southland Berries and he's now looking down on me as his supplier.

"Where would we exchange it if not at school?" I asked.

"At your home!" Shu Zhe said as a matter of course, "It's safe and easy to pick up new goods. I'll go today and can also give you the embarrassing underwear I'm wearing right now&"

Shu Zhe wears women's underwear everyday to school now, the underwear that even he finds embarrassing is a thong that reveals his ass cheeks.

"Are you not going to eat the dinner your sister made?"

"Tsk. My sister had to go with Loud Mouth to see a classmate who's on sick leave. She actually told me to first eat the bread in the fridge and she will cook after she gets back. Who wants to eat those bread she bought when it was all heavily discounted?"

So, you call Loud Mouth by her name in front of her, but with her nickname behind her back? I hate two-faced people like you, I always call her Loud Mouth even to her face.

I calculated the time. If we were fast, I could bring him home, exchange the underwear, and maybe even get him to blow& a few balloons. It's fine as long as I kick him out before 7:30.

"Then come with me. But I don't have anything to eat at my place, how about I cook an egg for you."

"Who wants to eat your eggs? As long as you pay me my wages, I'll go eat fast food by myself."

"Well, what would your sister do if you already ate?"

"She can cook herself if she wants, and there's still bread in the fridge&"

I hit Shu Zhe on the head with a knuckle.

"Ow, why did you hit me?"

"If you're going to eat out, then bring some back for your sister. If she knows you already ate, then she won't have any drive to cook and might actually eat some bread as a meal."

"That's fine." Shu Zhe felt the bump on his head, "But you have to give me money to call a ride, I don't want to walk home carrying heavy bags&"

Is one serving of takeout really heavy? There's no limits to your laziness! You might be smart, but I find it hard to imagine you would be able to hold a job in the future. Or are you expecting your sister to raise you? Do you want your sister's husband to add an extra vow on their wedding day that says 'I promise I will care for your younger brother'?

Who wants to take care of him! If he's still depending on his sister as a grown man, I'll give him to Director Cao and ask if he needs an extra actor for gay films.

When Shu Zhe was changing in my washroom, he realized I had already fixed the lock and it gave him a sense of security.

"I used to be always on edge when I was using the washroom&"

What are you on edge for? Do you think I would run inside and rape you? If that was the case, why would I have to wait while you're in the washroom, I don't have those kinds of tastes!

Since I wasn't willing to do a sloppy job and sell underwear worn by Shu Zhe for one day as three day olds, Shu Zhe stuck with the plan of never separating from girl's underwear to maximize his income. He would wear a new pair every time he took off a pair and he had the same plans at my house.

"Bro Ye Lin, I heard from Xiong YaoYue that your cousin Ai Mi is actually a famous American singer?"

"Why are you calling them by their full names when they want to be called by their nickname?"

Shu Zhe unnaturally adjusted his pants. The new spider webbed style underwear is probably even more uncomfortable.

"Then I'll call her Winnie. She said she's going to follow Miss Ai Mi and if she ends up leaving the country, she will use it as her English name&"

"Why did Winnie tell you all that?" I asked, "Does she not suspect you as the underwear thief anymore?"

"Huh, weren't you the underwear thief?"

"No, are you saying I'm an underwear thief simply because that video got a lot of views? I'm the hero who fought against the underwear thief, or simply known as the conqueror of the underwear thief, understand?"

"I understand." Shu Zhe nodded, "So you're the conqueror of underwear&"

I hit Shu Zhe's head with my knuckles again.

"Bro Ye Lin, don't hit my head. My sister will hate you for life if you give me a concussion."

"Hmph, have you not heard of Darwin's theory of evolution? The more I hit you, the sturdier it becomes. If I hit you a hundred times everyday, you will quickly learn the iron head skill and you wouldn't even have to pay money to go to the Shaolin temple."

"If it's the iron head skill, you can learn it. It's best if you can master it and be able to block bullets& stop, don't hit me anymore, I won't say anymore."

"Back to my earlier question, why did Winnie tell you about Ai Mi?"

Shu Zhe covered his head as a preventative measure, "Because I promised I would do her math homework today&"

How embarrassing, Shu Zhe's one grade lower than you, but he still makes less mistakes?

"Brother Ye Lin, if you're cousin is that awesome, how come you don't get any benefits?"

Shu Zhe's first reaction is to try and get benefits from his relatives. His head is full of the notion of reaping without sowing and also money.

"No reason." I replied coldly, "It's because I'm not on good terms with Ai

Made in the USA
Las Vegas, NV
21 December 2024